A COUP

A TURKISH TRILOGY - 3

PHYLLIS M SKOY

Black Rose Writing | Texas

ISBN: 978-1-68513-209-5
PUBLISHED BY BLACK ROSE WRITING
www.blackrosewriting.com

Printed in the United States of America
Suggested Retail Price (SRP) $21.95

A Coup is printed in Chapparal Pro

*As a planet-friendly publisher, Black Rose Writing does its best to eliminate unnecessary waste to reduce paper usage and energy costs, while never compromising the reading experience. As a result, the final word count vs. page count may not meet common expectations.

For all those who have suffered under tyranny.

The mighty gray wolf is the Turkish national animal.
Legend says that the ancient Turks were raised by gray wolves.

ACKNOWLEDGEMENTS

Reagan Rothe and Black Rose Writing for publishing *A Turkish Trilogy*.

Lynn Miller: I thank you for your continuous critique and careful coaching over the years.

Joan Schweighardt: Thank you for always pointing me in the right direction and for your careful, excellent reading.

Kathryne Andrews: Thank you for a meticulous editing and helpful ideas.

Lynda Miller: Thank you for reading and your helpful critique.

Arthur R Skoy: Thank you for putting up with me. These books would not happen without your ongoing support.

Rabia Sahin Orhan and Necip Orhan: I thank you for your ongoing support and the support of The Raindrop Foundation.

A COUP

CHAPTER 1

Nuray Demir slows her pace, adjusts her headscarf, and glances behind just long enough to ascertain whether she is being followed. The streets of Istanbul are bustling. Turks are heading home, exhausted from a long day of work. Tourists, loaded down with market deals, stumble back to their hotels to shower and nap before dinner. Mothers herd small children home, carting their daily groceries. In the amber evening light, their misshapen shadows fall across Nuray's path. Their silhouettes increase the sense of foreboding she has attempted to ward off all week.

Internet chatter has put her on edge. Perhaps, Nuray thinks, it is my journalist's intuition, but I sense something big is at risk. I can feel it. I don't just imagine these things.

And what does it matter if I am being followed, she considers, but still she accelerates her stride. They know where I work, where I live, who I eat with, who I sleep with, every move I make, most of which is far less interesting than they might wish.

Nuray is on her way to her friend Adalet's apartment just off Taksim Square. It is just after 5:00 p.m. on the evening of July 15, 2016. The air is warm and somewhat sticky, without a breeze. Nuray carries a small backpack with her laptop, a change of clothes, a toothbrush, an overnight sleep shirt, and a small camera. She has not seen Adalet in months, and this is planned to be a catch-up sleepover.

"Stay the weekend," Adalet encouraged her, "We never see each other anymore."

1

"I can promise Friday night. We'll have to see about Saturday. I might have to work."

"You are married to that magazine. Okay, stay as long as you can," Adalet agreed. She knew it would be useless to argue any further. "We'll talk away the night. I'll have lots of snacks. Are you drinking these days?"

"I'm a journalist," Nuray laughed. "What do you think?"

"I thought you were a hijab-wearing journalist."

"Please, let's save this discussion for another time. Which way is the wind blowing these days?"

"You would know better than I," Adalet muttered into the phone. "See you when you get here. Text me and I'll come down to open the door."

At this hour, the tram is bursting with bodies of all shapes and sizes. Nuray is lucky to find a metal pole to grab onto in between the tightly clutched grips of other unseated passengers. She removes her backpack with her free hand to position it in front of her. She has learned through hard experience and the loss of valuables not to leave it on her back. Pickpockets are not so common, but when they do exist, they are highly skilled .

Three heavy elderly women in headscarves sit in front of her. Shopping bags are nestled between their long skirts. A young girl in a low-cut blouse and miniskirt sits flanked by two of them. They lean over her, deep in conversation. The girl ignores them, staring straight ahead into space. She must be one of their granddaughters, Nuray reflects, smiling. The girl does not belong with them. And yet, it is a mistake to think so, Nuray knows. The mixture and blend of old and new, religious and irreverent, often coexisting, often battling with one another, has been the state of being and the culture of Istanbul for some time now. Nuray wears a headscarf and dresses conservatively. When she dresses this way, men tend to leave her alone. There is no religious intention on her part.

A group of soldiers gets on at the next stop. They are unusually quiet, Nuray observes, none of the customary light banter occurring between them. Their silence, and what Nuray suspects is a collaborative sense of purpose, heightens her awareness. One of them looks in her direction.

"Where are you all going? Is there an event happening?" Nuray asks the soldier.

He looks away, and then glances back at her again. "Heading home," he tells her. "Nothing special."

"Nothing special," Nuray repeats. "So why are you all armed?"

"And why is this any of your business?" A wiry soldier asks her, standing within hearing range of the first soldier.

"We're coming back from an exercise," the first soldier responds before purposefully looking away again, to end any further discussion.

The Funicular 1tram stops at Sirkeci, just a few minutes-walk from Taksim Square. Nuray is surprised to see that the soldiers also disembark there. As far as she knows, there is no barracks anywhere near Taksim. So much for them going home.

Nuray alters her route to avoid walking with the soldiers. The winding and hilly streets leading to Adalet's home are fairly deserted. Other than slumbering feral cats, drugged from the still stinking offal left in the street for them by the local butcher, and a couple of stragglers rousted from the few cafes that will not open again until 8:00 p.m., Nuray doesn't see a soul. But when she begins to climb Steep Street from the Bosphorus, where Adalet's house sits halfway up the hill, she can hear shouts and loud pops of some kind coming from Taksim Square which spread out at the very top of Steep Street. Gray clouds of smoke hover over screeching gulls attempting to flock to safety.

The grating static of loudspeakers pierces Nuray's ears: *Good citizens, leave your homes now! Go out to defend your government!* The mechanical voice continues: *Save your government! Come out now! President Erdoğan asks you to fight, to save his government!* An aircraft of some kind hovers over the Square. She can hear the wind rushing against it. A helicopter? What is going on?

The noise accelerates, and Nuray runs up the hill towards the shouts and pops. The hill is steep, but Nuray is still young and in good shape, and so it only takes her a few minutes to see the outline of the shops surrounding the Square. A smokey cloud cover hangs over everything. Through the haze, Nuray can see armed soldiers surrounding the area. Nuray approaches one near the perimeter. Unfortunately, she sees that it is the unpleasant wiry fellow from the tram.

"*Selam*. I am a reporter. Can you please tell me what is happening here?" Nuray takes the camera from her pocket, along with her press card.

The soldier barely looks back at her. "You again. What the hell are you doing here? You need to get out of here. Go back where you came from if you don't want any trouble." He takes the rifle off his shoulder and makes a pushing back motion with it. "Go back."

Nuray tries to show him her press card. "I just want to be able to report what is happening here. Can you tell me anything?"

The soldier takes a look at Nuray's card. "Give me this." He yanks the press card from her hand. "Some people are trying to take over the government. For all I know, you could be one of them. Go back where you came from before I take you in right now."

"Give me my card back," Nuray insists. She can feel the sweat of her trepidation breaking through her skin and pressing against the fabric of her blouse.

The soldier puts the card into his jacket pocket and points the barrel of his gun at Nuray. "Come and get it," he says deliberately taunting her. Nuray feels her stomach turn over with fear. Is he really pointing a gun at her? Would he actually shoot her? She has heard of such things.

But then the soldier lowers his gun and puts it back on his shoulder. This interaction has caught the attention of several of the other soldiers who have been busy moving a small group of protesters from the Square. When Nuray sees them turning in her direction, she quickly flashes a photo of the soldier and the men behind him. Before

Nuray can put the camera back into her pocket, the soldier takes his gun back off his shoulder and knocks her camera out of her hand with the tip of the barrel. He smashes it with his rifle. "Get the hell out of here," he shouts.

Nuray turns on her heels and runs.

CHAPTER 2

Nuray does not stop running until she is halfway down Adalet's street. She pulls her phone from a pocket in her jacket and pushes Adalet's cell number. The phone only rings once before Adalet picks up.

"Where are you?" Adalet says whispering into the phone, as if someone else is with her and she doesn't want them to hear.

"I'm almost downstairs. Please be quick and open the door. Something is going on in the Square." Nuray can barely get the words out, as she gulps for air and listens to her heart pumping. She stops in front of Adalet's building and struggles to catch her breath. She hears Adalet's footsteps sprinting down the stairs.

"Hurry, get in here!" Adalet grabs Nuray's arm and pulls her into the vestibule, slamming the heavy door behind and almost catching Nuray's jacket in the frame. The women hear popping sounds. They both take a minute to breathe before Nuray grabs Adalet's wrist and wrenches her up the stairway. "Come on," she gasps. "It's not safe out there. I think we are in a coup again."

"Yes, that is exactly what I heard on the news." Adalet rushes beside her, pressed against the wall on the narrow curving staircase.

The women kick off their shoes outside Adalet's apartment, and place them on the rack Adalet keeps there for that purpose. Adalet owns the building she inherited from her dear friend, Fatma, but she lives only in her apartment on the second floor. She rents out the other three flats.

Inside the smells are tantalizing. Good to her word, Adalet has been making snacks for several hours. In fact, she's assembled a feast of mezza dishes, cheese *börek*, a smoky eggplant dip with flatbread, a cucumber and walnut salad, one of Nuray's favorites, a spicy barley and hot pepper spread salad, one of Adalet's favorites, hummus, black oil-based olives and two varieties of dolmades, one stuffed with rice, one stuffed with spicy bulgur.

Nuray surveys the low table spread with all of these delicious treats, along with a bottle of wine with two stemmed glasses. Next to that, Nuray sees that Adalet has placed a bottle of raki, two drinking glasses and a bowl of ice sitting next to a pitcher of water.

"Wow, *Mashallah, elinize sağlık!* Health to your hands, God willing!"

"Take off your jacket and put down your things. If you'd like to wash up, I will pour the drinks. Do you want to start with the wine or the raki?" More insistent loud popping sounds can be heard.

"I have to find out what is happening. I've been holed up in my dark, little office all day. Those sound like gunshots!"

Adalet takes Nuray's jacket from her and hangs it from a hook by the door. "They are gunshots. Believe it or not, we're in the middle of yet another coup."

Nuray grabs her jacket off the hook. "I have to go. I have to get back out there and report all of this for the magazine. I'll be back..."

Adalet seizes the jacket from Nuray's hand and hangs it back on the hook. "You're not going anywhere. Those are real bullets and it's impossible to say who is doing the shooting. From what I saw on the news a few minutes ago, it looks like the soldiers are fighting themselves. It's crazy. Really, Nuray, it's very dangerous. There's an angry mob all around them, pushing and pulling. Then *they,* whoever *they* are, seem to be also firing from the air, from helicopters or small planes. I don't know, but it's really not safe. Please don't go back out there."

Nuray stares at her jacket hanging by the door. As much as she is drawn to the Square and the action, she knows Adalet is right. The chances of her getting hurt or being dragged off to jail are pretty high. She doesn't choose to consider the possibility of being killed. She's been a journalist too long for that.

"Okay, but I will have to get on the phone and the computer later to get the news." Just as she says this, the electricity dies. In one big sigh, all the lights swoosh out, along with the air-conditioning. Yetim, the orphaned cat Adalet adopted so long ago, carefully jumps down from her perch on the windowsill. She stretches her body into a yoga-like position and disappears behind a stack of pillows where she likes to hide from visitors. Yetim is close to twenty years old now and such disturbances are unwelcome.

Adalet lights the candles she has already set on the table and slightly opens a window on the alley side of the room, not on the open street, just to get some air in the room. She has recently lost weight, giving her already slight body the appearance of a wraith. Her wild dark mane and wide almond eyes deny this apparition. She has no one to cook for now, this evening being a rare exception, and so she tends to throw together light salads for herself.

Nuray and Adalet have known each other since they were at the university together. They lost touch during Adalet's marriage. After Adalet's divorce, they ran into each other by chance in the Sunday market. Since that encounter, they have become close again, or as close as anyone ever can get to Nuray. Adalet has learned to respect Nuray's privacy and way of distancing herself. It is the only way, she quickly discovered, that one can maintain a relationship with Nuray.

Nuray goes to the bathroom off the bedroom that Adalet has not used since Meryem and Isha went to live in New York. This has become her guest room and guest bath once it became clear that Meryem, Fatma's granddaughter, and Isha, her partner, would not be returning to Turkey any time soon. The shifts in government and attitudes have cemented this, as it is no longer safe for them here. The more radical Islamists are in the forefront these days, and Meryem and Isha are two women living together, life partners.

"Do you miss them?" Nuray asks upon returning from the bathroom and settling down on the pillows Adalet has arranged as seating around the low table. Nuray is also a slender woman, but her bone structure is larger than Adalet's, giving her more of a presence. Her light brown hair is hidden in a tight cap made for the purpose of keeping her hair contained in her purple silk headscarf. Her eyes are a much lighter brown than Adalet's, her nose wider and shorter. Nuray's family is mixed Turkish and Kurdish, and she clearly takes after the Kurdish side.

"Do I miss them? Meryem and Isha?" Adalet sighs. "Of course I do. But to be very honest, I'm glad they went and I'm glad they stayed. Things would have become so difficult for them. In this climate, they would have had to hide their relationship. In New York, they're a married couple. And Meryem is becoming known. Her paintings are selling anyway. Her work is in a good gallery in Soho now."

Adalet sinks onto a couple of pillows next to Nuray. She reaches up for the bottle of raki, plunks several ice cubes into each glass, and pours in a slight portion of the thick licorice-like liquid. "Water?" she asks Nuray?

"Please," Nuray answers. Both women watch the ice cubes dance in the foggy mixtures.

Adalet lifts her glass. "To peace in the empire and to our enduring friendship."

"I can definitely drink to that." Nuray raises her glass and both women sip with some caution, setting their glasses back onto the table. The effects of raki can be surprising, sneaking up abruptly on those who don't give proper respect to its potency.

Rapid loud bursts of what sound like fireworks or worse, gunfire, bring both women to their feet.

"Get down," Nuray says grasping Adalet's arm as she kneels back down on the floor. "That sounds like gunfire, and it's really close."

"What do you think is going on now?" Adalet crouches by her friend, afraid to move but tempted to run to the window. Not able to resist, Adalet pulls on her friend's arm. "Let's look outside. We'll be careful to stay low."

The two women creep slowly to the street window. When Adalet pulls the curtain aside, they can see plumes of smoke rising over the direction of Taksim Square.

"What do you think?" Adalet asks her friend.

Nuray reaches over and takes a sip of raki. She sets her glass back down and reaches for a small plate.

"I think I'd better eat something. I haven't eaten since breakfast, and suddenly I'm feeling faint."

"Sit. We can't do anything right now anyway."

The women sit cautiously back onto the pillows and begin to place bits of food onto their plates. Nuray takes several bites before she places her dish back onto the table.

"This is crazy," she says getting back on her feet. "I can't just sit here eating and drinking as if nothing is going on out there. Let me try my computer and see if I can get a signal."

Adalet takes another sip of her raki and tosses a couple of olives into her mouth. She pushes herself up and joins Nuray at the dining table in the next room where she has opened her laptop and set it onto the table. Nuray turns the computer on and struggles for a few minutes before turning it back off. "No WIFI. The government probably shut it down again."

CHAPTER 3

Nuray turns reluctantly to Adalet. She knows that Adalet tries to avoid confrontation and thus, she shies away from politics. Nuray does not wish to frighten her, but she feels compelled in the moment to tell someone what she has just experienced. "He actually broke my camera!"

"Who?" Adalet asks.

"I don't know. Some soldier on the Square. I took his picture, and he knocked the camera out of my hands and smashed it. He stole my press card, too."

"Are you going to report him?"

"I'm not sure what to do. There were a bunch of soldiers at the Square. They were on the tram I took over here, too. I heard some people at Taksim Square shouting that there was trouble at the bridge, the Bosphorus Bridge, but I was a little shaken after that soldier refused to give me my press card back."

"Why do you think he kept it? It's of no use to him."

"I think he wanted to rattle me, show his authority and make me afraid. It made me angry, and that's why I took his picture. Then when he smashed the camera, I did feel afraid. When he told me to get out of there, I admit it, I ran."

"I would have done the same, but I would not have taken his picture." Adalet shook her head at her friend's foolhardy behavior. "He could have hurt you or arrested you."

"Well, he didn't." Nuray feels a sticky sweat on the back of her neck. Adalet is right. She could have been arrested. Nuray does not want to think about that now. "Let's try the WIFI again." She sets her glass back down on the table.

"Okay," Adalet answers. "The signal seems to be going in and out."

"Let me try." Nuray retrieves her plate of food from the table in the living room and sits down at the dining table. She starts her laptop back up and gets a live stream of the Bosphorus Bridge. "Oh, my, look, Adalet. They're killing each other." And then as suddenly as the picture comes on, the signal is lost and the screen turns black.

Adalet's phone starts to buzz. "WhatsApp is working." Adalet recognizes the caller. "It's Mark calling from New York."

"Good news spreads quickly these days," Nuray comments. She goes back into the living room to replenish her plate while Adalet takes the phone call. Although Nuray feels that she should be out there, right on top of whatever is taking place, she is shaken by the loss of her camera and press card, to say nothing of having a gun pointed straight at her.

"Yes, I'm okay." Adalet responds to Mark. "Your voice is vibrating. We have a bad connection." Adalet pauses to listen.

"I'm not sure what's going on here," Adalet confesses to Mark. "Nuray is here, and we've been trying to figure it all out. We're inside and okay. There were gunshots earlier, but the street seems quiet now. I think they've gone to the bridge." Adalet pauses.

"No, don't worry, I have no intention of going anywhere. My friend Nuray is the one you need to talk to. She's already been out and gotten into trouble. She had her camera smashed and her press card taken. Let me go to see if I can find out more information. I'll try to call you back when I do, but you know how the phone lines can be, especially when there's trouble. Don't worry if you don't hear from me immediately. Our WIFI has been in and out, and I'm not sure how long we'll have WhatsApp." Adalet pauses again. "I love you, too," she says before sliding her finger to shut off the call.

"Do you still love Mark?" Nuray asks, eating a piece of bread covered with *ezme* with one hand and trying to get online with the other. A smudge of the spicey pepper spread has leaked onto the edge of her hand. Nuray licks it off, undeterred.

Adalet takes her glass and plate and joins Nuray at the table. "Love turns out to be a complicated matter," Adalet sighs. "Like the WIFI, the signal comes and goes. He's the only man I've been with since my divorce, but he lives in New York."

"And why didn't you go with him?" Nuray pumps her finger up and down on the computer keys without any luck.

"I don't know. I wish I did know. That would make things so much easier. He's such a good man, and I know he loves me."

"So?" Nuray pushes the computer aside in disgust and swallows the last sip of raki from her glass. She is not normally much of a drinker, but raki has a way of settling her nerves.

"We're from such different worlds. And New York scares the hell out of me." Adalet gets up and goes to the living room to retrieve the bottle of raki and the ice bucket. "More?" she asks Nuray.

"Just a tiny bit, there, that's good." Nuray takes a couple of cubes of ice and lowers them into the almost negligible amount of raki. "New York isn't scary."

"How would you know? You've never been there."

"You were there right after September 11th. Of course it was scary. If a New Yorker was crossing the Bosphorus Bridge right now, she'd think Istanbul was scary. Things happen everywhere." Nuray pulls the laptop back in front of her and tries to get online again.

"That's not what I find scary. Oh, look. You're online again. Oh, no, there are bodies lying there. People are being killed. There are army tanks. Oh, Nuray, this is awful."

Nuray pulls her cell phone from another pocket in her jacket. "I'm going to call the magazine to see if anyone is there now. Maybe Mohammed is working late. If he is, he'll know what's going on. Maybe I'll just try his cell phone first."

Adalet tries to slow down the rapid beating of her heart. She is frightened. What is happening in her city? In her country?

Adalet has found the past three years difficult. Mark was unable to renew his temporary position at the university, and so he went back to New York. The truth was that Mark became uneasy with the upheaval of the political situation in Turkey, the looming autocracy of the Erdoğan government. As sympathetic as Mark was to their plight, he felt overwhelmed by the huge influx of Syrian refugees from the civil war. Their presence was changing the very nature of Istanbul. The ongoing conflict with the Kurds presented constant political pressures, as Mark had so many creative Kurdish friends who were artists and performers, people he met through the university. At one point, there were also suspected terrorists living in Adalet's neighborhood. When their landlord began to hear rumors, he had kicked them all out. But Mark did not feel it was safe for him to remain in Turkey, a Jewish man who was then unemployed.

Mark had asked, actually begged, Adalet to marry him and come to New York to live with him, but she had hesitated.

Adalet fiercely loves her country and Istanbul. She is Turkish down to the core. She cannot imagine herself living anywhere else. Even when her contract was not renewed with the school for the deaf, as they were in the process of shutting down (although Adalet hadn't known it at the time), she had no thoughts of leaving her home. The income she receives from the three other apartments in her building generates enough cash for her to live quite comfortably, as long as her tenants can continue to pay the rent. In a city like Istanbul, where comfortable apartments aren't so easy to find in good neighborhoods, Adalet has been lucky to find good tenants. If only her luck will hold, she is content for the most part, except for the separation from Mark. And he has visited.

Nuray speaks quickly on her cell phone. "Okay, good. If you find out anything more, call me. I'll have my cell on. Hopefully, you can get through. I'm staying at my friend, Adalet's tonight, just off Taksim

Square. I'll be there first thing in the morning. Please be careful to lock everything up before you leave. See you tomorrow."

Adalet groans. "So much for our girlfriend time together."

"What can I say?" Nuray puts her cellphone down on the table. "I'm a journalist and this is big news. Mohammed is unsure of the story. Like everything in this country, there are a dozen rumors. I have to try to get to the bottom of things. I'll try to make a few calls later tonight, but now, tell me about Mark."

Adalet leans back in her chair, runs a hand through her hair and sighs. "I don't know what to say. I wish he could live here. I don't know if I can live there. I don't think I can."

"Your English is good enough." Nuray spoons more bulgur salad and *ezme* onto her plate. "This is really good, Adalet."

"It's not about language, not really, anyway. I don't think like an American. And there is the religious difference."

"Oh, come on, Adalet. You're not observant." Nuray wags a dismissive finger at Adalet.

"No, but I do believe, and I am Muslim in my own way. And I think the same is true for Mark, even though he wouldn't admit it. He's not observant either, but he is Jewish in his own way." Adalet takes an olive and pops it into her mouth. "I love these things. They're so oily and salty."

"I'll say." Nuray puts several olives on her plate. She fills her empty raki glass with plain water and ice. There is a whooshing sound and the air conditioning comes back on.

"Electricity!" Nuray exclaims. "Yes! Let's try to get some news." Nuray goes back to the living room, takes the television remote and switches it on. "Ah, Adalet come, we have live news."

The two women stand in front of the television. The scenes being shown are chaotic. It is difficult to ascertain who are the putschists and who are the defenders of the government.

"How do they know who they're fighting?" Adalet asks.

"I don't know." Nuray shakes her head in confusion. "It looks like people are fighting the soldiers, but then they all look like soldiers. I have no idea who is on what side."

A commentator's voice comes over the chaos: *Some factions of the military have attempted a coup to take over the Erdoğan government. President Erdoğan is denouncing this and states that he has control of the government. Vacationing with his family, he has come on social media and local channels to ask the people to take to the streets to fight for his government. President Erdoğan is charging the Gülen movement with the attempted coup. Many are being arrested.*

Nuray grabs the remote and shuts the television off. "This is crap. Erdoğan is seizing the moment to take advantage of his enemy. It's going to be a terrible time, Adalet. He's going to get back at Gülen any way he can. They used to be the best of friends, but now Erdoğan is trying to seize absolute power. There is nothing like perceived disloyalty to set him off. Gülen is a mere cleric, not a politician. And he doesn't even live here anymore. You can bet if he did, Erdoğan would have the police at his door right now."

"I don't know too much about that," Adalet confesses. "I try to stay away from politics. All Mark talks about these days is Trump. He says if Trump is elected, the U.S. is in big trouble. Mark knows him from New York and the things he's done there. He really hates him. And here, I am never sure who is in favor of Erdoğan and who is against him. People have become afraid to even talk about it. Remember when the cafes were filled with young people talking?"

Nuray sighs. "Now we're too afraid of being arrested. Even saying something bad about him in public can be enough to put you in jail. I don't know why you didn't go to America."

"From what Mark is telling me, immigrants aren't welcome there now. And if Trump is elected, he threatens to send all the Muslims back to where they came from."

"Trump won't be elected, *Inshallah*." Nuray waves her hand dismissively.

"Mark thinks he will."

"Well, then maybe we can put Erdoğan, Trump and Putin together in a leaky boat in the middle of a stormy Black Sea. Let's hope none of them can swim!"

Adalet laughs. "I'll have to tell that one to Mark."

Nuray's phone bings. "Oh, I have a text." Nuray looks at her phone and drops it on the floor. "Praise be to Allah, what is this?" Nuray hands the phone to Adalet.

CHAPTER 4

"What is this?" Adalet repeats, holding the phone in her hand. "It looks like a photo of your press card."

"Look at what's written below." Nuray takes the phone and scrolls down. She hands the phone back to Adalet.

Adalet reads: *If you want this back, meet me at 8:00 tomorrow night at the Café Lale just off İstiklal Cadessi by the large pastry shop. If I don't see you there, I will turn it in to the police.*

"Oh my, Nuray, what are you going to do? He found you so quickly." Adalet hands the phone back to Nuray, as if she is purging live flames.

"All my information is on the press card. Fortunately, my address isn't, but my cell phone is there." Nuray sees that her hand is beginning to shake. She sets the phone down on the table and rubs the shaking hand with the other. "I will go, of course. I will ask Mohammed to follow me. It's a public place. I can get Mohammed to photograph him secretly with his phone." Nuray picks up her cell and begins to text immediately. Her hand is still shaking slightly. She waits for the text back from Mohammed and then nods to Adalet.

"It's okay," she says. "He will do it. I can't tell you how valuable Mohammed has been to me. He is such a good friend."

"Any romance there?" Adalet asks, trying to lighten the mood but so fearful for her friend.

"He's married with two small children, a boy and a girl, so no. If not, I might grab him up in a heartbeat. The good ones are all taken by now, dear girl. I don't expect romance is on the horizon for me. Anyway, all of this is exhausting. I hate to ruin our evening, but if you don't mind, I'm going to turn in now. Tomorrow promises to be a very long day. I'll have to get to the office early, and I'll probably need to spend some time on the computer tonight before I get any sleep. I need to start composing, and then I'll clean up the facts once I get more information in the morning. Too much is rumor right now." Nuray picks up her phone and computer and her backpack and heads for the guest room. She turns back to Adalet. "Do you mind terribly?"

Adalet stops to assess her friend's mood. Nuray will go into the guest room and work. She is not going to sleep for several hours, but she will not spend this time with Adalet.

"It's okay," Adalet concedes. "Take some goodies with you, and more raki, if you like."

"I'll just put these things down and then I will make myself a plate and one more small shot of raki. It will help me to sleep."

Adalet smiles. "More like it will help you to work. I'm going to check the news and will be up for a bit before I put things away and go to sleep. Feel free to help yourself to the refrigerator and to anything else you need."

Nuray takes her things to the guest room. Adalet has laid out bath towels, a hand towel and washcloth. She is always so thoughtful, Nuray thinks. I can learn these things from her. Nuray's home is always so cluttered, she cannot imagine having Adalet stay there. She opens her laptop and returns to the living room for more food. Her nerves are too frayed to eat much, but she knows some nibbling will help her to concentrate. Adalet is lying on the couch with the television turned on softly to the news.

"Anything new?" Nuray asks, filling her plate with hummus, olives, and bread. She hesitates before adding some walnut salad.

"No," Adalet tells her. "They keep repeating the same information, and they add that it isn't confirmed. They've managed to secure Erdoğan and his family and whisk them off somewhere. He's scheduled to speak tomorrow. But there's all this chatter, and so who really knows what's what."

Nuray splashes a small amount of raki into her glass. "That's what I'm going to try to find out. Sleep well, my friend, and thank you for everything." Nuray starts to make her way back to the bedroom.

Adalet calls out to her, "Try to get some sleep. See you in the morning."

Nuray calls back, "Good night." She does not tell her friend that she has no intention of seeing her in the morning. As soon as it is light outside, Nuray plans to be on her way to the magazine office. She is too tired to argue with Adalet about staying for breakfast. Nuray loves her friend, but now is not the time to linger over idle conversation. Adalet does not have the same thirst for causes that Nuray possesses. Adalet's heart and mind are on the right side, but she is not there when it comes to action.

Nuray sets her plate and drink on the small table alongside her computer. Her hand begins to shake again. Oh, yes, she can understand why Adalet hesitates to become involved. The world is a dangerous place, and Turkey becomes more so every day. Nuray sits down at her computer, presses on her hand until it stops shaking, and hits her online function. She goes to some of the more obscure newsrooms that she has for just such purposes.

There are no signs that her magazine has been mentioned or raided. Nuray breathes a bit more freely. Some of her friends and colleagues have recently expressed fears that they will be shut down and silenced. She knows of journalists who have supposedly been threatened. Most of these are Kurdish publications, and they are used to it, but Nuray is outspoken on women's issues and her feelings about a woman's place in Islam.

Although Nuray has never been physically recognized in public, her magazine has become better known over the last couple of years. But since she has changed the name a couple of times, it is sometimes thought of as several different publications, if people know of it at all. But what started as a small student newspaper at the university has grown into more than Nuray ever hoped or anticipated. *Turkey's New Woman*, as it is now called, sells enough copies for Nuray's salary, Mohammed's salary, and a modest office with a small staff of student volunteers. Nuray pays Mohammed twice what she takes herself, as he has a wife and a family.

Nuray sees troubling chatter. Clearly, the attempted coup has failed. There is word that the Erdoğan government is controlling the outgoing news. There are rumors that WhatsApp and other communication sources are being shut down either temporarily or permanently. She is tempted to contact Mohammed again but restrains herself. Mohammed's wife is a generous woman who likes and respects Nuray, but Nuray would like to keep it that way. She has already texted him and spoken to him tonight. And it is only some solace that she is after.

Typing in letters reluctantly, she goes to a site to see if her name or her magazine's name is listed there. No, there is nothing new, but she will continue to check. There has not been enough time for the news media to be targeted, but without any doubt, it will happen soon. Of this, Nuray is confident. This coup, or whatever it is that is happening, will be just the excuse that Erdoğan and his supporters need and will use to obliterate their enemies. Nuray does not consider herself important enough to be an enemy of the government, but she is all too well aware of what can happen in a massive sweep. She takes another sip of raki and scoops some *ezme* onto bread. She is tired, and there is little she can do tonight other than getting her own experience down on paper. She will not write about her encounter with the soldier, not yet anyway.

Nuray logs off of the Internet and goes into her word program. She types rapidly, date, time and facts only. Once she is satisfied with her details, she saves and closes the file. Briefly she thinks about seeing if Adalet is still awake but decides against it. Sadly, Adalet cannot bring her any comfort. She will only try to discourage her friend from doing anything that might bring her trouble. Adalet has not done anything smacking of courageous since she went to the site of the Twin Towers after September 11th. Nuray has tried many times to get Adalet to write about that, but Adalet has always refused.

So instead, Nuray takes her plate and glass of raki and sets it down next to the bed. She lays the towels and washcloth across the chair by the table and crawls under the covers without changing. She finishes the food and raki slowly, wondering what will happen when she meets the soldier tomorrow. Placing the empty plate and glass on the floor, she scrunches the pillow under her head and pulls up the covers. A few hours of sleep will help her get through tomorrow whatever it brings.

But Nuray tosses and turns in the unfamiliar bed. Finally, she gets up, turns on her phone and examines the text from the soldier once again. What is it that he can possibly want from her? Perhaps he regrets his behavior and will just return the press card. Nuray does not really believe that this is the case or he would seem more friendly in his text. But then, texts are hard to read in terms of mood or intent. Maybe it is foolish to have asked Mohammed to come there, to take him away from his family in the evening. Is she being silly, paranoid for no reason?

Sitting on the edge of the bed, Nuray asks herself this question. She turns the phone off and sets it next to her computer. She wanders over to the door to the balcony and opens it onto the now quiet street below. The air is warm and there is a slight breeze. Nuray steps outside. She has always envied Adalet this balcony, this way of stepping out of doors and viewing the street without really being outside. Nuray sits down on the white plastic chair Adalet leaves out there for just this purpose. She wishes she had a cigarette, but she is in one of her periods of quitting and so has none. Instead, she massages her hands, first one then the other.

What will tomorrow bring? What will the new day mean for her as a journalist? What will it mean for the magazine? What new problems will this soldier bring with him? She is familiar with the café where he has asked her to meet. The outside is decorated with the tulips from which it gets its name. It is not unlike many of the small establishments in the same neighborhood.

Nuray spies a cat sleeping in the seat of a motorcycle parked below. She remembers Adalet's cat, Yetim. Yetim is probably hiding from her, as she is known to do, especially from visitors who are infrequent. Nuray feels a pang of guilt for not coming to see Adalet more often. Ah, this is the way that it is. Nuray isolates from her few friends. She is not a social creature. She smiles. She is like Yetim in many ways, an orphan who hides from people. Yetim is wise, Nuray reflects. Keeping people at a certain distance guarantees a certain degree of safety. Nuray regrets telling Adalet about the soldier. Whatever happens tomorrow evening, she thinks she will not share with Adalet, unless it is simply to tell her that he has returned her press card and all is well. Adalet is prone to worry and will only add to Nuray's anxiety.

Not expecting to get any sleep now, Nuray closes her eyes on the balcony and waits for daylight to come. If she drifts off for some moments, so be it. Any rest at all will be welcomed.

When Nuray next opens her eyes, still sitting out on the balcony in the white plastic chair, patches of red and blue are breaking through the charcoal sky. She is surprised to have slept and finds her body stiff when she pushes herself up from her sitting position. She lets herself back into the guest bedroom, careful not to make any noise to wake Adalet. She gathers her things and tiptoes through the living room, not even stopping to use the bathroom. She will do that at the office.

The street is eerily silent. The tailor across the way nods to her as he sweeps the walkway in front of his shop. The cat is still asleep in the motorcycle seat and does not stir as Nuray walks by. The early call to prayer has come and gone, and Nuray is surprised to have slept through it. Other than the rustling of floating papers and garbage debris, there are no signs of the activities of the previous night.

Nuray decides to text an Uber.

"Kadıköy," Nuray tells the driver, settling into the seat. "I'll show you how to go when we get there."

CHAPTER 5

Nuray directs the driver through the winding streets of Kadıköy to her office which is located above a small grocery store.

"Were you out driving last night?" Nuray asks the driver, a young fellow with a full head of black hair and a mustache, which he more than likely sports to hide his youth.

"For a while. But when I saw all the soldiers, I took off and went home. I didn't want to be involved in any trouble."

"You were at the bridge?" Nuray hopes to get something useful out of him.

"Only for a minute. One of the other drivers told me that some of the military were trying to overthrow the government. I got out of there as fast as I could." He hesitates before he says, "They couldn't do it, though."

Nuray does not comment. She has no idea what the driver's thoughts are on the subject, whether he is happy or upset that the coup has failed.

The day is fully alive now with street traffic and open markets. Horns honk steadily; hawkers call out their wares. A party of seagulls is scavenging tidbits from the sidewalks that the morning sweepers have missed. Nuray makes a note to herself to take a break at some point and wander through the local neighborhood market to pick up some fresh fruits and vegetables. She hurriedly pays the driver and runs up the back stairway, stopping on the landing to pull out her keys, when the door opens. Mohammed pulls the door back to let her in. His expression is grim.

"*Merhaba*. Glad you're here early," he says. "Did you see what happened at the Bosphorus Bridge?"

"Yes. We are in a mess." Mohammed watches as she puts her things down on her desk, lowers her backpack and removes her jacket. She settles into her desk chair.

"We have to be careful now," Mohammed finally speaks. "The failure of the damned coup has created a lot of chatter in the media and the press. Raids are expected any time. The Kurdish presses and anyone who is in any way associated with Gülen is going to be targeted. Your father was Kurdish?"

"If he's still living, he's still Kurdish." Nuray curls her lower lip in disgust. "He left as soon as my mother got sick. He disappeared, and we never heard from him again. He was in the import and export business, tourism stuff, dishes, decorations, some small prayer rugs and a few carpets here and there, nothing to do with the press or politics."

"Do you know if he's had anything to do with the Gülen organization or any folks associated with it?" Mohammed is staring at her intensely now.

"I have no idea. I was only twelve when my mother got sick, and we've been estranged since then. But I know people in the Hizmet movement, don't you? The people I know are concerned with spreading good education and Turkish culture. They aren't terrorists. Why are you asking?" Nuray opens her backpack and pulls out her overnight cosmetic bag. She hasn't even brushed her teeth yet and needs to use the toilet.

"The Erdoğan government is going to go after everyone associated with them. The police are starting to show up to arrest people, accusing them of being traitors and plotting the coup, people who have clearly nothing to do with it. And just who is this guy with your press card? How did that happen?"

Nuray gets up from her chair and waves her cosmetic bag at Mohammed. "I need to freshen up. I didn't want to wake my friend, so I snuck out without her knowing and didn't even brush my teeth or wash my face. Let me go to the bathroom first and then we'll talk." Nuray leaves Mohammed standing there, exits the overcrowded, tiny office, and walks down the hallway to the toilet closet.

Adalet was on to something. Certainly, if Mohammed were not married with two children, he might be the sort of man to inspire interest from her. He is tall, muscular, with a full head of black wavy hair, large brown eyes and olive skin. He is, by any standards, a handsome man. But the thing is, Nuray has often reflected and does so now, she is not so interested in a relationship with a man or a woman. She has had only a limited experience of intimate relations with both, not feeling particularly fulfilled or desirous of repetition. And she doesn't feel there is anything wrong with or lacking in her. This is just who she is.

The office is in an old building, poorly heated with ancient plumbing, but the rent is cheap. The grocer lives with his wife and adult daughter on the floor above, so the bathroom is really only used by Nuray, Mohammed and the in and out volunteers to the magazine. They have a key and can keep it locked, but it is more trouble than it is worth, so they leave it open for ease of use. They are the only ones to use the second floor.

Nuray looks into the cracked and somewhat distorted mirror. Aside from the faults of the mirror, she looks weary. She throws cold water on her face and brushes her teeth. She readjusts her headscarf. Only a slight improvement, she thinks. Well, it will have to do for today.

Nuray wonders if her pallor reflects the anxiety she is feeling. When she really thinks about it, the political scene has been worsening for some time now. People have been lowering their voices when expressing their opinions, if they dare to express them at all. She knows that there have been arrests for speaking out against Erdoğan and his policies. The climate has been dangerous for many months, even for several years. But I am insignificant, she consoles herself, why would they even bother with me?

Nuray smooths out her wrinkled clothing, zips her cosmetic bag and heads back to the office. She is surprised to see the two student volunteers have arrived. They are already busily working at their laptops. Nuray nods hello to the young man and woman and motions to Mohammed to step out into the hallway with her. Mohammed shuts the door behind them.

"I'm sorry to involve you in this thing with the soldier," Nuray says.

"He's a soldier?" Mohammed shakes his head back and forth in irritation. " I don't like this at all. Who knows what he's up to. Why did you even speak to him?"

"He was standing to the side, not in a group. I thought I might get him to tell me what was going on." Nuray plays with a button on her blouse. Mohammed is so tense. Should she be more worried about this than she is already?

"And so, you took his picture?" Mohammed's large hands are gesturing his question. "What were you thinking?"

"That was after he pocketed my press card. I only wanted to show him that I was press, and he grabbed it out of my hand. Taking his picture was a reflex. I didn't think about it at all. I just wanted to get my card back." Nuray realizes she is loosening her button and lowers her hand. "I'm so sorry, Mohammed. I really am."

"*Tamam*, okay. There's nothing to do about it now except to get the card back. He said 8:00?"

"Yes, I'm sorry again. That is probably when you eat dinner."

Mohammed doesn't respond to another apology. "I'm thinking I should get there early, take a seat and order something, just in case he is already there and sees me come in so close to 8:00. It might make him suspicious."

"That's a good idea, my friend. Thank you. And please, not a word of this to anyone."

"*Tabii*, of course. But if this goes any further, we go to the police."

Nuray knows better than to argue, but she has no trust for the police. Knowing Mohammed, she finds this ultimatum unexpected. Right now she just needs him to show up. If anything goes awry, they can argue it out later.

When they go back into the office, the two students are in conversation.

"Do you really think we need to worry?" the young female student, Zeynep asks. She is tall and slender with long, dirty blond hair. She reminds Nuray of a young willow tree.

Alp, a short, stocky young man, lowers his voice when he sees Nuray and Mohammed enter. "Yes, I do think so."

"But we're so small and insignificant," Zeynep protests.

Alp lowers his head and returns to his laptop screen.

"Okay," Nuray calls to everyone. "Let's talk. Let's have a meeting. Here, pull up your chairs around my desk. Mohammed, you sit next to me over here. One by one, I want to know what you know and what you are thinking. Alp, it looks like you have been searching and reading online, so we'll start with you. And please be honest with me and tell me exactly what you are thinking and feeling. These are dangerous times. We need to be—no pun intended—on the same page."

The meeting goes on longer than Nuray intends. At some point, Zeynep gets up and puts water and tea into the *çaydanlık,* the double boiler teapot used for making Turkish black tea. Both Alp and Zeynep have been online most of the night prior and this morning. No one has had much sleep and they are all highly charged and anxious. Alp expresses more apprehension regarding their safety than Zeynep who in her youth and naivete is full of bluster and rebellion.

"You really ought to be more aware," Alp tries to warn her.

"Please, Alp. Don't you think he's overreacting, Nuray? No offense, but we're not *The New Yorker.* Erdoğan doesn't even know we exist. Gülen doesn't even know we exist. They're going to go after the Kurdish press first, the pro-Kurdish papers, and we're a women's magazine." Zeynep turns to Nuray for support. When Nuray does not respond, Zeynep gets up to pour the tea. She returns with four glasses on a tray with a bowl of sugar and a tiny sugar spoon.

After they are settled with their tea, Alp persists. "But we do print articles that can be considered political. That's the only reason I'm even working here. I wouldn't be working for a simple women's magazine." Alp's expression of disgust at this idea is clear. "And Nuray did a couple of pieces on Erdoğan, you know that, and they certainly weren't complimentary."

"No, they weren't," Mohammed interjects, "but would the government take the time to read our little magazine? We're insignificant compared to the larger presses. I can't say that we should not be careful from now on, and I wouldn't want to promise that no one will come after us, but right at this moment I'm not terribly concerned."

"Look," Nuray says, noting that her left hand is beginning to twitch again and stilling it with her other before she can spill her tea; she refuses to allow her magazine to fall apart. This is her life in the balance. "I can't afford to pay you much, but if you're willing to stay, I'll come up with something. It's a lot for us to handle by ourselves. We do appreciate all that you do. But if you're worried for your safety, I don't blame you. And if you do have any connections to the Gülen people, you might want to think twice before committing to staying on here."

"I'm not going anywhere," Zeynep proclaims, "but a few lira won't hurt."

The room is silent. Alp rubs his forehead. "I have to think, Nuray. My *anne* cleans houses for rich people to pay for my school fees. You know, my *baba* died many years ago, and she never remarried. I'm her only child. If anything happens to me—well, I just have to think about it."

"We understand," Nuray nods to Mohammed.

"Of course, we do," he agrees.

"Let me know what you decide when you're ready, Alp. Okay, let's get back to work. We have an issue to get out by the end of the month, and this coup will be the feature story, naturally. We need to get to work on the facts. We're getting a lot of conflicting information."

Nuray ends the meeting and settles in to do some research and writing. Mohammed leans down to whisper, before he returns to his own computer, "I hope Alp doesn't quit, *Mashallah*."

Nuray smiles but does not respond. Alp quitting or not, there is much work to do. And Zeynep will find a friend as enthusiastic and unwitting as she is to join their team. She already offered a month ago. Nuray told her no, as the office is too small for even four people. But if Alp does decide to leave, Nuray is confident that he can be replaced. Maybe not well replaced, but replaced.

The magazine has always had a high turnover of student volunteers. Although Nuray could not get along without them, she has learned not to get too attached to any of them. They come for the experience, ask for a letter of reference, and move on to jobs that actually pay. The turnover is a nuisance, as the students need constant training, but Nuray is reluctant to hire when she is never confident of sales and revenue. Her mother left her the house and enough funds to live on, albeit not extravagantly. Nuray is frugal by nature; buying books is her largest expense. If she has to forgo more salary, so be it.

The day passes with much frustration. Nuray knows that there are two sides to every story, but this failed coup of 2016 has two definitive scenarios that are extraordinarily different. Erdoğan and his supporters are insisting that the attempted coup originated with now American-based, neo-Ottoman cleric and scholar Fethullah Gülen and his followers. Of course, Gülen and his followers deny any such involvement. As far as Nuray understands, the Hizmet movement is an organization focused on education and culture based on Sufi and Muslim teachings. She has not known them to be political in any way.

Nuray's phone buzzes insistently. She really does need to change her ring tone. Adalet's name and number pop up on the screen. No time for that now, she thinks. I'll talk to her later.

Nuray knows many reporters with connections to the Hizmet movement, and she begins to put in calls to find out what she can. She is only able to get one person to answer his phone.

"*Merhaba,* Ahmet. How are you?" Nuray asks, relieved to hear a human voice after leaving a dozen messages.

"*Merhaba,* Nuray. Things are pretty chaotic here right now, as you can imagine. What can I do for you?" Ahmet's voice indicates that he is unwilling to linger or exchange pleasantries.

"What can you tell me about this craziness? What do you know?" Nuray is persistent.

"I don't know a hell of a lot about the actual facts. We're trying to get them. What I think is that a faction of military tried to overthrow the rest of the military and army behind Erdoğan. The Gülen people haven't had anything to do with it. It's just a golden opportunity for Erdoğan to get back at his one-time best friend and now his best enemy. He's playing his political cards. That's what I think, anyway. Truth may be hard to get at. I've got to run, friend. The phones are ringing off the hook here and my cell has dozens of messages. Stay safe."

"Thanks, Ahmet." He disconnects the call before the "Ahmet" is completely out of Nuray's mouth.

What do I print? Nuray asks herself. Two sides, two interpretations of the truth. Okay, I'll write them both, even though it does seem a prime reason for targeting Gülen. The Muslim Sufi cleric was smart enough to get out of Turkey when he did, Nuray thinks. If he were not in Pennsylvania now, in the United States, the police would be bringing him lunch in jail.

Nuray looks over and sees that Alp is deep into a conversation on his cell phone. He is arguing with whoever is on the other end of the line. She is unable to read lips and cannot hear what he is saying, but he hangs up rather abruptly and walks over to her desk.

"That was my *anne* on the phone. She is begging me to come home and to stay out of all of this."

"So what did you tell her?" Nuray asks, deleting a line from her script before looking up at him.

"You know, Nuray, I am a good son. I only do one thing my *anne* disapproves of and that is studying to be a journalist. My *anne* is very conservative. For her, being involved with politics is equal to death. How, she asks me, can I avoid politics as a journalist? I tell her, I cannot. This is our quarrel. She is always afraid for me."

"I understand," Nuray says. "Don't worry."

"No, no," Alp tells her, one hand gesturing in the air, to his mother or to Allah, Nuray can only guess. "I have made a decision. This is a time that will not come again. I am going to stay."

"Good," Nuray claps her hands. "Now get back to work. And Alp, don't be too sure about this time not coming again. Think of history. We've had more coups in this country than I can count on one hand. It seems to be the only way we know to change the government." Nuray gives Alp what she hopes is an ironic grin and returns to her computer. Well, that is one problem solved, she supposes. There are too many not so easily resolved.

CHAPTER 6

Alp has left the office early to pick up office supplies for everyone. Zeynep is gathering her things to leave. Mohammed is buried behind his small desk in one small corner. Nuray looks up at them.

"I'm not getting many return calls," she announces.

"If they're smart," Mohammed quips without looking away from his screen, "they're all on their way to the airport or have left the country. I wish I could leave."

"Don't be silly. You would never want to leave in the middle of all of this action."

Mohammed gives Nuray a long, hard look. "That's you, my friend, not me. I have a wife and two children to consider."

Nuray starts to say she is sorry again and stops herself. Mohammed is a grown man. He is able to make his own decisions. She cannot continue to feel guilty for involving him. He certainly has the capacity to say no.

Nuray shuts down her computer and decides to go home for a shower and a change of clothing and perhaps a real meal. The clothing she brought with her to Adalet's was meant for hanging around the apartment and is not at all suitable for going to the café tonight. A shower and a nap, if she can allow herself to sleep, would go a long way towards giving her a better edge against the evening's challenges.

The streets have returned to normal for the time being. Erdoğan is holding on to his government and beginning to arrest everyone suspicious of trying to upend it. All Nuray can hope for is that her magazine is not on anyone's target list.

What was once Nuray's mother's apartment and now is hers alone, is on the Asian side of Istanbul, not too far from the magazine's office. Tired and grubby from lack of sleep and a shower, Nuray takes a taxi back to the modest two-bedroom home in which she has lived her whole life. Surrounded by similar structures, hasty wooden construction, just five-stories tall, Nuray's apartment is situated on the third floor, most convenient for when the elevator is not working. Fortunately, today it is working and empty of passengers.

Nuray drops her belongings on the floor in front of #3C. She searches for the housekey in her bag which she has hooked onto a large blue *hamsa* with an eye to ward off evil glued onto the middle. This is, she acknowledges, a silly and superstitious sort of keychain, but one that makes it so much easier for her to find her keys.

The apartment is stuffy in the summer heat, and Nuray opens a window and turns on a fan to refresh the living room. She now occupies what once was her mother's bedroom, using her old one as an office/guest room, although she has never had an overnight guest. She dumps her laptop and knapsack on the desk and goes straight to her bedroom to strip off her clothing and get into the shower. There is only one bathroom in the apartment, as it is an older building. A master bath in the bedroom is a thing of the future in this neighborhood, if it is ever to be. There is no fan either, and so Nuray must leave the door ajar if she wishes to be able to see in the mirror after she showers.

Inconveniences aside, Nuray is grateful for her home. The maintenance is very low and affordable. The kitchen leaves a lot to be desired in terms of modern appliances, but Nuray rarely prepares food for herself. She brings in prepared food or cooks very simply. Her mother was an astounding cook. Nuray does not know how she managed under such primitive conditions. Oh, how she misses those homemade dishes. But Nuray has neither the time nor the inclination. This is why she so appreciates Adalet's efforts.

Nuray prefers living on the Asian side of Istanbul, in any event, as tourism has saturated the European side. She could never afford to live there, even if she wanted to do so. Adalet had offered her one of her apartments, but it had made no sense to Nuray. She lives and works on the Asian side where she, honestly, feels more Turkish. She is more able to avoid the Europeans and Americans who frequent the other side.

And the Russians, Nuray reflects, as she allows the shower jets to massage her body. There are so many of them living in Istanbul now. Well, not so many in comparison to the influx of the Syrians. So many Syrians. Suddenly there are all of these groups of women in burkas parading through the streets of Istanbul. The Syrian civil war has changed Istanbul forever. She has seen little Syrian businesses growing up all over and realizes that these refugees of war have no intentions of returning.

The shower feels so rejuvenating on her skin that Nuray hesitates to end the pulsating flow of water. Well, she reflects, I wouldn't want to go back to that ravaged country either. I can hardly blame them. Syria is done for. She finally turns off the water, pushes back the shower curtain and steps out of the tub to dry herself. The tub is old and stained from hard water. It has not been used since her mother died six years ago. When she wants a soothing bath, she visits the *hamam*.

Nuray wraps herself in a terrycloth robe and soft slippers and makes her way to the kitchen. She opens the refrigerator to a series of containers that have accumulated from takeout food over the prior week. Some okra and green beans will work mixed into some scrambled eggs. Since she never made it to the market, whatever is around will have to do. Nuray chops some garlic and slices an onion into a frying pan with hot olive oil. She cracks two eggs into a bowl, scrambles them and tosses them in with the garlic and onions. Nuray pinches off some oregano, red pepper, cumin, and sumac. This will do. When the eggs are just about cooked, she throws in the leftover okra and green beans. Not bad, she thinks, as she pours it onto a plate.

Settling down at her small table in the adjoining dining area, Nuray checks the laptop that she has carried in from her home office. She opens it to the various newspapers she reads on a daily basis. The newspapers are still operating, although there is chatter of pending raids. The Internet is filled with chatter. Opposition television stations have been shut down or taken over. Nuray pushes the laptop aside to attempt to concentrate on her food. She hears her mother telling her to do this. She takes several bites and pulls the laptop back over. She works through most of her meals, she acknowledges, mother's lecturing voice or not. This is who she is.

When her *anne* was living, Nuray tried her best to adapt to Sema's ways. When Sema became ill with both rheumatoid and osteoarthritis, Nuray's father disappeared. His beautiful Turkish wife was suddenly bent over and disfigured. He packed one suitcase of clothing, shoes and toiletries, nothing else. Sema was too incapacitated to look for him, and she told Nuray that if he wanted to be found, he would turn up. He never did, even when Sema passed away. Nuray hates her father for abandoning them, and so she has never attempted to locate him. But Sema became so frail and vulnerable that Nuray adjusted her life to make her *anne* comfortable in every way that she could. Now she finds herself sometimes listening to her *anne's* voice, even though she is no longer there.

"Please hang up your jacket, Nuray dear. There's no need to leave it thrown over the chair."

Nuray hangs up her jacket these days as if her mother is standing there asking her to do so. She washes her dishes instead of leaving them in the sink and makes her bed, actually taking more care with certain aspects of the apartment than she ever did when her mother was alive. But there are towers of books and articles piled everywhere, much like the columns of blocks Nuray once created as a child. This was something she could not do when her mother was living. The piles have grown with every passing year.

Nuray knows that she inhabits a cloister of collecting irrelevance, even to her, but to sort it out now feels beyond her. Almost nothing ever makes its way to the trash bin. And she has to admit that there is something comforting in the accumulation of books and papers. You never know when you might need something.

The shower, combined with the food, soothe both Nuray's mind and body. She stretches out on the couch in her robe and falls into a deep sleep. When the phone begins to beep, Nuray reaches out, thinking it is her alarm, and tries to shut it off. Just before the disconnection occurs, she sees that it is Mohammed and immediately calls him back.

"Where are you?" he asks.

"On my couch," Nuray almost shouts into the phone, still not quite awake and jolted by the nerve-wracking sound of her phone ring—she really must change the ring to something less jarring—she lowers her voice. "Sorry, Mohammed, I was sound asleep. What time is it, anyway?"

"It's after 6:00. You'd better get ready to leave for the café."

"You're right. I just need to throw on some clothes. I'm so glad you called. I might have slept through the meeting."

Mohammed grunts. "That might not have been a bad thing. So he has your press card. So what? He could have found it on the ground where you dropped it."

"But I didn't drop it, did I? Are you backing out? I would understand if you did." No, I wouldn't, Nuray thinks. But she has to say so anyway.

"No, I'm not backing out. I told you I'd be there, and I will. But please don't pull any funny stunts and whatever you do, do not leave the café with him. I can't follow you all over town." Nuray can hear one of Mohammed's children in the background not sounding very happy about something his mother has said.

"I have no intention of going anywhere with him. I'm not stupid." How stupid is she being at this very moment, Nuray wonders? She takes a deep breath. Should she tell Mohammed to forget the whole thing? He is right, after all. She could have just as easily dropped the press card. She could just apply for a new one. What is the big deal?

But instead, Nuray says rapidly into the phone, "See you there," and presses the phone off. There is something more in it for her. She is curious. Her curiosity is her biggest asset, as well as her biggest downfall. She almost got thrown in jail once before when her curiosity took her to a protest for women's rights. She ended up with a black eye—that same eye also stung with tear gas—as well as a very sore knee that took a hit from a policeman's night stick. She had barely managed to escape being thrown into the police wagon.

She forces herself up from the couch and into her bedroom closet to find something appropriate to wear. She selects a pair of wide purple silk pants, a long-sleeved matching purple jacket, a white shell to wear underneath it, and a purple head scarf just a shade lighter. Satisfied that her outfit is sophisticated without being flashy—or sexy; Nuray actually has nothing in her wardrobe to qualify in either category—she finds an innocuous pair of black flats to finish off the outfit. She sets the shoes down by the door and returns to the bedroom to survey her appearance in the mirror that is attached to the back of her bedroom door.

Liking what she sees, her slim figure gracefully carrying the silk fabric, she smiles and then frowns. For Allah's sake, she admonishes herself, this isn't a date. It's a blackmail.

Nuray returns to her closet, pulls out a simple pair of black pants, a long gray jacket and changes. She substitutes a gray scarf with a slight pattern to cover her hair. What was I thinking? she scolds herself. I was getting dressed up to be blackmailed? Is Adalet right? Do I need a man in my life? Certainly not a Turkish soldier. No, no, she shakes her head. What she needs is to read more good literature and watch less soap opera-like series on television.

She stands again in front of the mirror. Now she looks like a journalist scurrying off to collect a story. This is who she is. She gives herself a cocky smile, grabs her purse and keys from the table, slides her phone into the purse, slips on her shoes and is out the door. It is just 7:15, and she has a full 45 minutes to get to the café. She could make it in time taking public transportation, but the last couple of days have cramped her style and her mood. Instead, she walks to the taxi stand and climbs into a cab. "Istiklal Street," she directs the driver. She is blowing her whole budget on taxis today, but the whole country is coming apart. What one does in a coup is not the same as what one does in normal times.

CHAPTER 7

The streets are quieter than usual. *İstiklal Caddesi* is normally bustling at this hour, as the avenue is lined with side streets of cafes and restaurants and bars usually packed with tourists and residents alike. Although, Nuray reflects, the surge of Syrians and the complications and dangers of the war are changing the face of Istanbul. American tourism is all but disappearing. European traffic has slowed considerably. The long, flowing garments of the devout Syrian women give the city a more exotic but darker quality. What was becoming Western is now becoming more Eastern. Some of these women are still out in fashionable heels, but more and more can be seen in worn and torn sneakers. The sign of refugee is clearly written there, as are the signs of desperation and poverty. Nuray understands that she is losing the Istanbul she loves.

The café that the soldier has selected is almost empty. A couple of German tourists are having tapas and beer. Nuray worries that Mohammed's presence will stand out here. They do not acknowledge one another as she passes. He is sitting at a table by the door.

The maître d', a tall, slender well-dressed man in his forties, Nuray guesses, greets her and tells her to sit wherever she would like. She takes a table off to the side and towards the back. She has not thought of this until now, but she wonders if the soldier will be carrying a gun. When the waitress comes over, she orders a hot *çay*. Since it is the hour for tapas and drinks, the waitress gives her a questioning look as if to say, is that all? But Nuray looks away and makes no comment.

Nuray pulls out her phone and glances at the time. Ten minutes after 8:00. There is no sign of him. The tea arrives and she sips it slowly. She glances around at the café. The photographs lining the walls speak to earlier times. A man who Nuray guesses to be the owner is shown in several photographs, one by himself and one with a beautiful woman Nuray supposes to be his wife. In both photos he is wearing the same dark suit. His thick head of dark hair and full mustache depict the concept of the typical Turkish male. The man and woman do not look at each other, but straight ahead at the camera, an old-fashioned portrait photo. On the other side of the wall is a photo of Erdoğan. Nuray is not sure why, but she instantly thinks of Chairman Mao, a fleeting thought but one that makes her smile. Perhaps it is the solid posture of utter confidence. Does the café owner think that displaying a photograph of Erdoğan will keep him from harm? Probably. The café does serve liquor, so the owner is a businessman, whether he himself drinks or not. These distractions do not lower Nuray's anxiety for long. She folds her napkin into a smaller and smaller square.

Nuray startles when the door abruptly opens. Two husky young men rush in, arguing, shouting too loud about a recent soccer match. The waitress knows them and tells them to sit where they like. Nuray speculates that the waitress is probably a member of the owner's family. The young men order drinks and tapas and continue their heated discussion.

It is now 8:20. Nuray looks over at Mohammed. He has ordered something, she cannot tell what it is. He has opened a book and appears to be reading. Good, Nuray thinks. He doesn't look in the least suspicious. When she thinks about it, she is the only suspicious looking person in the café.

The door opens again. Nuray catches her breath. There is her soldier, dressed as a civilian, in jeans and a black t-shirt underneath a black nylon windbreaker. He looks even younger than he did on the Square. Feeling all of her thirty-eight years pressing down on her, Nuray watches the soldier walk toward her, pull out the chair across from her, and seat himself. This close, his youth makes him appear a bit nervous, less confident than he seemed at the Square. In place of any facial hair, his chalky complexion is dotted with several angry-looking pimples. But his eyes are cold, unreadable.

And now, as he speaks, he dispels any impression of youthful innocence. "So, here you are. You are looking for this." He reaches in a jacket pocket and places the press card on the table, closer to him than to Nuray. She has to lean across the table to recover it. As she extends her arm, the soldier presses his hand down on hers.

"Not so fast," he says.

Nuray snatches her hand away in obvious anger. "Okay, what do you want?"

"You can have it," he says, pushing the card over to her.

Nuray snatches the card up before he can reclaim it. She puts it away in her purse.

"Yes, put it away. I have all the information I need, anyway." He is smug now and confident. Whatever minimal boyish good looks he possesses are lost in his demeanor. All Nuray can think of is a Nazi white supremacist, even though he is clearly Turkish.

Nuray looks directly at him and repeats, "What do you want?"

He stares at her. "I want to come to your apartment."

Nuray glares back at him. "And what would you want in my apartment?"

He laughs, a nasty sound that further distorts his face.

The waitress comes over to the table. "What can I get you?" she asks the soldier.

He slowly shifts his gaze from Nuray to the waitress. "A Pilsner," he says, immediately looking back to Nuray. The waitress leaves to fill his order.

"So," Nuray repeats, "what do you want?"

"I will be blunt," the soldier tells her. "I want to sleep with you."

"And if I refuse?" By this time, Nuray has figured out that she is being sexually harassed. She is being blackmailed for sex. This seems so impossible as to almost feel ridiculous. So why is she feeling afraid?

"Your father is an interesting fellow," the soldier smirks. "I looked him up."

"My father?" Nuray is shocked. "I haven't seen or heard from my father in years."

"That makes no difference. You are all on the same side now. You are both with Gülen. You are both against Erdoğan. This I know."

"I don't know anything about my father." Nuray can hear her heart beating. Her left hand begins to tremble again. She moves it to her lap and covers it with her other hand. This situation is more dangerous than she first thought. Has her father gotten himself into some political difficulties that are going to affect her? She never even thinks about him anymore.

"But I do know things about your father," the soldier says.

The waitress returns with the soldier's beer. "Do you want a glass?" she asks.

"No, thank you." He flashes a charming smile at the waitress. The waitress smiles back and leaves them.

"You will not be coming to my apartment," Nuray hisses at him. "If my father has done something wrong, he will have to pay for it. You can't protect him anyway. And I have done nothing illegal. I am not associated in any way with Gülen, or with my father."

"Maybe I can't protect anyone," the soldier says as he swallows a gulp of beer, "but I can bring something to someone's attention that wasn't there before. That is easy these days. You don't care about your father, but the police will. And if he is arrested, anyone with subversive ideas and connected to him will also be arrested. You can bet on that. You may not know that now, but you will." He takes another drink from his beer and sets it down emphatically. He signals for the waitress. In the meantime, he takes a piece of paper from his pocket and sets it on the table near Nuray. "This is how you can reach me," he tells her.

"Separate checks," he informs the waitress when she comes to the table. He pulls out a credit card which he hands to her. She looks at Nuray.

"I'm fine, too," Nuray says. She reaches into her purse and pulls out a credit card which she hands to the waitress.

The soldier and Nuray stare at one another.

"You'd better take that with you; then destroy it." He looks at the untouched paper on the table. "Your magazine is insignificant and might go unnoticed now. But police are getting perks for bringing in people sympathetic to Hizmet and people speaking out against Erdoğan, not that you would do that, of course." He grins sarcastically.

The waitress returns with their checks. The soldier signs his, pockets his credit card and drains the last of his beer. He pushes himself up from the table, leans over it threateningly, and says, "I'll give you a few days to think it over. You'll see what's happening and come to your senses. Just one night, and I won't bother you anymore. I promise." He pushes in his chair and turns and walks away before Nuray can respond.

Mohammed meets Nuray outside of the restaurant. "Let's walk," Nuray says, trying to regain her breath and slow her rapidly beating heart before speaking. Mohammed adapts his stride to hers and is silent, waiting for Nuray to gather her thoughts. Finally, she blurts out, "He wants me. He is threatening me for my body. He says we're too small to be noticed by the government, but he will bring us to their attention. He also seems to have some information about my father being some source of concern to me. I have no idea about any of that. I haven't seen or heard from my father in years."

"He's doing all this to have sex with you?" Mohammed is incredulous. "Why?"

"I have no idea," Nuray's hand begins to shake again. "I must be ten years older than he is, and I don't kid myself into thinking I'm some great beauty." She stills the shaking hand with the other one, but not without noticing that Mohammed has observed her gesture. He watches but does not comment.

"It's not about the sex," he says finally. "It's about power. If you give in, he'll never leave you alone, no matter what he says."

"I have no intention of giving in to him," Nuray says, releasing the now stilled hand. "But I do want to find out about my father. Let's do some research on him tomorrow and on this soldier. He gave me his information, so let's see if we can dig up anything useful. Maybe we can find something to use against him so that he will decide it's best to leave me alone. In these times, we don't want the unnecessary attention. It could prove to be damaging to us and to the magazine."

"I agree," Mohammed tells her. "Let's see what we can find. We don't need a raid, and we definitely don't want to be hauled off to jail. They have much bigger fish to fry, but they don't seem to care these days. I can't afford to be arrested."

"Me either." Nuray stops at a taxi stand. "Do you want to ride with me to the other side?"

"Thanks, no," Mohammed replies. "I have a few things to pick up for dinner before I go home. I'll see you first thing tomorrow. Text me the soldier's info when you get home so that I can get to work first thing."

"I'll text it from the taxi," Nuray says, waving a hand at a cab by the curb. "Be careful, my friend, and thank you for being there tonight."

"No problem," Mohammed retorts, already turning and walking in the opposite direction.

Nuray climbs into the taxi, gives the man her address, and texts the soldier's information to Mohammed. She takes in a deep breath. She is truly afraid.

CHAPTER 8

There is a bit of comfort in being back in her home, although Nuray finds herself nervously pulling up Adalet's number. The hour is late, but she needs a friend. Adalet's hello is sleepy, but Nuray relaxes at the sound of her voice.

"Did I wake you? I'm sorry. Do you want me to call you back tomorrow?" Nuray is apologetic.

"No," Adalet says, "that's okay. I was worried about you. I tried to call you earlier, but you didn't pick up. The police have been arresting all kinds of people, anyone they think might speak out against the government. It's really scary now. I hope you are being careful."

Nuray immediately decides not to tell Adalet anything, especially not over what may be a compromised line. She has not thought about this possibility until this moment, and even now it seems silly, but her level of suspicion is increasing steadily. She must be judicious in how much she reveals to Adalet. It is enough that Mohammed is questioning her safety.

"Of course, I am always careful," Nuray responds. "I just didn't want you to worry. We are a small-time publication. We aren't *Cumhuiyet*. They might have something to be concerned about, but we are tiny. They won't waste their time on us."

"Well, please be cautious in any event." Adalet admonishes. "I don't want to have to visit you in jail."

"No chance of that," Nuray says, thinking to herself that there might be more chance of that than she could have imagined just twenty-four hours ago. "Go back to sleep," she adds. "I'll call you tomorrow. Good night."

"Good night," Adalet mumbles.

Nuray switches off her phone. No matter what the cause, she wants an uninterrupted night's sleep. She must be thinking clearly tomorrow. Perhaps more editing is required on the coup article she has planned to publish. She might need to tone down her condemnation of Erdoğan's government and his tactics. Even though this is just the response the government hopes to achieve, she has to stay out of jail in order to continue to publish. The magazine will die without her. She has worked too hard and too long.

The soldier knows where she lives. He has successfully raised her anxiety. This is just what he wants. Would he try to break in and rape her? Nuray double locks her door, but just in case, props a kitchen chair under the knob. She puts a kitchen knife under her pillow and places her cell phone there as well. She feels that she is overreacting, behaving something like a character in a bad Turkish soap opera. But isn't it better to overprepare than to fall prey due to her lack of precaution? She does not believe that sleep will come easily, but as soon as her exhausted head hits the pillow, she is sound asleep.

There is a loud crash on the street outside that jolts Nuray upright and out of bed. Doors slam and there are raised voices in the building next door. Nuray throws on a robe and makes her way to the window and watches two policemen walking an elderly man in pajamas and a bathrobe to a police car. She sees that he has been handcuffed. There isn't enough light for her to recognize the man, if she even knows him, and things happen very quickly. He is pushed inside of the car, the door is slammed, and the officers climb in and drive away. She is unsure from which building he was taken.

Nuray checks the time on her phone display. It is 4:10 a.m. She has only been asleep for a few hours. Why was her neighbor arrested in the middle of the night? And who is he? What did he do, or what do they think he did? Why didn't they even let him get dressed before taking him in?

Nuray lies on her bed, flat on her back, still wrapped in her bathrobe. How can life be one thing one day, and without any warning, become something else the next? No, she cannot fool herself. The warnings have all been coming for some time. She has simply pushed them aside, refusing to see them. Why has she ignored this possibility until now? She is a single woman, educated yes, but in a male-dominated profession that is now being overtaken by an autocratic regime.

Nuray folds her arms behind her head. What are her options? She has no family other than a missing father. There are no wealthy friends of influence to buy her way out of a jam, if in fact she is in one. She can appeal to no one to pay a bribe should she be arrested. She hesitates. Perhaps her father does have money now. Would he help her if she needed him? What would he say if she contacted him at his company? Would that only make things worse for her if he really is connected to a Kurdish movement?

This is all a terrible waste of time, Nuray chides herself. I know absolutely nothing at this point except that I am being sexually harassed. That is enough to deal with for the moment. I hope Mohammed can dig something up on this guy. Maybe he's done this before, and charges have been brought against him. Not likely the courts would do anything, though. Men always get away with this sort of thing.

Maybe I will confide in Adalet, she reasons. Adalet has had to deal with many things in her life, surviving the earthquake and those terrible burns, losing her baby and her husband. Maybe she will have some idea of what I can do. I will try to meet with her tomorrow.

Nuray turns on her side and feels the knife under her pillow. She pulls it out and starts to set it on the floor next to the bed, but just as quickly, she changes her mind and places it back under her pillow.

If I am being silly, no one will know it but me.

CHAPTER 9

Mohammed is worried, a state of mind to which he is unfortunately too well acquainted. He leads a simple life, a family life, devoted to his wife and children. Working with Nuray has been challenging economically but stimulating and free of political infighting and frictional scrambling to get to the top.

Mohammed considers himself to be a good journalist. He knows he could be earning more and possibly making a name for himself. In fact, he was on his way to achieving just that when a colleague made several sexual advances. When he refused her, she became angry and took revenge. She falsely accused him of plagiarizing her work. Although ultimately the woman was unable to prove her allegations, the accusation itself, along with the prolonged time of the incident, left its mark on Mohammed. In his humiliation that he had even been accused, he determined thereafter to maintain a low profile.

Mohammed met Nuray in a journalists' and writers' rendezvous. Café Smyrna, in the midst of this well-known Cihangir neighborhood, is a known hangout for writers and journalists from around the world. Mohammed figured he could possibly run into someone there who could lead him to more obscure work. Mohammed ran into a mutual friend who knew Nuray was searching for someone to help her with her magazine.

Nuray's no nonsense directness and her professionalism impressed Mohammed immediately. He never imagined himself working for a women's magazine, but the advocacy of women's rights attracted him. At first, he struggled with his own history and the concept of working for a woman, but Nuray, with her straight-forward manner and businesslike persona, put his doubts to rest. Mohammed knows that he is attractive to women. He is a tall, slender, but muscular man, with a full head of dark hair and striking features. His large dark eyes and long lashes convey a sexuality that Mohammed does not intend. He understands too well the wrath his rejection can incur. He feels safe with Nuray. And even though his role appears to be shifting somewhat from friend and colleague to protector, he would do the same for a male colleague in a fix. And Nuray is certainly in a fix.

Mohammed takes the soldier's name and does a Google search. Safak Aksoy is easy to find but yields no information of any use. He is twenty-seven and single. He attended an *imam hatip* religious school before entering the military. Mohammed will have to find a way to search out both his school and military records for any possible infractions. Mohammed finds a Safak Aksoy listed as currently residing at the Selimiye Barracks on the Asian side in the Üsküdar district. Mohammed fantasizes hacking into Aksoy's computer. Surely he must have one. He wonders if Alp or Zeynep know anyone who could run a search and do this. Zeynep is a more likely choice. He will speak with her tomorrow.

Mohammed shuts off the desk lamp in his tiny home office. His children share a room in order for him to have this space. Soon they will be too old for this arrangement. Azra is eight, and her little brother Necip is six. They will either have to move or Mohammed will have to give up this tiny allotment of privacy. His wife, Ayşegül, is a secondary school history teacher who had been planning to return to work this year, once Necip settled into school. But the world has just flipped on its side, and Mohammed frankly has no idea what their future will bring.

The children are in bed, and so is Ayşegül. She is reading by the light of a small table lamp. It is another novel by her favorite Turkish writer, Elif Şafak. She places her bookmark in the page and shuts the book.

"Is it a good one?" Mohammed asks.

"She is wonderful. And she is so beautiful, look." Ayşegül shows him the photo on the inside cover.

"Yes, she is pretty, but she cannot hold a candle to you."

Ayşegül switches off the lamp as Mohammed sheds his clothes and slides into bed next to her. They quite naturally gravitate into each other's arms.

Mohammed allows his mind to empty of his worries. It has taken some time to heal the humiliation that the false accusation cost him. He has finally been able to regain some peace of mind with Ayşegül, and with finding work that sustains him. How serious can things really be?

CHAPTER 10

Nuray is the first to arrive at the magazine office the next morning. She is about to call Adalet when she is surprised by her landlord, Mr. Ekmekci, who hesitates halfway into the doorway.

"Am I disturbing you?" he inquires politely.

"No, not at all. Please come in." Nuray is curious, as Mr. Ekmekci is never to be seen other than in his store. Nuray leaves the rent check in an envelope at the register once a month, when they nod to one another and Mr. Ekmekci says thank you.

"Have a seat, please. What can I do for you?" Nuray gestures to a chair on the other side of her disk.

"No, thank you," Mr. Ekmekci says. He is a man in his early sixties who has not taken good care of himself. He is short and stout with unkempt graying hair, a thick mustache and stubby beard. He is always in a grocer's apron over a thick shirt and sloppy loose-fitting trousers. The trousers are often spotted with grease. He steps in closer to speak.

"The newspapers are in trouble," he says. "Offices are being raided and people are being taken off to jail. I hope we're not going to have any of that kind of trouble here." He looks directly into Nuray's eyes. He has never done so up until this moment.

Nuray feels her stomach churn. Mr. Ekmekci is the last person she would ever guess to be questioning her business. He has never taken a bit of interest in anything other than the rent. Nuray's hand begins to tremble. She cannot lose this office space.

"I certainly am not expecting any trouble, Mr. Ekmekci. Do you believe there is some reason I should?"

"No, no. It's just that the government is arresting people everwhere over this attempted coup. All kinds of people. And they are going into businesses and homes and ransacking them looking for evidence. I just don't want any kind of trouble. You can understand. This is my home and my business. I am a simple grocer. I've been here for years, peacefully."

"Of course, I understand. I don't want any trouble, either. I'm a very small publication. I don't think the government even knows I exist, never mind thinks I am plotting against them. That would be ridiculous." Nuray mentally goes over everything she has ever written or said about Erdoğan. But she quickly recovers from this exercise. "I can assure you, Mr. Ekmekci, there won't be any trouble due to my little magazine."

"I am glad to hear that," he says as he backs away from her desk.

Just then Mohammed comes bustling into the office. He stops short at seeing Mr. Ekmekci.

"*Günaydın*, good morning, Mr. Ekmekci."

"*Selam*, Mohammed. Okay, I am leaving now." Mr. Ekmekci negotiates his awkward frame around Mohammed and is out of the tiny space.

"What does he want?" Mohammed asks. "I've never seen him in here before."

"That's because he never comes in here," Nuray replies. She realizes her hand is shaking again. What is this about? Is there something physically wrong, or is she merely reacting to stress? Mohammed is standing in front of her waiting for an answer.

"He's nervous," she finally says.

"About what?" Mohammed moves over to his desk and places his bag down. He throws the light jacket he's wearing over the back of his chair.

"About the coup. About Erdoğan. About us being raided and hauled off to jail. He's afraid of being involved with us because he's our landlord."

Mohammed settles into his chair and begins to remove papers from his bag. "Is he serious? We're such little fish, less than sardines. We have nothing to do with any of this."

Nuray feels that twinge of nausea hitting her again. "Maybe you should have a look at that piece I did on Erdoğan a few months ago and see if I should be concerned. It wasn't complimentary."

"No, it wasn't. But it wasn't suggesting a government takeover either." Mohammed tosses his now empty bag onto the floor. "I don't know, Nuray. I'll have a look at it, but we can't let this stuff make us crazy."

"But with the soldier—"

"I found him," Mohammed interrupts. "Nothing much yet. He's living at the Selimiye Barracks. No criminal history that I can see, but that doesn't mean he's not a criminal."

"Can we find out anything more?" Nuray asks.

"As soon as Zeynep gets here, I'm going to see if she knows any hackers. I'll bet she does." He winks at Nuray.

Nuray laughs. "I'll bet she does, too. Thanks, friend."

"You don't think Mr. Ekmekci will throw us out, do you?" Mohammed asks as an afterthought.

"I hope not," Nuray sighs, then smiles. "Who else is going to rent this dump?"

"Good point." Mohammed turns on his computer and rifles through his papers.

The office is quiet and the two colleagues work steadily for the next hour until Nuray gets up to heat water for çay. When Nuray sets a steaming cup next to Mohammed, she sees that he is reviewing the article that has been concerning her. The article is titled: *Where is Turkey Headed Now?* Nuray received some very positive tweets on the piece, along with a few threatening ones. At the time, the threats were not alarming. How quickly things have changed.

The *çay* helps. Nuray feels her strength returning. She goes to Google and types: Arman Demir. She hesitates for a minute and a sip of *çay* before she hits return. And there it is. Nuray flinches before the more recent photo of her father. Then she stares, transfixed. Her *baba* is definitely older; a thick gray beard now covers his chin, and a salt and pepper mustache overlies his upper lip. His hair is as thick as ever, quite stunning with its silver and black overtones. Nuray has forgotten how handsome her father almost is. His nose, like hers, is thick and distorts the better features. She wonders yet again if it is this nose that has kept her from being pretty. She shakes her head dismissively. What does it even matter? She reads on:

Arman Demir is a rug merchant, importer/exporter of Turkish goods. He travels the silk road where he purchases items for resale in the Western markets. He exports carpets and assorted Turkish goods to Europe, Canada and the Unites States. His distribution center is Tekstil Demir—

Nuray stops reading in amazement. Is her *baba* now a wealthy man? He must own trucks if he is sending carpets to Europe and the United States. He could barely manage the mortgage payments on the apartment when she was a child. She would hear her parents arguing, her *anne* pushing her *baba* to get a regular job. Had her mother been wrong? Her mother never talked about him once he'd gone. Nuray was still uncertain whether he'd abandoned them or her *anne* had asked him to leave. Her *anne* was open and loving on all accounts except for the topic of her *baba*. Nuray understood not to question her *anne* on that subject.

There is contact information for the company listed below and a photo of an elaborate Turkish wedding carpet, maybe eighty or one hundred years old, Nuray guesses. She knows only a little about carpets but enough to know that the one shown is quite valuable.

Nuray plugs in several search engines and finally comes up with an older photo from 1998 that is much more recognizable to her. Her *baba* is clean shaven, looking much younger. He is featured with several others in an article about Turkey's import/export business and how well this business is doing in the western markets. Apparently, he was just establishing himself. Eighteen years ago, Nuray calculates. We sure could have used some help from him in those days.

And then it is as if two wires have connected in her brain. She never questioned how they were able to live in their own apartment when her mother was unable to work. Her mother had been a high school history teacher before she became ill, but certainly it had not been long enough for her to receive benefits. There were government disability checks that came every so often, but surely they could not have paid for the apartment. Had her *baba* contributed? Now she has to wonder. Money was always tight and her *anne* worried a good deal, but they always had enough food and the roof over their heads.

Nuray saves the older of the two photos and goes back to save the first. She wonders if there could be others of him online that would not come up under his name. She googles the company but only gets the same photo and company description. She googles under Turkish textiles. There are hundreds of responses. She stares at the screen before taking some cooled down sips of *çay*. She is getting a completely different picture of Arman Demir. How could he be such a loser in business and have become so successful?

The door to the office bursts open and Zeynep comes through carrying bundles of packages in both arms. Alp follows behind her, equally burdened. Zeynep catches her breath before she says, "We ran into each other downstairs. He was trying to carry all of this by himself, silly man. I don't know how you managed without me." She looks back at Alp and grins, and then drops everything in a pile on the floor in one empty corner.

"Ah, Zeynep, what would any of us do without you?" Alp drops his packages on top of hers. "We have paper now," he says.

Mohammed looks up. "Oh, very good, Zeynep. I've been waiting for you to come in. I need to talk to you after you settle in."

"Sure," she says. She drapes her coat over the packages and pulls up a folding chair next to Mohammed. They proceed in whispers. Nuray knows he will not divulge the situation with the soldier to Zeynep but will quietly extract the name of a good hacker. They are used to private conversations taking place in such small quarters and do not pry unless invited to engage. Alp sorts the packages into piles, proceeding then to stack the supplies into the corner cubbies where they belong.

Nuray returns to the textiles. She scans through them before finding a meeting and a photo that stops her short and sets her heart racing. Arman Demir is shaking hands with an editor from *Zaman*, a newspaper known to have more radical leanings and support for the Kurdish movement. On the other side of her father is another well-known editor from *Zaman*. What is this gathering? Why is her father there? What does this all mean? Her hands dig into her thighs. Nuray reads on:

At a meeting held in Istanbul in September 1999, media and merchants meet to discuss how Turkey is moving ahead in the International market scene, how Turkish goods are becoming so popular to Westerners and how the media can encourage the Turkish economy to succeed. Merchants and the media working together to promote the economy is the idea of one up and coming Istanbul merchant, Arman Demir.

The article goes on to say that Demir approached *Zaman* and was able to arrange for this meeting with several other merchants and media outlets in order to promote sales and for appeals to sponsor events for tourism. *Let us take the tourists to the factories and villages and interest them in how these goods are made. We can show them how our village women are able to make a good living by producing these carpets and other goods. The history of the carpet making process will be of compelling interest to them, and they will want to bring them back to their countries.*

Not a bad idea, *Baba*, Nuray thinks. I wonder, do the tourists know how many lira the women are earning and how many hours they are working? Now you are going to encourage strangers from other countries to stare at them while they work? Will you pay them additional money for that? The exploitation of women in Turkey is her magazine's prime raison d'etre. And her own father has been exploiting women to enrich his pockets. *Zaman*—she considers. They have been outspoken against Erdoğan and his policies. Perhaps this is what the soldier meant when he brought up her father. Is he actually connected with Gülen?

Nuray closes the site, afraid that she might see more incriminating information. This has been enough to set her on a precarious and jagged edge. What a dreadful couple of days. And suppose Mr. Ekmekci does decide to evict them? Can he? Of course he can. She doesn't even have a legitimate lease. What so recently felt like solid ground is quickly erupting into an earthquake.

CHAPTER 11

Safak Aksoy wrestles with the laces of his right boot. His time in the military is not easy. He has never been any good at following orders. Continuously in trouble at home and in school, not particularly talented at anything, he finds he can just about tread water well enough to remain afloat in the army.

Safak's father used his calloused fists on him regularly, so he is no stranger to violence masquerading as discipline, not that he has ever responded well to this technique. He knows that the physical beatings from his *baba*, or the recurrent fear of them, has never successfully taught him the lessons for which they were supposedly intended. He doesn't learn from the abuse he receives in the army either, but he takes it like a man (his father's words). He has no expectations for promotion. Staying alive and getting out with his honor reasonably intact are his only goals.

On the other side of the Safak persona, he has been pampered and spoiled by his *anne*. She continues to indulge him when he is able to go home. Now that he is too big for his father to manhandle him, the two men create as much space as is possible between them. While his *anne* is busy preparing all of his favorite foods, his *baba* either slinks off to another room to sulk, or he wanders off to the closest coffee house.

Safak's parents still live in the apartment where he was born, the same rickety house in which he and his older brother were raised, in the old neighborhood of Kasımpaşa. His father, Ali Aksoy, worked on the docks in the harbor there for many years until his overused and injured back left him dependent on disability. Safak's mother, Zehra, has only worked cleaning houses or babysitting. She does very little of that now.

Safak's older brother by two years has slipped away from all contact with the family. After some petty, and then not so petty thefts, along with unfortunate ill-conceived schemes to depart single women from their money, Altan did a couple of years in prison. Safak could not believe how quickly his brother became radicalized there. He was out only two weeks before announcing he was leaving for Syria to train for ISIS. Safak wonders if either of his parents tried to stop him. Safak certainly did not. If he is honest with himself, he was glad to see him go. He never liked Altan anyway. The two boys used to vie for their mother's attentions, each brother thrusting the blame on the other for anything that could result in a thrashing from their father. This has never been a loving or happy household. Safak knows his *anne* only remains with his *baba* because she has nowhere else to go.

Safak sees the plight of his *anne* and resents women like Nuray Demir all the more for it. Why should that woman have a job, a business of her own, while his own mother remains uneducated and without means? His *anne* is forced to accept all the degradations her husband dishes out just to have a roof over her head and food on her table.

Safak tightens the laces of his other boot and pushes himself up from the lower bunk he has claimed since its occupant was called to the fight in Syria. Safak hates the barracks, hates the other men with whom he is relegated to sharing this space, hates his superior officer, hates his father, his brother and almost every aspect of his life. But right now, he is focused on hating Nuray Demir.

Why does Safak wish to have sexual relations with this woman he despises? He simply wants to humiliate her. And why? Not even Safak can give a good answer for that. The hatred itself is enough.

Safak pulls out his laptop computer from underneath his bunk. He sets it on his lap and turns it on. When he presses his online server, he waits and waits some more. Why is it taking so long, he wonders? Finally, a pop-up for Viagra flashes on his screen with a full-breasted naked woman smiling at a cartoon drawing of an erect penis. What is this? Safak swears at the screen. He tries to delete the ad which refuses to go away. He shuts down the computer and reboots. Again, he waits, becomes impatient, and juggles the computer up and down on his knees. As soon as he is online, another equally lascivious ad pops up onto his screen. In under a minute, the first ad pops up again. He is unable to delete either of them.

"*Orospu çocuğu,* son of a bitch," Safak shouts. "*Orospu,* the bitch hacked me."

One of Safak's bunkmates looks up from the book he is reading while lying on his bed. Other than this one fellow, all the men are out on duty. Safak is supposed to be with them. "What's going on, Safak," he asks, "computer problems?"

"Nothing," Safak grumbles. He has not noticed this man until now. Safak thought he was alone which is why he has chosen this time of day to be here. He checks for an email from Nuray Demir. There is nothing. He slams the computer closed knowing he must now choose another form of encryption and protection to keep her, or whoever has done this, from breaking in again. Whoever did this is pretty damned good, he begrudgingly must acknowledge. He is so careful.

Safak thrusts the laptop into its case, lifts himself up from his bunk, grunts a "*görüşürüz,*" "see you," to the reading man, and he is out the door. He will take his computer to his tech genius both to beef up his security and to see if he can return the hacking favor to Nuray Demir. This *orospu* needs to be taught a lesson.

CHAPTER 12

Adalet rereads the letter her tenant has enclosed with her rent check. Marta has been an excellent tenant. She came from Ukraine three years ago to study art history and language at the university. She is quiet, polite and entertains very few guests. Her rent is as reliable as the arrival of the first of the month. Now she is leaving to go back home. Her mother has sent for her, as afraid of what might happen to her in Istanbul as she had once feared might happen to her in Kyiv. Her mother's rationale is, "at least we can be together."

This is not good news for Adalet. She is dependent on the rent she receives from the other three apartments in her building. She will have to find another tenant immediately. The third apartment is rented to a young couple who are also quiet and pay their rent on time. However, the wife is five months pregnant, and Adalet suspects they will want to move to a larger apartment. Whether this is something they are considering, or even can afford to do, she does not know. But this has been on her mind and is now more so with the arrival of Marta's letter. Adalet has not asked for more than two months' notice, and Marta has given that now.

In the past, Adalet has rented to graduate students and young couples. As her building is located close to the universities and Taksim Square, she has never had a problem finding new tenants. People have come to the building looking for an apartment when she has had none to rent. Adalet never considered the possibility of worrying over an empty space she could not fill. Now she already has an empty that she has had for several months. The tenant was a German student who went back to Berlin to continue his studies.

Istanbul is changing. The truth is that her beautiful city has been changing for some time now. This breaks her heart, and when it is not absolutely necessary, she tries not to think about this fact. She sees the Syrians filling her streets. Adalet knows people are in fear for their lives under the weight of the Erdoğan government's arrests. The husband of the pregnant tenant is a high school math teacher. Teachers are being purged and jailed. If he is arrested, who will pay the rent? Adalet admonishes herself for having such selfish thoughts, but she is a woman on her own and must think of her welfare. She will put notices up at the graduate departments of a couple of universities. She will also ask Nuray if any of the journalist students working for her might need an apartment. No, she thinks, too many journalists are being arrested. Even Nuray could be one of them. That is a terrifying thought, and Adalet banishes that from her mind immediately.

Nuray is avoiding her, Adalet thinks. She is not telling her anything. Adalet is sure of this. Nuray is her closest friend. After Meryem and Isha moved to New York, and then Mark was forced to leave as well, Adalet began to rely more and more on her friendship with Nuray. But this is not true for Nuray. She is so deeply involved with her work, and she is often secretive and elusive. Adalet wishes for more from Nuray, but she also wonders if that is not because she feels Mark's absence so much. If Adalet would only have listened to Meryem and Isha's advice, Adalet reflects, she would be in New York now, married to Mark. Adalet smiles. Perhaps it is time already.

What is keeping her here anyway? Everything she knows. Adalet sighs. No, it is everything she once knew. Everyone she has ever loved is gone or dead. Her parents are long gone. They both perished in the 1999 earthquake in Duzçe. That disaster also cost her the life of her unborn child, to say nothing of the pain and suffering from the terrible burns to her legs. She has not seen or heard from Yasar, her ex-husband, since that one day so long ago when they ran into each other in the market. The divorce would have come anyway without the earthquake. His infidelity would have come to light eventually, Adalet believes. She could never have accepted his betrayal.

Adalet will always be grateful that her old friend, Fatma, left her the apartment building in her will. It has been a steady source of income. But now this building has a chokehold on her. Maintenance costs are always rising, and then there is the problem of finding people to do the work. How can she just walk out on these responsibilities? Ah, she reflects, responsibilities for what and to whom? Even Nuray has urged her to leave Turkey and marry Mark. Mark has told her it is her turn to propose to him. He is tired of asking. She does not blame him for this.

Adalet would never have to worry about money again if she married Mark. Mark's wealthy and rather annoying mother died of a sudden heart attack last year, and she left everything to him. He sold her Manhattan apartment for a small fortune and followed his dream of living on the water. He bought a house in Northport, on the North Shore of Long Island. The sprawling colonial house sits right off the bay. The pictures he sends are stunning. "Please, Adalet," he has asked her so many times, "come here to live with me. Marry me. We can listen to the gulls and the sea birds singing and shouting to each other every day and evening. We can drive into the city whenever we wish. It's not so far. New York is filled with Turkish people. You won't be lonely here."

What is she so afraid of? Is it change? Well, she decides, that is foolish. Change is happening all around her and has been happening to her all of her life. Perhaps Mark is right. Maybe she should speak to a therapist about her decision to leave Turkey and marry Mark. Therapy has become so much more popular among young women in Turkey today. But if she is to do this, she'd best hurry before Erdoğan has all the women back in veils again. Or, she thinks smiling, she could just hop on a plane and see someone in New York. There are more than enough therapists there.

Adalet does what she always does when she cannot come to a decision. She fills the *çaydanlık* with tea and water, sets it on the fire and picks up her cell phone. If she cannot reach Nuray, she will just have to make the trip over to the Asian side to her dreadful office for a visit.

CHAPTER 13

Nuray has changed the annoying shrill signal of her cell phone to a chirping bird ring, and so she does not hear Adalet's call. Two hours later, while she is checking her phone and finally hears Adalet's message, Adalet is already stumbling into the overcrowded doorway of the magazine office. A large water delivery bottle has been neglected there, and a stack of newspapers has accumulated close by. Adalet is dismayed by the disorder, remembering how neat and clean it looked after she helped Nuray clean the space when she first rented the office.

Nuray removes her reading glasses and stares at Adalet. "Selam, Adalet. Whatever are you doing here?" Nuray sets her glasses down on the pile of newspapers stacked on her desk.

"Selam," Adalet replies. She is upset with Nuray for not answering her call, especially when she sees her sitting there so casually. Does my concern mean nothing at all to her, Adalet wonders? "Why don't you answer your phone? I was worried, so I came to see for myself."

"Oh, Adalet. You worry too much. I changed the ring tone on my phone, and I didn't hear it. I was just checking my messages when you walked in the door. As you can see, I'm fine. I'm sorry you came all this way, but I'm not unhappy to see you. Here, let me clean off this chair." Nuray pushes a pile of papers and books to the floor. "Come, sit down. Do you want some tea?"

Adalet sits. "That would be nice, but only if you're not too busy."

"My dear friend, I am always too busy. You know that by now. But I need some tea myself. Zeynep? Where are you?"

"I'm back here heating the water for *çay*. I'll bring some when it's ready."

"Thank you. Two glasses, please."

Nuray watches Adalet surveying the office with what she surmises is a distasteful and critical eye.

Adalet catches her gaze and laughs. "How do you get anything done here? How do you even know where anything is?"

"You may not believe this," Nuray replies without returning the smile, "but we all know where everything is."

"Where is that piece you wanted me to look at by that Kurdish journalist who was just arrested?" Mohammed calls out from behind his own mountain of papers on his desk.

"Well, almost everything," Nuray mutters and then bursts into laughter herself. "See?' She pulls a newspaper from under the mess on the floor and waves it in the air for Mohammed to see. "It's right here."

Mohammed gets up to retrieve the newspaper, and he notices Adalet for the first time.

"You remember my friend, Adalet, don't you?"

"I've heard lots about you, but I don't believe we've ever met." Mohammed extends a hand in greeting.

"No, we haven't." Adalet extends her hand and Mohammed takes it lightly. "Pleased to meet you," she says.

"I'm pleased to meet you, too. May I ask why you are here in the midst of our chaos?"

"Please tell my good friend to answer her phone, and then I would still be on the other side of the Bosphorus."

"Take this and go away!" Nuray hands the newspaper out to Mohammed.

"Yes," he says, nodding to Adalet, "she is always like this. And these days, she is more like this than she ever was before."

"Go!" Nuray warns Mohammed. He laughs and takes the paper from her hands. He nods to Adalet and returns to his desk.

"Aren't you afraid he'll quit?" Adalet whispers to Nuray.

"You, my dear, know nothing of how we operate in this business. Mohammed is not only my colleague but my dear friend. He knows how much I value him. Ah, here is Zeynep with our *çay*."

Zeynep approaches with a small tray with two glasses of tea already poured and a bowl of small cubes of sugar. There is no room on Nuray's desk for the tray, so each woman takes a glass and places the desired number of sugar cubes in her glass with the tiny spoon provided.

"Zeynep," Nuray says, "this is my friend, Adalet."

Zeynep grins mischievously at Nuray. "It's good to know she has some. Nice to meet you." She immediately slips away before Adalet can respond.

"You're right, my friend, I do not understand your business at all." Adalet sips her tea. "Seriously, Nuray, how are things going?"

"Okay, okay. I got my press card back."

"Well, that is good news."

Nuray's phone begins to chirp. She recognizes the number as a friend from one of the local Kurdish papers.

"I've got to get this," Nuray says, picking up the phone. "*Merhaba,* Yasemin. How are you?"

"No time to talk, Nuray. Get the hell out of there. You are going to be raided. Don't ask me how I know this. Please just go now!" The phone clicks off before Nuray can respond. She whispers to Adalet, "Get the hell out of here. We're going to be raided."

Nuray shouts, "Everyone get out. We're about to be raided. If you can take your computer, do so right now. Don't wait to pack up." Nuray throws her bag over her shoulder and lifts her computer off her desk. Adalet, momentarily frozen to her chair, rises quickly and follows Nuray to the door. But before any of them can leave, they hear the sirens, the heavy footsteps running up the stairs. They are too late.

"Put your stuff back quickly. We'll all appear guilty running out the door with our computers. Better to look like we know nothing." Muhammed looks about to protest, but he realizes quickly that compliance makes more sense. He sets his computer back down, as do Nuray, Zeynep and Alp. Nuray motions them to sit back down at their desks which they do, just as the pounding on the door begins. Adalet watches, and startled by the banging and trembling door, finally falls into her chair. Why did I ever risk coming here, she asks herself? What is going to become of us all?

"Open up, it's the police!"

"I'm coming. No need to break the door," Nuray shouts above the furious clamor of fists against wood. She makes a sign for everyone to be calm, although her own heart is beating like a giant drum, so loud inside of her that she fears it might be heard outside of her. She also wishes Adalet had not come.

There are six policemen who almost cascade into the room when Nuray opens the door. "You are all under arrest," the smallest of them all announces, clearly the one in charge. The other police begin to handcuff everyone.

"But she doesn't even work here." Nuray points to Adalet. "She just came to visit me."

"We'll sort all of that out at the station. Our order is to bring everyone in and to confiscate your computers, phones, and documents. The office will be closed and sealed while we examine the documents. Please cooperate and things will go smoothly. No one will get hurt. If your friend is not involved, as you say, she will be released."

"What are the charges?" Mohammed inquires, as his hands are being secured behind him.

"You'll find that out at the station as well," the one in charge responds. "Get the computers and phones," he instructs his men. "Put everything in the vehicles, including them, and seal off the place. Oh, you, Ahmed, go let the grocer know what is happening."

Nuray cannot help but to struggle against her handcuffs. "Did Mr. Ekmekci report us? What for?"

"Mr. Ekmekci is the owner of this building, and therefore, he must be informed. As I said, you will find out more later, more than likely in Court."

After they hand over their phones, they are marched down the stairway like common criminals. At least no guns have yet been drawn, Nuray considers. This is all her fault. She should have shut down the paper until things eased up.

They are all shoved into a van, along with two of the officers. The inside of this vehicle is too warm and stuffy. The steel bench seats feel damp. Nuray catches a quick sight of their computers being loaded into another vehicle before the back doors are shut. She tries to catch Adalet's eye, but Adalet does not look up. Nuray is more disturbed for her friend than for herself. Adalet has done nothing to deserve this treatment except to be acquainted with her. Guilt by association must now be a crime in Turkey. Nuray hopes they will let Adalet go quickly.

Nuray does catch Mohammed's eye. She abruptly looks away. His expression is more forlorn than she has ever seen it. This makes her stomach turn. She guesses he is wondering how his family will survive. Nuray has no one to worry about her other than Mohammed and Adalet. This is not the case for Mohammed. What grief has she created for these people?

No, Nuray counters, they've all accepted that this might be a possibility except for Adalet. She is not responsible for any of their decisions, including Adalet's foolish decision to come into the office. She looks at Alp whose eyes are on the floor. His mother will be horribly upset. Zeynep catches Nuray's eye and smiles, even if a bit off kilter. Nuray gives her a full smile, not without some effort. Thank goodness for brave, if not reckless, Zeynep.

They are immediately separated in the police station.

CHAPTER 14

Adalet stares at her name written in various loops and scrawls on the filthy cell walls. My name means "justice," she reflects. I wonder if there is any to be found here. She finds seeing her name written by so many in this deplorable place is disconcerting, disturbing. She hopes that one of her tenants will feed Yetim.

The police station holding cell is tiny. Adalet knows that there are women living together in large dormitory-like cells. She has read this in the newspaper. She so wishes that Nuray were here with her. If only they could be together, this would not be so terrifying. Adalet cringes, thinking about the beatings and rapes she has heard of occurring not infrequently in Turkish jails and prisons. And Mark, he will be so worried when he tries to call and is unable to reach her. If only she had her phone. Before she sits, using only her bare hand, Adalet wipes the dirty bench that is attached to the wall with a chain. Will she have to sleep there? She cannot imagine this. The Turkish squat toilet is stained with urine and worse, has a trickle of feces running down the inside. A large cockroach darts across the wall from behind the sink, scuttling across the floor to whatever crack its friends are occupying.

Not having seen a soul since she was placed here, Adalet has no idea of the time that has passed. She places her head in her hands and begins to quietly weep. What if this is to be the rest of her life? Suppose no one notices her disappearance and Yetim starves alone in her empty apartment? Her tears come faster as she pictures poor Yetim alone and confused, just as she is now. Adalet reaches for a tissue, but of course, there are none. She has not been fingerprinted or told why she is being held. Although, she reflects, there is little to be left to her imagination.

Why did she leave her apartment so thoughtlessly and go to the magazine office? Now she wonders if it was worry about Nuray that motivated her, or was it anger at Nuray for not picking up her call? Since this has happened several times recently, she now realizes her frustration with Nuray has been building. Does the friendship mean less to Nuray than it does to her? Does Nuray not trust her? Now that her thoughts veer from Yetim's fate to doubting her relationship with Nuray, her tears slow and finally cease.

Adalet remembers conversations she's had with Mark about relationships, and one, specifically, regarding Nuray. Mark said something about people viewing friendship differently.

"Not everyone sees friendship entailing the same commitments and principles, Adalet," he'd told her. "You always think of Meryem and her commitment to you. That is something very unique and precious. Nuray is not Meryem. Her first commitment will always be to her politics, her advocacy, and to her writing. You have to decide if the friendship offers you enough to accept this." Adalet wipes her face dry with her sleeve. Mark is absolutely correct.

Adalet decides that reflecting is not wise in her current situation. Better to take each moment as it comes. She cannot bring herself to get on the gruesome floor to pray, but she beseeches Allah from where she is sitting. At the same time, she berates herself for only praying when she needs something so desperately. For some months, Adalet has not been to the mosque. She does not beg for forgiveness though, as she is not sure she will correct her behavior if or when released.

Who is this person I've become, she wonders? Why am I retreating from my religion, questioning it really, when I need it the most? Why does Allah allow this evil man, this Erdoğan, to do all of these horrible things and get away with it? He is destroying my beautiful country and the lives of so many people. Why doesn't Allah stop him? Why does my name mean justice when there is none? How did my *anne* and my *baba* come up with a name that means something that doesn't exist? Oh, this is dangerous, Adalet chides herself. I am thinking too much.

To keep her thoughts from despair, Adalet tries to recall poems she once learned and song lyrics she loves. She practices remembering synonyms and antonyms for a variety of words, her intent being to go from the beginning of the alphabet to the end and then start over again. At one third of the way through the alphabet, Adalet loses patience with this invented game of hers. When will someone come, she wants to know? At the same time, she fears when someone will come. Will she be beaten, raped? Adalet has heard too many stories.

CHAPTER 15

Mohammed tries to pray. Even though his holding cell is filthy, he does get down on his knees. He prostrates himself. This is the only way he can keep from obsessing about his wife, Ayşegül, his daughter, Azra, and his son, Necip. If he pauses in his prayer for only a moment, their images invade his heart and his mind.

Why didn't he quit *Turkey's New Woman* while he still could? Why did he quiet the warning voice of the danger he might be in if he continued at the magazine? Gratitude to Nuray for hiring him? Loyalty to her? Did he enjoy being a male advocate for women's rights? Yes, that was certainly true. But what will his family be going through when he doesn't return home this evening?

Mohammed forces himself to recite his prayers and rejects the doubts and suspicions that threaten they might not do him any good. Who would have ever thought that the government would mess with this small-potatoes publication? Then he remembers the soldier, Safak Aksoy. He compels himself to return to his prayers. But when he is finished, now what? He has nothing to read, nothing to distract him from his predicament. Reading has always been his way to divert his attention from unpleasantness. He smacks his forehead in frustration. He feels the tears welling up in his eyes and smacks himself again to control them. If he loses his strength now, he cannot imagine what will happen. He expects to be beaten. In his life, he has never been beaten. He must stay strong. He must not let them see his weakness.

CHAPTER 16

Nuray paces the floor that is covered with layers of dirt and something sticky and unidentifiable near one corner of the narrow bed. She cannot bring herself to sit down, partially due to raw nerves and partially due to the yellow stain in the center of the mattress.

Well, this is it, she thinks. This is the end of my life as I have known it. The worst of it all is that I have dragged my friends into this. Isolated from them, she now accepts all the blame. The only good she can derive from this is that Safak Aksoy cannot rape her here. As soon as this thought passes, she realizes that now many other guards can rape her. She knows so many stories, too many. These are stories she has been covering for some years now. She thinks back to the stream of women who have sat in her office revealing the nightmares of their jail experiences. "Allah, help me now," she says in more of a cry than a prayer.

Swiftly, Nuray's mind reverts to Adalet. If only she were here now. How can she possibly be coping? Sweet Adalet who always seems so vulnerable, so innocent. Then Nuray reflects back to all Adalet has told her of her history, waking up from severe burns in the earthquake to find she had lost her baby and soon after, that her husband was leaving her. She has managed to survive all of that. But these filthy and frightening cells would surely shake her being, her soul. I know what I am feeling. I can only imagine what this is doing to her.

Her thoughts fly to Mohammed. He has been split, courageous in one moment and in fear for his family the next. Alp has been equally on the fence, worried about his mother. And with all her show of bravery, what could Zeynep be feeling now? And why had they separated the women? Were the men separated as well? No one comes to answer her questions.

Hours, or what seem like hours, pass with absolutely no human face to consult. Time drags on. It is like a watching a worker ant drag a piece of food up a wall, so slowly you want to pick him up and take him wherever he is going. If only the ant were there to watch.

Something scurries under the bed. Nuray hates rats. She truly fears them. She turns around and paces the few feet available to her in the opposite direction. She cannot bring herself to look. The picture of a pack of rats overcoming and eating the flesh of a character she once saw in a horror movie assails her mind. She cringes and hugs herself tightly. She must get a grip on her emotions, or she will not last here very long. If only she were not so aware of the things that happen to women in Turkish jails.

Oh, my poor Adalet! You did nothing to deserve this. If only I had answered my phone, you wouldn't be here now. I am so self-centered, and she only wants to be a good friend. I am not a good friend. I only hope I can speak to them, let them know she is just a friend who came to visit me; that she has nothing to do with Turkey's New Woman. *Why the hell did I ever come up with that name? Oh, Allah, please let me wake up and discover this is all a nightmare, and then I will make everything right again. Somehow.*

Nuray hears the creaking of barred doors moving. Someone is coming. She braces herself and whispers, "Please, Allah, be kind."

CHAPTER 17

Safak Aksoy grins into the small mirror hanging on the wall by his bed. His nemesis is in hell. What could be better? Like an annoying mosquito, he has buzzed his poisonous accusations into the ear of a superior he knew would follow through.

Safak laughs aloud. He wonders if he could have even gotten an erection if she had agreed to have sex with him. She's not his type at all. He is not attracted to women in hijab. If he'd tried to rape her, maybe. The excitement of her attempting to fend him off might have aroused him. But he isn't so sure, and now he is rescued from having to do anything. He does not want to think about how she might have mocked him if he'd tried to force her, and then he was unable to perform. That had happened to him once recently, and in his fury, he'd beaten the stupid girl unconscious. He'd left her lying in a pool of blood in her own bed. He never saw her again.

Safak wonders what Nuray must be thinking now. Is she sorry she didn't agree to his demands? Does she even know that he was the one who reported her? When he knew the raid was happening, he'd ducked into the tiny laundry across the street from the magazine to watch. Just as Nuray was being led out in handcuffs, the owner of the laundry had come out from the back of the shop to ask him what he wanted. This had distracted him from seeing them put Nuray in the wagon. He was sorry to have missed the best part.

Safak slicks back his hair, grins at himself in the mirror, and thinks of his brother. He likes to think Altan would approve. Altan the terrorist. We're not so different after all, Safak thinks. He wonders if the stories he hears are true. For all he knows, Altan now has one of those young, captured brides that seem to be part of the perks of joining up with ISIS, or so they say. Safak plops down on his bunk and sighs. A ripe young thing would suit him so much better than that frumpy Nuray.

"Aksoy. Now!"

Safak snaps up and off his cot. His superior officer stands in the doorway.

"Yes, sir."

"My office."

Safak reluctantly lets go of the erotic image he has conjured and follows the officer into the hallway.

"Sir?"

"We'll talk in my office. Not here." The officer is a small, wiry fellow. He seems in a hurry and unhappy in his mission, whatever it might be. Safak is equally unhappy to be disturbed from his reverie and has to increase his steps in order to keep up. The office is down a long, narrow corridor with a sharp turn to the right, and then halfway down another corridor. Safak loses him for a moment when the officer veers to the right. When he catches up, the officer is already in his cubicle with the overhead light turned on. As soon as Safak enters, he motions to him to shut the door.

"Sit down," he motions to the hard wooden chair positioned on the other side of his metal desk. The room is barely large enough for the two men to occupy at the same time. The walls are bare, with the exception of a poster of Erdoğan tacked loosely onto the wall.

The officer does not look up at him but scratches a pen across a messy and overwritten piece of paper he has pulled from a thick file. He thrusts the paper in front of Safak.

"What can you tell me about these people?"

Safak scans the names, but the only one he recognizes is Nuray's.

"Nuray Demir. She is the one who runs the magazine."

The officer snatches the paper back. He glares at Safak.

"Don't you think I know that already? Give me something I can use, some dirt, on any of them." The officer makes a fist and pounds it onto the desk, shaking the metal structure and the papers loose from the fat file.

Safak squirms and finally, he shakes his head. This is unexpected. He knows nothing about these people.

"This one. This Adalet Ulusoy. Who is she?" The officer's face is red, and spittle sprays from his mouth with the force of his words.

Safak is clearly dismayed. "I'm sorry, Sir. I have no idea who she is."

The officer rises from his chair, lifts the file and smacks it back down onto his desk. "Useless, Aksoy! You are useless. You have me arresting five people, and I can only hold four of them. In reality, I can only hope to convict one of them. Why do you waste my time like this?" Safak's superior sucks loudly on the tip of his pen. "Aksoy, you make me wish that you'd taken the other side, backed the coup and betrayed Erdoğan. Then I could lock you up now with the rest of them!"

"But this magazine publishes articles that condemn Erdoğan," Safak protests.

"Yes, yes. But the rest of them. Really, Aksoy, this is small potatoes. I have whole staffs I can arrest. You waste my time with this. Go! Don't bother me again, or I will find a way to lock you up, too."

Safak starts to say something more. He wants to address the officer's ingratitude but thinks better of it. He pushes out his chair and rises.

Without looking up at him, the officer shouts, "Go on, get out of here before I throw you out."

Safak wants to slam the door behind him, but he thinks better of that as well. No wonder Altan ran from military duty to join up with the terrorists. They probably show his brother some respect, something Safak has certainly never gotten here, even after sticking his neck out to add some names to his superior's arrest record.

Safak sulks back to his bunk. It is almost time for the lights to go off for the evening. Men are congregated here and there, playing cards or games, gathered in group conversations, or just winding down for sleep. No one approaches Safak. He has no friends here.

Well, Safak reasons, removing his boots and then his pants, at least I fixed that Nuray. He swings his legs up onto the bunk and chuckles. I bet her friends are all getting a good scare, even if they can't hold them. They're probably not getting much sleep where they are tonight.

And with that thought, Safak closes his eyes. He dreams about Altan. *Altan greets him in the terrorists' camp with three young brides for him, one more beautiful than the next. "Take your pick," Altan tells him, "anyone you like. Nothing is too good for my brother."*

CHAPTER 18

Adalet's head has begun to itch. She has only closed her eyes for mere seconds. There are no windows in the small cell where she is being held, and since they have confiscated her phone, she has no sense of time. She scratches her head, wondering if there are lice in here. Can she get them if she is alone, or do they need a body to survive? She has never had to even think about such things until now. Suddenly her whole body is itching.

There are some sounds of doors opening and shutting, the pipes whistle and then screech, but all human voices are at a distance or too muffled for her to hear. Adalet has never felt so alone. Again, she wishes that Nuray had been held in the cell with her, even if Nuray would have cursed her for coming to the magazine office in the first place. Well, her current circumstances certainly prove that she was right to be concerned for Nuray's safety.

Adalet is hoping to get out of here before she is forced to use the grungy squat toilet. There is no paper or any bucket of water to clean it afterwards. She tries not to focus on what she believes might be the remains of blood and vomit encrusted on its sides. Adalet attempts to block out any bodily functions or needs. Another cockroach, this one the size of a water bug, darts by her foot, hesitates in a small collection of dirt, and then continues on its journey, disappearing as quickly as it has appeared. Adalet shudders. How long will she have to be here?

Does anyone even know where she is? Mark will be so worried when he is unable to reach her. Do the police answer her phone when it beeps? Do they just shut it off and throw it into a collective pile? Will they check all of her information on the phone and investigate everyone? This is all too awful to contemplate.

Adalet thinks briefly of asking for a phone call and making a plea to Ahmet, Fatma's son, and then immediately dismisses the idea. He is so judgmental. And who knows if the police would even allow her a phone call? She has never been arrested before, and she doesn't even know anyone who has. Adalet does not even know her rights well enough in order to know whether or not they are being violated.

Times passes, she cannot say how much, but the pressure on her bladder is increasing. She has no choice. Her fear is that someone will come just as she is using the toilet which is completely in the open. She pulls down her pants and crouches, closing her eyes and willing her urine to pass quickly. Her anxiety causes her muscles to contract. She forces herself to breathe deeply and finally, the flow begins. She shakes the wetness off the best she can and pulls up her pants. She is relieved that no one has come, although the indignity of this experience clings to her in the moistness of her underwear.

There is no way to occupy her mind. Once again, she tries to recall old song lyrics, poems she has read. She translates them into the sign language she once knew fairly well when she worked as a consultant to parents of deaf children, but which she is now losing through lack of usage. She gets stuck on several signs she can no longer bring to mind and becomes frustrated. The silence is such that she can actually imagine being deaf.

Time is so elusive that she could be encapsuled underwater, floating, completely out of touch with the world. Adalet attempts to conjure this image and to wrap herself within it, but the sensation is fleeting and gone before she can gain any comfort from its presence. She wishes now that she could run away in her mind. This would be a gift. But she is as much an emotional prisoner as she is a physical one. Try as she might, she is unable to escape.

What if I have to actually stay here? Adalet wonders this silently, and then, from an impulse she cannot explain, she begins to call out,

"How long do I have to stay here? Someone, anyone, please come and get me out of here!" She pounds the bars with her fist and cries out with the pain. There is no response.

Her mind travels to the unimaginable. She is so unimportant in all of this. What if they completely forget they even have her in here? If no one can even hear her, they could leave her here to die of thirst, of starvation. Adalet has a vision of Mark traveling to Istanbul to find her, weeks passing, rolls of red tape being unraveled, and no one even remembering what they've done with her. She pictures them finally taking Mark to see her, and there she is, skeletal, lying dead on the cell floor.

Stop this, she scolds herself. This crazy thinking won't get you anywhere. She tries to do the deep breathing exercises she learned when she was recovering from the leg burns she suffered in the earthquake. Breathe in on one and out on two. Breathe in on three and out on four. If I have any intrusive thoughts, start over at one.

But Adalet quickly becomes agitated. She is unable to get past two. The intrusive thoughts are sharpened arrows shooting mercilessly into her brain. There is no preventing them. She gives up on the meditation.

Adalet asks herself what her dear, departed friend, Fatma, might do in these circumstances. At last, she has to smile, even if for only a moment. Fatma would never find herself in such a predicament. Her attitude would have been, if Nuray chooses to be an idiot, well, leave it to her then. No need for me to get myself involved. Politics? Politics is for idiots. They are all stupid, she would say. And she would also say she would be a fool to join them. Well, now who is the fool? Adalet sighs heavily. If Fatma were still alive, as much as she would disapprove, she would get Adalet out of jail, even if she had to call on her equally disapproving son, Ahmet, in order to do it.

Adalet again begins to shout, "Water, please. I need some water. Please, someone, bring me some water."

Although she tries to prevent herself from yelling, she cannot seem to stop. "Water! Please, I'm so thirsty. I need water!" Over and over again, she cries out into unrelenting silence. Nothing.

Now reduced to angry and unwelcomed tears, Adalet plunks down on the bench. There is no point in any of this behavior, she decides. They will either come or they won't. My yelling is not going to bring someone here any sooner. Her resignation brings on a fresh burst of tears. Adalet sobs freely, for Fatma, for Nuray, for Mark, for her long dead parents and for herself. She stops long enough to remember Yetim, and she breaks back into sobs once again. Yetim might be more likely to starve to death than she is.

Time is interminable. After undetermined hours, perhaps only minutes, pipes hiss and screech again. Adalet is relieved to know by these sounds that there is life in this horrible place. Sometime after that, against all her wishes to remain alert, Adalet slips into a light doze. At some unknown interval later, she is jolted awake by a terrible grating sound. For a moment, she does not remember where she is, until she recognizes the jarring movement of the heavily barred doors that she was led behind in order to get to her cell. Someone is coming.

CHAPTER 19

Nuray sits up abruptly on the hard bench and contemplates the approaching footsteps with the dread of not knowing. Her life is not in her control. A skinny young guard with a face decked with angry red pimples opens her cell. He is alone and carrying handcuffs. He motions to her to put her hands behind her back so that he can cuff her. He does not speak to her.

"Where are you taking me?" she asks.

"You'll know soon enough," is his curt response.

"These are hurting my hands. Can't you take them off? I'm not going anywhere."

"Just follow me. No questions. Do as you are told."

The cuffs restraining her hands behind her back throw Nuray off balance. She is not used to walking in this position. Wobbling slightly forward, she stumbles on the stairway going up. The guard is behind her and his hand in her back keeps her from falling, but then he pushes her onto the next stair before she can reclaim her balance. She tumbles forward and smacks her head into a stair above. The guard grabs her cuffed arm and yanks her up.

"Get up, clumsy bitch. Don't play with me. Keep moving."

Nuray is silenced. There is no empathy to be found here. She restrains a whimper at the pain, now from her head and her cuffed hands.

As they proceed down a long corridor at the top of the stairs, the guard pushes Nuray forward with the back of his hand. Nuray's nose is running. When the liquid drips onto her shirt, she realizes it is blood.

"I'm bleeding from my nose," she tells the guard.

He whips her around to see for himself, and then spits on the floor in disgust. "Look at you, you pig. Just follow me. We're almost there."

He takes off at a clip. Nuray shuffles behind him, trying her best not to trip again and breathing as best she can through her seeping nose. The corridor is lined with offices on either side, and the guard finally stops in front of a door and knocks. A loud voice on the other side shouts, "Yes!" The guard opens the door into a chamber and shoves Nuray inside.

The room feels cramped and dark to Nuray. There is an immense man seated behind a table with a lone chair positioned across from him. The man is much too large for this room. A florescent light blinks over him, dimming and sputtering every few seconds. He does not look up but waves his hand to the guard, and the guard removes the handcuffs and leaves. Nuray stands where the guard has left her, blood streaming down her face and onto her clothing. She rubs her freed hands and grabs the end of her shirt to stop the flow.

The man finally raises a bloated, raki ravished face to survey what the guard has delivered, his eyes dark bulges that convey nothing, empty hollows without expression.

He finally says, "What happened to you?"

"I fell," Nuray manages to get out. "I tripped on the stairs. Do you have any tissues or cloth I can use to stop this?"

"Your shirt will do for now. This is not the infirmary. Sit." He motions to the chair.

Nuray sits, grateful that she is wearing a long shirt over a t-shirt. This is all she can be grateful for at this moment. Her heart is thumping so loudly that she is sure the man can hear what sounds to her like a chorus of African drums, every one of them signaling danger. In spite of how perilous she knows it is for her to show any fear, she cannot keep her shaking hand from betraying her. Nuray rubs the offending hand to hide its involuntary movement.

The man rifles through a folder of papers on the table in front of him. Nuray sees that the folder contains copies of articles from *Turkey's New Woman.*

"Your words are weapons against our Republic," the man's fat lips accuse. "Your words strike our President with venom. Do you realize how serious this is?"

"What are the charges against me?" Nuray manages to ask, her voice coming out in a childlike squeak that she detests.

The man grunts and stares at Nuray. "You are a traitor. You are a loser like your father. You will never see the light of day again."

Nuray is unable to speak. Her father. What does her father have to do with any of this? Why does he keep coming up? First the soldier and now this man who is not wearing a uniform but seems to carry much authority. They have both spoken of her father.

Nuray forces herself to ask again, "What are the charges against me, and can I speak to a lawyer?"

The man laughs, his red cheeks distorted, his face ugly and frightening, like a monster from a horror film that Nuray has seen somewhere but now cannot recall the circumstances. He continues, "First, you are accused of insulting the President. Second, you are accused of terrorism, affiliation with a terrorist organization, and inciting an insurrection with this terrorist organization against our government. You face up to life in prison. If you choose to cooperate by giving a written confession, you might be able to get a lesser sentence. There is no way that the Court will not convict you. The evidence is all right here. Do you wish to confess and to cooperate in this investigation? A confession is your only hope right now."

Nuray cannot speak. She fiddles with her blood-soaked shirt tail. At least the bleeding has slowed. She is dumbfounded. What terrorist organization? She has never belonged to any political or religious group, any group for that matter. Could he possibly mean The International Federation of Journalists? What is he talking about?

"Do you wish to confess and cooperate?" he asks again. He glares over at her, tapping the edge of his pen against the table in impatience.

"I won't confess to something I haven't done," Nuray tells him, her voice no longer squeaking. "I've never been affiliated with a terrorist organization. I haven't ever had anything to do with inciting an insurrection."

He raises his enormous frame from the chair, surprisingly agile, and thrusts an article in Nuray's face. "Did you or did you not write this?"

"I did, but when I wrote that it wasn't a crime to speak one's mind."

He deposits his bulk back down into his chair. "Tell that to the Court. If the judge will buy it, so will I. I'd be just as happy to get rid of you and your friends, but I can't do that now, can I? And what about Gülen? What about that group? Huh? Talk."

Nuray shakes her head in disbelief. "I tell you, I am not a member of Hizmet. I have never been a member of Hizmet. I have had nothing to do with them."

"Aha! See, you know who Gülen is!"

"Everyone knows who Gülen is."

"But your father has had plenty to do with them, and with Gülen, personally. We already know this."

"But I haven't seen my father in years. He is dead to me. I don't know anything about him." Nuray is beginning to realize that her protests to this man mean nothing.

"And that fellow who works for you? I suppose you don't know that his mother works for the terrorist organization?"

Nuray is unable to resist defending this. "But Alp's mother is only a cleaning woman. She cleans houses to put him through school."

"She cleans for the Hizmet schools. She takes money from them. She profits from a terrorist organization, and so does he."

"This is outrageous and ridiculous!" Nuray wishes she has not said these words, as the man's face explodes with anger. The red cheeks flare and flame as if ignited by dynamite. She should not have antagonized him.

"Okay, you just keep on with that attitude. Aiding a terrorist organization is no laughing matter. Neither is insulting the President of this country!" She can feel the spittle from the force with which he punctuates his words. "We'll see just how ridiculous you think all of this is when you are rotting away in prison for the rest of your life. So, you do not wish to confess?"

"No." Nuray manages a stronger tone of voice. "I have done nothing wrong."

The colossus slams his fist onto the table and pulls a cellphone from his pocket. He pushes some numbers and speaks into the phone. "Come and take her to the women's detention hold. She is refusing to cooperate." He clicks off his phone and stares at Nuray in silence. Nuray stares back. They remain thus for many minutes until there is a knock at the door.

"Enter," the frustrated official shouts.

This is a different guard, a woman. She is without handcuffs. She takes Nuray's elbow gently, helping to raise her from the chair and says, "Come with me."

CHAPTER 20

Adalet has no idea where in Istanbul she is. Taken from the appallingly foul cell where she has been held captive for she does not know how long, handed her phone and other belongings, she is simply told that she is free to go. No charges will be filed against her at this time. The "at this time" is not reassuring. A huge sliding door rolls open and Adalet finds herself in a deserted street in the middle of the night. She checks her phone, and it is 1:00 a.m. The sky is dark and the outdoor lighting dim enough that Adalet can glimpse a few stars.

Adalet's phone battery is so low that she is afraid she will lose the signal before she can contact an Uber or a Lift. There are no taxis in sight. She looks for a street and a building number. A brass name plate informs her that she is at the Vatan Police Headquarters. She automatically presses the number for Uber. She does not need a street number. The receptionist is aware of Vatan Police Headquarters. The night is quiet and still. A light breeze whispers against Adalet's cheek. Air. Real air. Non institutional air. Senses she has taken for granted up until this day. She holds back the tears she feels forming.

The sympathetic Uber driver who arrives explains that he and a few other drivers have picked up other fares from this place, and at all odd hours.

"They are arresting people, anyone, any place and anywhere. They arrested my cousin. She's a high school history teacher. Can you believe it? She's still locked up."

"I can believe it now," Adalet sighs. "My friend is still in there, I'm sure. She's a journalist. They won't let her go, I'm afraid."

They are silent for the rest of the drive. Adalet does not have enough cash on her to pay the driver. She hunts for her credit card. "I think I left in such a hurry that I left my credit card upstairs. Do you mind waiting while I get it? I don't have quite enough money on me to pay you."

The driver turns and looks at her. "Just give me what you have. I think your night has been difficult enough. You look like a nice lady who shouldn't be in jail."

Tears form in Adalet's eyes at this kindness. "Thank you so much," she whispers. "You are very kind."

Two cats are curled up asleep on the motorcycle parked on the street by her door. Immediately, Adalet thinks of Yetim, and she hurries her key into the lock. Once inside the vestibule, the outer door shut securely behind her, Adalet bursts into tears. The downstairs apartment door opens, and Marta, Adalet's tenant, comes out dressed in a heavy bathrobe and slippers. She wraps her arms around the sobbing Adalet.

"What's happened to you? What's the matter?"

Adalet is unable to answer. Marta's comforting arms around her only lead to heavier, more intense sobs. Some minutes pass before she can speak.

"It's okay," Marta consoles her, "take your time."

Adalet finally releases herself from Marta's grasp. "I was arrested, Marta. They arrested me."

"Come inside. Tell me."

"No, I must go upstairs and tend to Yetim. She hasn't been fed since early this morning."

"Shall I come with you?" Marta asks. "My key is in my pocket. I'll just lock my door and come up with you, if you like."

Adalet hesitates. She needs a shower. She needs to call Mark. But she also needs a friend. "Just for a few minutes, Marta. That would be very kind."

Marta locks her door and follows Adalet up the winding staircase. Yetim greets them at the door, meowing her hunger and annoyance at Adalet's disappearance. Where have you been? she seems to be asking.

"Shall I make *çay*?" Marta asks. "I know where everything is. Why don't I feed Yetim and put on the kettle? You take a shower and change your clothes. It's the first thing I'd want to do. Go ahead. Don't worry."

Adalet feels her eyes filling up again. "Thank you, Marta. I will." Marta's kindness moves her. She feels so alone. Nuray is in jail. Mark is thousands of miles away in New York. Marta has shared some of her life with Adalet, but Adalet has shared very little with Marta. She has wanted to maintain the landlord/tenant boundaries which are soon to be obsolete in any event. At this moment, she could care less about her normal concerns. She plugs her cell phone into a charger and goes back to her bedroom.

What does it matter that I own this building? Adalet thinks. Owning property is not going to protect me. What am I still doing here? The time to let go has arrived.

Adalet strips off her clothes and throws them into her hamper. She wraps a robe around her naked body and heads directly to the bathroom and the shower. She turns on the water with as much pressure as it is able to yield and steps underneath. The spray hits her body like hundreds of soft needles, erasing the dirt and smell of that awful place from her body. When she has stood there for some minutes, she pours shampoo onto her head, not the usual small amount she first pours into her hand, and attacks her head vigorously, first with her nails, and then her fingers. She does this for some time before rinsing out the shampoo and applying a conditioner. She fills a sponge with liquid soap and scrubs her body from top to bottom, once, twice, three times. Then she again stands under the full spray of water, rinsing both her hair and her body until her fingertips are wrinkled from the water. I may never feel clean again, she thinks.

Immediately, her thoughts travel to her friend and the staff of *Turkey's New Woman*, still in that awful place, as far as she knows. What can she possibly do? Well, she can get them a lawyer. She will ask Marta if she knows a good lawyer. And Mark. Mark did consult someone when he was trying to stay in Turkey. Yes, she was a clever and capable young woman, as Adalet recalls.

Adalet looks into the small bathroom mirror, partially covered in steam, and she is shocked by the face that looks back at her. Her complexion is almost white, gaunt, her beautiful cheekbones so amplified as to appear skeletal. This is only one day, she contemplates. What if I'd had to stay there? Poor Nuray. What is going to happen to her? She quickly brushes her hair into place and wraps her robe around her.

In the kitchen, Marta has fed Yetim who is now curled up on the kitchen window sill. Adalet scoops her up in her arms. "You poor kitty. I'm so glad you're okay. I didn't mean to leave you alone for so long." Yetim purrs loudly, her stomach full and her safety reestablished.

The *çaydanlık* whistles, announcing that *çay* will soon be ready. Marta has set out the tea glasses and a plate of cookies that were stored in a tin by the *çaydanlık*.

"I don't know how to thank you, Marta." Adalet sits at the small table Meryem left behind when she moved to New York. Adalet promised to keep the inlaid Italian table safe for Meryem. How grateful Adalet feels to be sitting here now, away from that awful jail cell. She is so glad that Meryem is safely in New York.

Marta sets the tea glasses on the table and pours the steaming hot beverage. "So what happened?" she asks. "How did you ever get arrested?"

Adalet shakes her wet hair. "It's a terrible story. I went to visit my friend, Nuray, who owns and runs a magazine called *Turkey's New Woman*. She wasn't answering my calls, and so I was worried. I went to the magazine's office. Such bad timing. I had just gotten there when the police arrived. They arrested all of us, put us in a police wagon, drove us to a jail and stuck us in different cells. At least Nuray and I were in different cells. I don't know about the other woman on the staff." Adalet takes a long sip of the tea. "The other woman was just a student volunteer. And I'm just a friend. I don't understand any of it."

Marta sets her glass down on the table and offers Adalet a cookie. "Here, please eat something." Adalet obliges her by taking one. Surprisingly, she is not hungry.

Marta waves her cookie in the air for emphasis. "This is not unusual circumstances for either of our countries. We Ukrainians broke from the Russians, and now they are back with a vengeance. We get a few minutes to breathe, and then another power-crazy guy comes along and we're back where we started. Putin is no good. Erdoğan is no good."

Adalet sets half of her cookie back down on the table. "We thought he might be in the beginning. He did good things in Istanbul. So many people went from poverty to middle class. Services improved. We thought he would be good for the country. He is much more conservative and religious than we thought." She picks the cookie back up and takes another nibble before setting it back down again.

Yetim, satisfied that her stomach is now full and that Adalet is at home, jumps into Adalet's lap for a pet and then jumps back down to perch on the windowsill. Adalet's cell phone begins to ring.

"That must be Mark. I have to get this, Marta. He must be so worried."

"Please, go ahead. I'll just be downstairs if you need me." While Adalet runs to get the phone, Marta sips the last of her tea and quietly lets herself out the door.

Adalet now sees that there have been several calls from Mark. He sounds frantic when she answers.

"Where have you been? I've been so worried about you. I must have called you half a dozen times."

"I'm so sorry, Mark. I couldn't help it. I wasn't able to call you back."

"Why not? What happened?"

"You won't believe it, but I was arrested."

"With Nuray?"

"How did you know?"

Mark sighs. "I didn't know. I just guessed. Why on earth would anyone arrest you? I warned you about this." Mark's voice conveys some disapproval.

Now it is Adalet's turn to sigh. "I know you did, but I was so worried about her. She wasn't answering my calls, so I went to the magazine office. I must have been there for ten minutes before the place was raided."

"How did you get out?" Mark's tone is softer now.

"I have no idea. They told me they would not press charges at this time. 'At this time' makes me nervous."

Mark is silent for a moment. "I think they must have realized that you were not connected with the magazine. They didn't have anything to hold you on. But now they have your name in their sights. I don't like that at all, Adalet. I think it's time again for you to consider leaving."

Adalet is surprised at her own response. "I do, too. I am thinking about it seriously, Mark. My life here has changed. Istanbul has changed. And Turkey is far from where I expected it to be. I really believed we would have a democracy here."

"You're not alone, my darling. I believed it once, too. Many did."

"Mark, if I say yes now, what is the question you will ask me?"

"Oh, Adalet. Are you very sure?"

"I am. I've already waited too long."

"Not for me," Mark laughs. "My dear Adalet, my one and only Adalet, will you marry me?"

"I've already answered that question." Adalet smiles. "Yes, Mark, I will. I will marry you and come to live in America."

"Even if we have to import your favorite red pepper?"

"Yes, my love, we'll find my red pepper somewhere."

CHAPTER 21

Mohammed tries to clean the dust off his shoes with his handkerchief before he faces Ayşegül. He and Alp were both released at about 10:00 in the morning. He does not know yet what has happened to Zeynep, but he does know that the police are holding Nuray. That damned article, he thinks. If not for that, she would probably also have been released. Or perhaps not. Everything is crazy, upside down. Before he can place his key in the door, Ayşegül opens it wide and pulls him into her arms.

"I've been so worried. Where have you been all night?" She releases him and stares directly into his eyes, as if she can hardly believe he is home and in one piece.

"I was arrested," he says. "I was just released."

"Allah be praised." She brushes her hands against his wrinkled clothing, as if she can iron out the marks of his evening with her hands.

"We were all arrested. They raided the office. Even Nuray's friend, Adalet, was taken along with us. She has nothing to do with the magazine. But they let everyone go, I think, except for Nuray. I haven't heard about Zeynep, but since they released Alp with me, I'm guessing she was also released. I need to get out of these clothes and take a good shower. Then I need to eat something. I haven't eaten in twenty-four hours."

"Of course, my darling. I will get you some breakfast. I'll make some *menemen* while you take your shower."

Letting the hot water spray over his entire body, Mohammed thinks that Ayşegül is taking his arrest unusually lightly, as if she has expected this to happen all along. There are times when Mohammed feels he knows his wife so well, and other times she surprises him, as if she might be a total stranger.

As the smell of the eggs, peppers, tomatoes and a whiff of paprika reaches him from the kitchen, Mohammed realizes that he is starving. He turns off the shower and quickly towels himself. He grabs some clean underwear and a clean shirt, pants and socks and heads for the kitchen where Ayşegül pours his Turkish coffee and piles *menemen* onto his plate. She joins him with a cup of *çay*.

"I'm surprised," Mohammed says in between bites of the spicey *menemen*, "that you don't seem more surprised."

Ayşegül sips quietly from her *çay*. "I do know what is going on around me," she finally says. "Many teachers from the Hizmet schools have been arrested, teachers, supervisors, principals, anyone under suspicion." She sets her tea glass down on the table. "Even though those schools are so good, I am glad I'm not teaching in one of them. I have already put in a request to return to work, my darling, so we will have an income. I will start next week."

Mohammed sets down his fork and stares at her. She has taken it for granted that he will not return to the magazine. How does she simply know these things about him? "How did I get so lucky when I married you? You continue to amaze me."

"You will have to get the children ready for school and be here to meet the bus afterwards. I will try to get home as soon as I can. My *anne* can begin to help us, but since she is caring for my *baba*, she won't be able to come every day."

"Of course." Mohammed picks up his fork and continues to eat. He is grateful, but he is unsure how to express his feelings. The recent stressful atmosphere in the magazine office, the political climate, culminating in the raid and arrest, all of this is weighing in to make him glad to stay at home for a while, to look after his children. He has spent too much time away from them.

Mohammed is no coward, but he is a family man. He believes in the principles that inspire Nuray, but he is not willing to go to prison for them. Mohammed is not optimistic that Nuray will be released any time soon, and he has no intention of carrying on there without her. Journalism in Turkey is just too risky for him now. He will have to find new work while he still can. If he returns to the magazine and is arrested again, he may have his passport and papers taken from him, and then he won't be able to work anywhere.

Mohammed's stomach turns over as he thinks of telling Nuray this news. If only she could be as perceptive and understanding as his wife. Well, this is why he is married to Ayşegül and not to Nuray. He has never been the least attracted to Nuray, although his admiration for her is without hesitation or question.

Mohammed looks up from his reverie to find Ayşegül staring at him intently. "I will have to go visit Nuray in jail to tell her."

"Is that a good idea? Why not send her a letter? Do you want to be seen associating with her?"

Mohammed is once again surprised, but this time he is shocked at her lack of sympathy for Nuray. "That is so cold, my love. I am at no risk, or they would have held me. I think that is the case, I am almost certain. I really do need to tell her in person. I should also see if she needs anything."

"You could send her friend, the one who was arrested with you."

Mohammed looks at his wife and shakes his head.

Ayşegül gets up from her chair and goes over to Mohammed. She takes his hand. "I'm so sorry. Of course, you must go to see her. I am selfish and only thinking of you and of the family."

Mohammed strokes the hand she has given him, rises, and pulls her close. "You are right to think of the family. I will only go the one time. She knows my feelings about getting involved in anything provocative against the government, no matter how wrong I feel they are. I will not risk our lives together." He strokes Ayşegül's hair. "I am a husband and father first and a journalist second. If not for Nuray, I might never have gone back to being a journalist."

"Take your time, my dearest husband. Just be careful. We need you here."

Mohammed holds Ayşegül closer. "I know," he whispers. "And I need to be here."

CHAPTER 22

Nuray is startled to hear that she has a visitor. She is still being held in isolation at the Vatan Police Station, where she and Adalet and the magazine staff were all initially taken. She does not have a lawyer, and no one has spoken to her since her first interrogation. Her cell is quite small but cleaner than the awful place she was being held initially. There is a tiny sink with running water. A clean hand towel, albeit frayed with a couple of holes, has been thrown over a hook next to the sink. There is a hotel travel-size bar of soap, and a tiny flush toilet behind a half-wall. Nuray was happy to find a single bed attached to one wall with a mattress and pillow, no sheets or pillow case, but a vast improvement over a hard bench. Food and water has been slipped to her through a slot in the door. So far, she has been offered a cold cheese sandwich, a bottle of water and a wrinkled, worn-out apple. What she craves is a good, strong glass of çay.

It is odd, she thinks, that she is finding her new surroundings luxurious in comparison to her prior circumstances. She has not been able to change her clothes, and there are bloodstains on her shirt, even more on her pants, but she has been able to wash most of the blood from her face. Her nose is swollen and may be broken, she doesn't know. The pain is now a dull but constant throbbing.

The female guard, a different one, handcuffs her in the cell and leads her through several corridors to a large, open room with tables and chairs. She is relieved to see Mohammed seated at one of the tables. He starts to rise to greet her, but the guard motions him to stay seated. She removes Nuray's handcuffs. Nuray is surprised when the guard moves close to the door to give them some privacy.

Mohammed surveys her face. "What happened to you?" he asks, obviously shocked at her appearance.

"I fell down some stairs. I'm okay, really. I'm so glad to see that they let you out."

"I think everyone is out but you."

"That is a relief. Have you been to the office?"

Mohammed hesitates a moment before answering. "No, I wanted to speak with you first."

Nuray sighs. "Everything has been confiscated anyway. We will have to start from scratch."

Mohammed can hardly believe what he is hearing. "Start from scratch? Are you out of your mind? They told me you will be charged with terrorism, attempting to overthrow the government. Nuray, do you understand how serious this is?"

Nuray is silent. She stares off into space. Finally, she looks at him. "I need a lawyer," she says. "And I need some clothing and toiletries."

"I left some things for you with the guard. Adalet found me. She had packaged some things for you. She will come to see you herself, but I needed to talk to you. Adalet is working on getting you a lawyer. There is someone she knows through her boyfriend in New York. She has spoken to him and gotten the name and phone number."

Nuray rubs her wrists from the aggravation created by the handcuffs. "She is a good friend, a better one than I deserve."

"I might as well tell you. She said I could. She said it would make you happy. She's also hiring the lawyer to help her to leave Turkey, if a lawyer becomes necessary. She's decided to go to New York and marry that guy. Things being the way they are, I'd say it's a good decision."

Nuray fights back tears. She nods to Mohammed, "Yes, I am happy that she's going." Nuray takes a deep breath. "What about the magazine? What will we do?"

Mohamed has dreaded this moment. "I'll go settle up with Mr. Ekmekci. What do we owe him?"

"We don't owe him anything, Mohammed. I've always paid him on time. In fact, we're paid up for this month and next." Nuray's hand begins to shake, and this time Mohammed notices.

"What's that about, your hand?"

"I don't know. It just happens lately." Nuray halts the shaking with her other hand. She immediately diverts Mohammed's attention. "This might be asking too much, and I doubt that he'll do it, but see if you can convince Mr. Ekmekci to return the one month's rent. That money could help me to pay a lawyer. I don't really have much put aside. To be completely honest, I have nothing of value but my apartment."

"So," Mohammed says with much relief, "you are prepared to close the magazine."

"What else can I do? I'm so sorry, Mohammed. This must all be awful for you."

"Your being locked up in here is what is awful for me." Mohammed can say this quite truthfully. He is still somewhat afraid that Nuray, in her stubbornness, will attempt to continue the magazine from jail, expecting him to manage everything on the outside. He thought he might have to talk her out of doing that, or flatly refuse to continue. He is relieved that things do not seem to be heading in that direction.

"I'll go to see Ekmekci when I leave here, and then I will send word with Adalet. Ayşegül is worried."

Nuray is puzzled for a moment until the realization hits her that Mohammed will not be returning to visit her in jail. His wife is afraid, and understandably, he does not wish to upset her. Again, she fights back tears. Nuray does not want to make Mohammed feel bad about things he cannot change.

Nuray shifts in her chair. She is hiding her hands in her lap, as they are now both shaking. How can she possibly say goodbye to Mohammed under these conditions? She cannot find the words she wants to say to him. Nuray does not wish to have him feel guilty, but she knows she has no control over his feelings. After some moments, she looks up at him.

"Thank you, my dear friend, for all you have done for me. You have always gone beyond my expectations. I cannot ask for anything more." Nuray sees the water forming behind Mohammed's eyelids. Her own begin to fill. She breathes in deeply, controls her trembling hands, and reaches for Mohammed's. Their hands clasp before the guard calls out, "No touching allowed."

"Selam Aleykum," Nuray whispers, rising from her chair.

"Aleykum Selam," Mohammed responds, "Peace be upon you, dear friend."

After her encounter with Mohammed, Nuray's cell no longer seems luxurious, even compared to the last one. Too much reality, she thinks, rubbing her wrists from the pressure of the handcuffs. What could she have been thinking anyway? She knows that Mohammed has been through a great deal and that the accusations that plagued him could have ended his marriage. Fortunately for Mohammed, his wife trusts him. He cherishes her trust. If she does not want him in contact with Nuray any longer, that is what will happen. Mohammed will not risk his family.

The guard has left a bag on her bed with the things Adalet packed for her. When Nuray unzips the bag, she smiles for the first time since her arrest. Adalet has not gone to Nuray's apartment, but she has gathered some of her own clothing and purchased new toiletries. Knowing that Nuray is a bit larger, she has packed two pairs of loose-fitting pants that tie at the elastic waistbands. There are four t-shirts, two short-sleeved and two long-sleeved, and two sweaters. Adalet also purchased new underwear and socks. Unbelievable, Nuray thinks, as she pulls out a long-sleeved flannel nightgown. A plastic case has soap, toothpaste, shampoo, and conditioner. There is also a new toothbrush, a hairbrush and comb. At the bottom of the bag, there is a copy of the *Quran,* the only book they would allow her to have.

Ah, my dear, dear, Adalet, Nuray reflects grinning, we used to joke about you bringing me cigarettes to jail. I'm glad I don't smoke. They are too expensive for you. But here I am, and there you are, out there, helping me. Ah, but soon you will travel to New York. And then, my dear friend, I will truly be alone.

CHAPTER 23

Safak Aksoy waits at a small café in Kilis, close to the Syrian border. The night is cool, and he zips his jacket. Altan has instructed him to wait there for the smuggler who will escort him to the other side, for the paltry equivalent of $25.00 American. He carries only a small backpack with absolute essentials.

He is by now, he guesses, an official deserter. Safak thinks nothing of the consequences. He does not consider the possible repercussions. He is a man of impulse. He does not contemplate what will happen to him if he returns to Turkey.

Not only is Safak a deserter, but he is now a thief. At the request of his brother, Safak searches his parents' bedroom and finds cash that his mother has hidden away in her underwear drawer, just as Altan has predicted. "She hides money so Baba can't find it and drink it up. She's been doing that for years. You'll meet me on the Syrian border. It's easy. There are photographers and journalists just hanging around out there. It's unbelievable. I'll send a smuggler to bring you across. You can join up. We'll train you. It's got to be a hell of a lot better than the Turkish army."

Safak has not given this a second thought. He is not a religious zealot, and he can hardly believe that Altan is either, but they share a mutual disdain for life as it is. Power is seductive. Guns, women, and control await him. This just might be the answer to a good life.

The café is fairly deserted. A few journalists sit around with their laptops, as the café also serves as a WIFI connection source. One of these scraggly men has a camera strapped over his shoulder. There are no women present here.

Safak has no idea how the smuggler will identify him, or even more important, how he will be assured that this is the smuggler Altan has sent. But he figures that Altan knows how these things are done, and so, he sits and waits. While he waits, he sips on a tepid tea and takes small bites from a sandwich filled with cheese and cut vegetables. He is not hungry, but he must do something to account for his presence in the café.

The minute hand on an old clock hanging on a paint-chipped wall defies time. For Safak, it takes five minutes at least for it to move once. He finishes his sandwich, orders some olives and bread and another cup of tea. He would prefer a beer right now, but the café does not serve alcohol. Well, he'd best get used to this. There is no alcohol in ISIS.

The café owner and waiter inform him that the café will be closing in a few minutes. Safak pays the tab and wonders what he will do now. Just as he is about to leave and head back to the hotel he checked out of earlier that day, the door opens and a scruffy man with a large bearing enters. He has a wide face with a thick and long beard, eyes that look as if he is just about to squint.

"Ah, my cousin," he exclaims too loudly, since the café is now empty, "I am sorry to make you wait so long. Let's go. I will tell you all about my delay as we go." He motions to the door, and then pushes Safak outside with a strong hand.

Once they are only a couple of feet from the observation of the café owner, the man grabs Safak's wrist. "Follow me quickly, and don't say a word. Just do as I tell you and quickly. No hesitation. I will get you over the border and to your brother, *Inshallah*.

"How do I know you are who you say you are?"

The hand grips Safak's wrist tighter. "I do not say who I am. You will never know who I am. You will simply come with me and do what I say. If not, wait here for someone else to come until you die. Your choice."

Safak grunts. This is not what he expected. But now there is little choice. "Okay," he tells the smuggler, and feels the grasp on his wrist loosen until it drops away.

"Then let's go." The smuggler heads off, and Safak follows.

The path is dark, and Safak stumbles a few times over loose stones in the gravel and dirt. A couple of times he is smacked by a branch that his guide has failed to warn him of or hold out of his way. Safak swallows his anger, as he has no idea where he is, and despite his nature, he knows this is no time to retaliate.

After what feels like an endless hike, his smuggler motions him to stay low and be quiet, even though Safak has not uttered a word thus far. The path is a bit more tangled with prickly brush, and the rocks are larger beneath Safak's feet. He has to slow down in order not to trip and fall. His guide motions him to hurry anyway. Just as Safak does trip and fall flat on his face, a hand pulls on his backpack and lifts him up. He is staring into his brother's eyes.

"Altan," Safak whispers, blood dripping from one of his nostrils from the fall.

"You're across the border now. You're in Syria. Ah, my brother, I would have to pick you up off the ground." Altan laughs, stepping back and surveying a dusty, filthy Safak.

"Where did that guy go?" Safak asks, wiping the blood from his face with his hand and brushing the dirt from his clothing.

"Never mind. He did what he was supposed to do. That's all you need to know. I can't believe you had the guts to desert. Wow. I am impressed. My little brother is growing up."

Safak smiles. "The military is shit. I help my officer make arrests, and he yells at me and wants to lock me up. Turkey is fucked, anyway you look at it."

Altan opens his arms and embraces Safak. "It's about time you got some sense. I'm sorry I had to ask you to steal from *Anne*, I know she's been good to you, but it took some cash to get you here. And that bum old man of ours would take it and spend it on booze anyway."

"He's worse than ever," Safak says . "But I'm too big for him to beat me up anymore."

"*Tamam*, okay, let's get to the camp. I have a jeep waiting just a short walk from here."

"Good," Safak tells him. "I've had enough of a hike for one night."

"Well," Altan replies, "you had better get used to hard work. ISIS training is no picnic."

CHAPTER 24

"Get up," the guard shouts as he holds handcuffs up for Nuray to see. She puts her hands out in front of her body, but he yells, "in back, in back." Nuray holds back tears, as this position is now painful when her hands begin to shake. Whatever has been going on with her one hand has progressed to the other. But there is no recourse, as she sees no compassion in this man's eyes. She places her hands behind her, and he cuffs them aggressively.

The guard is not tall and quite slender, but he pushes Nuray forward from the cell as if he is propelling a bag of garbage, something distasteful. She feels his disdain. They move along a dimly lit hallway, go up one flight of stairs, and down another hallway. The guard grabs hold of Nuray's arm in front of a door marked "Interrogations." When he opens the door, the room is empty. There is no desk or chairs. There is an overhead florescent blinking light and a cement floor. He pushes Nuray inside and leaves, locking the door behind him.

Nuray attempts to sit on the floor, but the handcuffs are too painful, as well as inhibiting her movement. Her cell is chilly, but this room is cold. The emptiness is forbidding. Nuray knows that nothing good can happen here. "Where are you, Allah?" she whispers. "Do you exist in such an awful place? Do you even know I'm here? Why is it that you seem to disappear when humans hurt each other? Please have some pity and help me now."

The floor of the room is filthy. Nuray is uncertain, but she thinks there are what could be blood stains in the cement. Will she be beaten? Or worse?

And there is no help. More than an hour seems to crawl by before there is movement, footsteps in the hallway, and the lock finally turns. Four guards burst into the room. They are all wearing masks. Instinctively, Nuray backs up against the rear wall. Her heart begins to thump. Her restricted hands begin to shake. She can smell evil approaching.

The tallest of the four steps forward. "Let's get her cuffs off. She can strip. That will be more fun. And if you fight," he warns Nuray, "we'll beat the shit out of you." He releases the handcuffs and pushes her back against the wall. "Take off your clothes," he sneers at her. And if you don't do it nicely, we'll rip them off. Your choice."

Nuray breathes deeply. She knows there is no way out of this. This nightmare has been pre-arranged. No one will come to save her no matter how loudly she screams. And she needs her clothes. She has only what is on her back and the things Adalet has brought her. She breathes deeply once again and tells herself, *Submit. Save whatever of yourself that you can and submit.*

Nuray slowly unbuttons her blouse. In a way, she has rehearsed this scenario in her mind many times. The rape of women in Istanbul, and throughout Turkey, is a depraved and immoral fact of life. She has often contemplated what she would do if she was not fortunate enough to make it through her life without facing this traumatic encounter. And here she is. Four of them and one of her. Will she even survive?

The men taunt her as she undresses. "Big, bouncy ones, eh? Come on, whore, off with the panties."

Nuray does not look at them. If there were only one, she might try to make herself more identifiable, more human to him, but there is no room for that here. Any words she might say will only be ridiculed and tempt more humiliation. Her only hope of survival is to submit. And for Nuray, submission is not easy. Completely naked, she tries to cover herself with her hands. The men laugh and move toward her. Nuray hears her mother's voice, *Leave your body, daughter. Leave your body and let your spirit soar.*

CHAPTER 25

Safak Aksoy is an extremely disgruntled young man. "ISIS is no picnic," Altan has told him from the beginning. That is putting it mildly. The Turkish army is easier than this, and there are always three meals available there. The food was not always the best, but he is starving here. His pants are already too big, but his upper body is increasing in muscle with the unyielding workouts and exercise he is required to do daily. But there's not enough fuel to keep him going.

He had a bunk in the army. There were four walls and plumbing. Now he sleeps where he falls, among many other filthy, tired men. They lie on the ground, rolled up in available blankets, wherever there is space. Sometimes there is water to wash; most often there is not. Rows of tents set on rain-soaked muddy ground house the fighters, their women, and their many children. On the go, on a mission, Safak understands that conditions are even worse. But Safak has yet to go on a mission. His commander will tell him when he is ready. First he must study his religion and be considered trained enough for combat on the front. He must be deemed emotionally and physically ready.

And women? The women in this camp are all taken, married off to others as soon as they've arrived on their own, or handed out to the men after raids. Many of them are pregnant. Safak has not yet raided a village, and so he is very much on his own. He barely sees his brother. Altan is, of course, higher up in the ranks, and Safak is at the very bottom. Altan is busy coordinating and planning with the commanders.

And praying five times a day? There is some discrepancy that he detects here, but if he wishes to pass his inspection without question, to remain and even advance in this group, he must appear to be devoted. His observance to his religion and its principles are scrutinized and noted. Altan tells Safak that he himself is now a believer. His faith is what carries him through. Safak, as of yet, has no faith, no principles. And yet, he does not seriously ask himself why he is here. His brother is here. Safak is AWOL from the army. He faces arrest, discipline, possibly worse. He has no place else to go. He has a gun. Soon he hopes to have a bride. He hopes to raid a village so that he can use the gun, capture the girl, and perhaps, find something better to eat.

And somewhere in the recesses of his mind, Safak wishes to belong somewhere, to fit in. This is an undeveloped, incomplete feeling that he has, a feeling that has no words as of yet, but this is what has driven him to be here. This is why he is so angry now. He did not expect the living conditions to be so primitive. Although Safak is not one to be overly meticulous with regard to his grooming, he is used to showering regularly, keeping his hair and beard trimmed, and cleaning his teeth and his nails. Already in just a few weeks, his beard is shaggy, and his hair is getting too long. Finding clean water to brush his teeth is difficult. He is out of toothpaste, and there is none to be found anywhere in this camp. He has only a tiny bar of guest soap that he found in his mother's bathroom and threw into his knapsack at the last minute. He wonders if he will get lice here.

He is up before dawn at the first call to prayer. There is a study group where he must learn to recite the principles of the *Quran* and of ISIS, not always exactly compatible, but interpreted as if they are written in stone. Then there are physical exercises before the morning meal which consists of some kind of porridge and coffee or tea. Weapons and marching are next. There is no midday meal, just tea, sometimes accompanied by a bit of bread. Tobacco is rolled and strong, but Safak finds himself smoking more and drinking more tea to relieve his hunger. Water is unsafe unless boiled. The afternoons are scheduled with a variety of military exercises, shooting skills, maneuvering in ranges designed to replicate the taking of villages, the making of bombs and suicide bombers, counterattacking aircraft, every possibility and every moment filled with the purpose and intent of the ISIS mission, to make the world into an Islamic State. By the end of the evening prayer, Safak can do no more than fall into the worn and filthy blankets on the dirt floor he now calls a bed. And when the rains come, and the floor becomes a muddy swill, he tries to find some plastic or a tarp to place underneath.

Days turn into weeks and then months. Somehow, having nowhere else to go and nothing else to believe, Safak finds himself no longer merely reciting words, but actually praying. His energy increases with his faith, and he begins to push himself to excel in the physical and military exercises, in the religious study, with a dedication he has never elicited, or even knew he had, to achieve any goal in his life. His hair and his beard grow long. He begins to wrap his hair in a scarf, like a turban. He begins to resemble the men around him. He can feel the emptiness within him being replaced with a new energy for this cause.

Altan greets his brother after some months one morning after prayers, and he hugs him close. "*As salamu alaikum.* Look at you, brother. You are a new man. You are coming along just fine. I am proud of you."

"*Wa alaikum asalaam.* Thank you, brother." No one has ever told Safak that they are proud of him. The words gush over him in a warm cascade of contentment. This is a feeling Safak has never known.

"Come with me." Altan tells him, "I'm going to introduce you to a few comrades."

"But I have morning exercises now," Safak replies.

"That's okay. You are excused to come with me. Let's go." Altan wraps one arm around his brother's shoulders and leads him off in the sea of tents.

"And how is your faith now, brother?" Altan releases his arm and looks Safak directly in the eyes.

"My faith is becoming strong. I hardly can believe it myself. I don't know—"

"Do not question your faith. Only question your lack of faith. There is no question. Allah is all and always there for us."

"Like *Baba* never was."

"Like *Baba* never was and never will be."

Altan directs Safak to a tent off to the side of the others, a bit larger and set up from the ground by wooden planks. "Here we go, Brother," he says, motioning to the tent.

"Altan?" Safak stops and puts his hand on Altan's shoulder.

"What is it?"

"Thank you for giving me this chance. I think you have saved my life."

"Saved it only to put it at a high risk again," Altan warns him.

"But for something. I feel I am something now. I was nothing."

The brothers hug again, and with no further delay, Altan calls out his name, pulls back the tent flap, and the brothers enter.

CHAPTER 26

Nuray opens one eye to a bright florescent light glaring down at her. The other eye, she soon realizes, is bandaged and will not open. Something serious has happened to her. She is not sure just what has occurred or where she is. Her arm is hooked up to an IV, and she is breathing oxygen through her nose. Beeping sounds indicate that her functions are being monitored. She is in a hospital. Some kind of tubing is in her mouth and throat, and she is unable to call out for help or to move her body. Her ankles and the arm not attached to the IV are chained to the bed.

She attempts to breathe in deeply and slowly, but she is immediately taken by a coughing fit. The beeping gets louder and more insistent, and that manages to get someone's attention. Nuray cannot clearly make out the person who comes to her bedside, as the eye that is not bandaged is swollen and images are ambiguous. She tries to ask where she is, but the tubing obstructs any words. All she can utter are grunts.

"It's okay, you are going to be okay," the figure informs her. "I am a nurse in the prison section of the hospital. You have had a bad accident and needed surgery. When the doctor comes, he will explain everything to you."

Nuray is foggy with drugs that she does not at this stage know she is being given for pain management. But she cannot remember any accident. In fact, she has no memory of anything happening to her that would have put her in the hospital. She tries again to speak, but the figure leaves the room. In any case, her efforts are useless.

The drugs take hold again, and Nuray drifts off into semiconsciousness. *She is in a dark tunnel, and she is not alone. Grotesque shadows loom over her, her body prostrate and naked on a cold cement floor. Cold and hard, bodies press her into the unforgiving cement. They enter her and leave her vagina, her anus, her mouth at once, not only with their bodies, their penises, but with objects, sharp and hard. Masked men turn her this way and that, prodding her, entering her, using her as if she were a thing, no longer human, no voice to protest, no soul to save.* Only the drugs keep her from feeling the pain.

Nuray screams awake, but nothing comes out except a gagging, a choking cough. A figure enters the room and explains in a male voice, "I'm going to remove the tube now." With no hesitation, the tubing is pulled from her throat, seriously scraped, and wounded, judging by the amount of pain Nuray experiences. Nuray has difficulty swallowing and chokes again. She tries to sit up in order to aid her breathing, but she falls back onto the bed immediately, coughing and choking into the sheets.

The blurry figure of a man in a white doctor's jacket stands by the bed. There is another figure next to him which must be the nurse, Nuray thinks. The man begins to turn pages on a clipboard and finally he speaks.

"You really did quite a bit of damage to yourself. Trying to abort a baby on your own is very dangerous. You could have died."

Nuray is stunned. She tries to speak. "No, no. I didn't. I wasn't." The sounds that come out do not fit the words intended.

"There was no way the surgeon could save your uterus. In order to save your life, he had to remove everything. Why did you think it would aid your abortion to puncture your anus and bowels the way that you did? The surgeon was really skeptical that you could have done so much damage to yourself, but that is exactly what we were told. You really made quite a mess. You have a temporary colostomy bag which the surgeon hopes he can reverse with another procedure before you leave the hospital. I must tell you, you will never be able to have children."

"Not pregnant, never," Nuray tries to tell them, but no one can make out what she is saying. Nuray cannot clear her foggy brain. There is a thick cloud covering her thoughts, smothering them, so that nothing makes any sense. The cloud thickens, darkness descends, and Nuray sinks back into a merciful unconsciousness.

When Nuray awakens again, the room is dark except for the lights flickering on the beeping machinery. She can almost open the unbandaged eye completely, although with some difficulty and sensitivity. Her right hand is attached to an IV needle, and the left is handcuffed to the bed. Even in her state of semi-drugged half consciousness, the irony of this is not lost to Nuray. She could not move even if her limbs were free.

An unknowable terror crawls from the recesses of her brain and into her heart and stomach. She can feel its motion, encapsulating every nerve and fiber of her being, slowly gaining in its momentum until her shackled limbs are shaking with fear. Her hands and feet are vibrating against the steel of the bed. Her heart rate climbs and pushes the needles on the machinery, the beeping increasing until an alarm is sounded. There is deadly silence and a sudden blackness to everything.

The room is flooded with lights and bodies. Nuray hears someone say, "She's back. We got her back."

A softer voice that Nuray can barely hear mutters, "Maybe better we didn't."

"Her heart rate is coming back. Blood pressure is down. Must have been the shock. Keep checking her vitals and let her rest for now."

The lights are turned off, and the room empties. Nuray tries to focus on her breathing. She attempts to count to ten in and count to ten out, but she is overcome by coughing and choking. For the first time, she feels the pain throughout her body. She cries out, and this time, she manages sound and is heard. A figure enters the room and comes to the side of her bed.

"Pain!" she screams, feeling it worse with her efforts.

"Okay," the figure says. "I'll be right back with your pain injection."

Nuray wants to go back into the fog. She yearns for the fog. But the masked men, they were there. Will they come back? Whatever this world is that she has awakened to, she wants to shut it down. Why is she here in this place? She knows, but she is unable to grasp onto the knowledge. Her mind is submerged in a swamp of confusion.

The figure returns, a syringe in her hand. "Get me out," Nuray struggles to cry. "Please, get me out of here."

"Now just relax," the voice tells her. "Here we go. You'll be asleep in a few minutes."

And slowly, Nuray slips back into the blackness.

CHAPTER 27

Mohammed Fetullah Gülen rises slowly from his prayer mat inside his apartment in the Chestnut Retreat Center. The Hizmet-affiliated compound is set in the Poconos in Pennsylvania, USA. Gülen resides here in exile. He occupies two small, modest rooms for which he reportedly pays rent from his publishing royalties. This is most certainly an improvement over the prison cell he would be occupying if it were up to President Erdoğan and the current Turkish government.

It is not as if this famous cleric has not had his freedom threatened in the United States. As reported in the news, notorious allies of President Trump, Michael Flynn and Rudy Giuliani, have not only urged Trump to give up Gülen in order to curry favor with Erdoğan, but hatched a kidnapping plot to extradite him. This is public knowledge. Along with his ill health, this has caused the cleric to be even more discreet about having visitors. His old age is thus fairly isolated.

Gülen is a man of deep religious and philosophical beliefs who has already spent time in prison. Who has not been imprisoned who has dared to object to government suppression in the many stages and reinventions of Turkish government? But one has to wonder how it might feel for anyone to spend the last years of their life sequestered away from their motherland and beloved country.

What is Gülen thinking? What is he feeling? What are his thoughts about his prior colleague and friend, Recep Erdoğan? Does he continue to contemplate this betrayal, or has he been able to leave it behind?

Mohammed lifts his hands from his keyboard. What is the point of writing this piece? He does not imagine that it will ever be published. And yet, there is consolation in the writing. But suppose the police aren't finished with him and seize his computer? Ayşegül is right to be worried. It is only weeks since he himself was released from jail.

But he has been thinking about Gülen. He is curious about the change that took place in his relationship to Erdoğan. How did it all come to pass? He is certain there is more to it all than what has been reported. And only these two men know the absolute truth.

And can a man ever put behind such a terrible betrayal? Mohammed wonders. Mohammed has not yet been able to forgive the woman who accused him of plagiarism and sexual harrassment, and that was minor in comparison. He would like to be able to forgive her and close that chapter in his mind, and so he is curious if this religious cleric has been able to do so.

Mohammed prints out what he has typed, and then erases the file from his computer. He copies his words onto a legal pad. He can hand write this piece if he chooses to continue, and then he can hide it somewhere. He considers for a few moments, and then puts the paper into his shredder. No, this is not the time to be writing a piece about the exiled cleric. What he is trying in vain not to be obsessed about is his own betrayal of Nuray.

To hell with it all, Mohammed thinks, I will go to see her, and let the fallout be what it will. I won't be able to live with myself if I abandon her. The children are in school and Ayşegül is substitute teaching where she may be able to get a permanent slot. He is on his own until late afternoon. He shuts down his computer and picks up his wallet and keys. He hesitates a moment before opening the door to leave the apartment, but only a moment. If I don't do it now, he reflects, I may not do it at all. The door slams shut behind him.

CHAPTER 28

Nuray forces her arms down to hoist her body from the hospital bed. This is not an easy task. Her temporary colostomy has only been reversed for a week, and none of her biological functions feel normal. She is still in a good deal of pain, both internally and externally. Walking is a strain, but she can manage with a cane now. Only a few days ago, she needed a walker, and every movement brought on sharp spasms. She is still being held in the hospital ward of the prison, but she anticipates that soon she will be moved again. Whether it will be into the general population or isolation, she does not know.

Nuray continues to struggle with the fact that her fate is not her own, along with the horror of what has been done to her. How could this possibly happen? And what could she have done to prevent it? She knows this thinking is crazy, and she would definitely confront it as such in anyone else, but she cannot seem to stop herself from the repetitive and unanswerable questions. There must have been something. What did she do to provoke them to such rage? Did she know them? Did they know her? They wore masks. She was unconscious much of the time. She did not recognize any of them. Did the soldier send them? Is it possible that he could have been one of them? Will she ever know, and what difference can it possibly make?

She wakes up screaming every night from a sweat-soaking sleep. Not one night has passed peacefully since—what to call it—the rape? Nuray has trouble naming it. Yes, she was raped brutally, but it was so much more than a rape. It was as physical as it was sexual, if not more so. Some object, and no one knows for certain what the object was, was inserted in her rectum and repeatedly forced inside of her. What would make someone do such a terrible and pointless thing? If not for a decent and sympathetic surgeon at the prison, she would have permanently had to wear a colostomy bag. He said he worked hard not to allow that to happen.

The staff refer to the incident as her assault. They are finally forced to accept that she could not have inflicted so much damage to herself, even if she had been pregnant. She was assaulted. Somehow the word is not descriptive enough or violent enough to embody what occurred. An invasion? An act of violence? Grievous bodily harm? All of these things? What to call it? What to name it? She is at a loss for the right word or words. Life altering event? Yes, most definitely that. The once confident Nuray, who felt her life was in her own hands, is gone now, perhaps gone forever, she does not know.

In the act of pushing herself from a sitting position to a standing position, she is once again aware of her vulnerability. Nuray remembers now that once, when she was a child, maybe five years old, a neighbor boy pulled a single leg maliciously from a spider's body. When Nuray questioned him as to why he would do such a thing, he explained to her that he simply wanted to see what would happen. Nuray had been horrified and fascinated at the same time. The spider had initially struggled, off balance, not quite able to right itself. After a few slides downwards, the missing leg seeming to have been forgotten, the spider ambled away from them, moving along as if nothing at all had happened. The boy had wanted to amputate yet another leg, but Nuray had stopped him. In fact, she now remembers slapping his hand away from the spider as it made its way along the cracks in the sidewalk, and then finally disappeared into one of them.

The act of disengaging the spider from its leg took a fraction of a second. Nuray replays that instant in her mind. In mere moments, how long she cannot say, her very being has been forever altered by inexplicable acts of violence and rage. It is impossible for her, as a woman, to conceive of the state of mind that would bring a man to commit such a crime alone, never mind in a group. She is quite certain that there are men, as well as women, who could not imagine being in the psychological state that would lead them to perpetrate such acts. She must believe this, if she is ever to trust a man again.

Nuray wants to understand. She desperately wants to know. She searches for a rational answer, a logical reason for what happened to her. To have to accept that this was all an act of random fate is inconceivable. The soldier must have instigated the assault. A random attack without explanation would mean that she might be vulnerable to anything and anyone at any time. Nuray cannot accept this. And yet, this is what she has been told. Women are raped here. It happens. No one is caught. No one is punished. It is like the rain. It just comes when it comes.

Nuray uses her cane to walk slowly around the bed. Her vagina is still raw, and it burns when she urinates. Having a bowel movement is excruciating, but she has been told this will heal and improve. She is not used to paying such close attention to her body's physical functions, but now they are primary. They take all of her concentration, all of her energy.

The sound of approaching footsteps breaks her train of thought. The interruption is both welcomed and rejected. She is drawn to embrace anything that pulls her thoughts away from this trauma at the same time that she wishes to resist everything that turns her scrutiny away from it.

One of the nurses who has been attending Nuray enters the room. "Are you up for a visitor? Good to see that you're out of bed."

"A visitor? I'm not sure I want to see anyone just yet. Who is it? Do you know?"

"A man. He says he's a friend. He's insisting on seeing you. I told him you'd been in the hospital, and I didn't know if you'd see him, but he didn't want to take no for an answer."

"I guess I can manage. I have no idea who it might be." Nuray takes tentative steps alongside the nurse. Since the incident, she has walked no farther than the bathroom until now. She suddenly realizes that she has not looked in a mirror, washed her face, or straightened her headscarf. She touches her head to ensure that she is still wearing one, even though she resists a temptation to tear it off and to leave her hair exposed. After all, she is not a practicing Muslim. She has only wished to appear to be a practicing Muslim. Well, whoever it is will have to accept her as she is. There is little she can do to improve her image right now.

Nuray is not surprised to see that the room is vacant except for the one guard assigned to monitor her, as it is not the official time for visitors. Nuray is not sure why she is even being allowed this interview, but she knows not to question something that could be positive and could be taken away.

When she sees that her visitor is Mohammed, Nuray is relieved. For some inexplicable reason, she had thought it might be her father. In the past weeks, he has been on her mind. Why she even thought he might visit her, she cannot say. Even worse, she thought it might be a complete stranger wanting her to talk about her situation, a journalist seeking a story. Somehow stories continue to emerge even with all the shut downs. She hears these things whispered around her.

Mohammed is clearly shocked at her appearance. She can read his expression so easily.

"What happened to you? Oh, Nuray, you have been beaten. Your eye has green and purple around it. I am so sorry. Are you okay?" Mohammed sits down across the table from Nuray. She slowly adjusts into the chair and leans her cane against the table. Mohammed eyes the cane but says nothing.

"I'm fine. Please, I'm asking you, let's not talk about it anymore. I'm okay now. But what are you doing here? We agreed you would not visit me. Does Ayşegül know that you're here?"

"No, I haven't told her yet. I made up my mind and came straight here once I decided."

"But you decided before not to come. I understood, my friend. You don't have to do this. You don't have to prove anything to me."

"Maybe it isn't you I have to prove myself to. I have not felt right about that decision even before I told you. I could not live with it. So here I am. I know that Ayşegül will come to understand. She is a good woman with a kind heart. She is just afraid. Fear makes us act in funny ways. I see that now."

Nuray adjusts her body in the chair. This is not a comfortable position for her. She longs to lie back down, but she knows that Mohammed has put his very marriage on the line to see her. She resists the pain.

"I am so very glad to see you," she tells him. "Thank you for coming."

"Have you seen anyone else?" Mohammed asks.

"No. Adalet was here, but they didn't allow her to see me. You must let her know it's okay for her to visit. I am pretty sure she will be leaving Turkey now."

"You think her arrest will have convinced her to go?" Mohammed asks.

"Yes, I do. I have encouraged her to get out of here. I am sorry that she was arrested, but I think it is just the incentive she needed."

"That would be a tough incentive, but now I am twice as glad I changed my mind about visiting you. Losing Adalet will be hard." Mohammed looks so deeply into Nuray's eyes that she is forced to look away. She stares down at her hands, folding one onto the other and pressing them down against the table.

"Yes, losing Adalet will be very hard. I didn't realize how much she means to me. I don't have many friends, Mohammed. In fact, Adalet is my only woman friend. And you are my only other friend. I'm afraid that I have spent no time at all in cultivating relationships."

Mohammed forces a smile. "I don't have friends, either. You are my only friend, other than Ayşegül, and she is my wife as well as my friend. She is in a difficult position. Please don't judge her too harshly."

"I don't. I completely understand. Perhaps I would feel as she does if I were in her shoes." Nuray tries to move her body in the chair with her hands, and feels a slight momentary relief.

"You are in pain," Mohammed says, shifting his own body in sympathy without realizing that he is doing so.

"I'm fine," Nuray insists, not wanting the visit to end, but wishing she could lie down somehow.

"Where will Adalet go?" Mohammed asks.

"She will marry Mark and go to America. She already has friends there. Meryem is there, the young girl she looked after, and Isha, Meryem's lover, so Adalet won't be alone. Even though I will miss her terribly, it is the right thing for her to do. And I know I'm only going to miss her so much because I am stuck here. If I were out of this prison and living my normal life, I would feel differently about her going. I would think about her from time to time, but actively miss her? I don't think I would so much. I've never been good at close relationships. And now because I need them, I can't expect people to suddenly show up for me. That includes you, Mohammed. I mean that."

"Well, I consider you to be my friend, whether you wish to accept it or not." Mohammed gives her another piercing stare and elicits a smile from Nuray.

"You don't choose your friends wisely, but I will accept. I have little choice, I suppose. " Nuray reaches for her cane. "And now, I must cut this visit short. Please forgive me. I must lie down for a while. Please come again, if you like." Nuray begins the struggle of getting herself out of the chair and standing. Mohammed stands up with her, so as not to stare.

"I will come again," he says. "I will be here for you. Is there anything you need?"

Nuray leans on her cane. "I would very much like to have a novel to read. If you can find a copy of *The Forty Rules of Love*, Elif Şafak is the author. I would like to reread it now. Do you know it?"

Mohammed shakes his head that he does not.

"It is a lovely book. Her best, I think. It is the story of Rumi."

"Ah, yes, of course. Ayşegül reads Şafak, and I have seen the book on her shelf. I will get you a copy."

"I thank you, my friend." Nuray motions to the guard that the visit is ended. She begins to walk away with carefully and cautiously placed steps. She turns her head to Mohammed. "Good-bye, dear friend. I thank you for coming. I will see you again, *Inshallah*."

"Yes," Mohammed tells her, still standing by the table, "I will see you again soon, *Inshallah*."

CHAPTER 29

Adalet runs her fingers over the lace of her *anne's* wedding dress, the one thing she has salvaged from the wreck of the earthquake. She hurt her *anne's* feelings deeply when she rejected wearing the dress for her first wedding, her marriage to Yasar. There are soot and water stains along the bottom edges of the lace, but the dress remains incredibly intact. Is it a crazy whim to pack this bulky dress to wear in America?

Adalet and Mark have made no actual wedding plans yet, other than to set the wedding in his gardens on Long Island. And although no one knows it yet, and they don't plan to ever inform anyone, Mark already flew into Istanbul a couple of weeks ago to marry Adalet in order to make the necessary papers legal for her to easily emigrate to the United States. Mark's Turkish attorney arranged everything, and the attorney brought her own witnesses. The marriage ceremony itself only took a few minutes. The attorney told Adalet, "Your passport will be in the name of Adalet Aronson, and there won't be any questions about it." But this is Mark's first marriage, and he wants a real wedding, even though he no longer has any family to attend the event.

Almost four months have passed since her horrific jail experience, and Mark is anxious to get Adalet out of this rapidly changing country as quickly as he possibly can. Adalet is as reluctant to leave as she is to stay, but she shares as little of these feelings as possible with Mark. He has waited years for her. She does not wish to give him reasons to doubt her decision.

. . .

The attorney had suggested that they leave Istanbul for New York together after the marriage was completed, but Adalet did not feel ready. "I still have so much to do before I leave. There are things I need to settle." Adalet asked the attorney to arrange papers for her to turn the building on Steep Street over to Fatma's sons. "I would like to do this in person, if it is at all possible," Adalet told the attorney. Mark said that he understood and did not press Adalet to change her mind. Adalet did not feel that a few more weeks were going to make a difference.

Can the wedding dress be cleaned? Adalet wonders. She can take it to the dry cleaner across the way and ask him if he thinks it possible. Perhaps she can put it into a garment bag and carry it separately onto the plane. But it might turn out to be too formal for the wedding, and then she will have gone to so much trouble for nothing. If the dress is ruined, she will feel easier about leaving it behind.

Adalet finds a large, clean garbage bag and stuffs the wedding dress inside. She makes her way across an unusually quiet Steep Street. Although Adalet has used this facility before today, the man who owns and operates it has spoken only a few words to her, and they have been to let her know the cost of her articles. He spends some minutes examining the dress.

"Very beautiful," he finally reports.

"But can it be cleaned?" Adalet asks.

"I don't know. I can try."

"And if it doesn't come clean?"

"Then I won't charge you very much, but I will have to charge you something. It will take time. It's very difficult, the lace."

"And if you get it clean? Will it be very expensive?"

The old man surveys the dress again. His worn hands and unclean fingernails work over the lace. "I will be honest with you. The cost of cleaning this will buy you another dress. It will take some work by hand. The lace is fragile. It might even tear in the process. It is valuable to you?"

Adalet fights back tears. "It was my *anne's*. It survived an earthquake."

The old man fingers the lace again. "Hmmm," he mutters, "maybe not so well."

Adalet takes the dress back and stuffs it back into the garbage bag. "Okay, let me think about it." She decides to take it somewhere else and to get another opinion and perhaps, a definite estimate.

"Wait. Why don't you let me see what I can do? If I can't get the stain from the lace, I will stop there, and I will not charge you. Come back in two days. If I can get it out, we can agree on a price. How does that sound?"

Adalet smiles. Why does one always have to be prepared to walk away in Turkey? "*Tamam*, okay. Thank you." She sets the garbage bag back onto the counter. "I'll check back with you on Thursday." For some reason she cannot explain, Adalet now feels determined to get the dress cleaned. It is as a tribute to her *anne*, but there is also something she does not quite understand herself that is linked to her leaving Turkey. This hurts her heart.

And she must go to visit Nuray. The last time she tried, she was informed that Nuray was in the hospital and could not be seen. This has been of great concern to Adalet. She has not stopped worrying about her friend.

When Adalet goes home, she is surprised to see a note has been left taped to the door with her name on it. She pulls if off and races up the stairs to see who it is from. She flings off her shoes and quickly unlocks the door. The handwriting of her name on the envelope is unfamiliar.

Adalet,

I am sorry to have missed you. I was on my way home from visiting Nuray. She wanted me to let you know that she is better, and you may visit her now. Please give me a call after you have seen her. I would like very much to speak with you.

    Mohammed

Mohammed has carefully printed his phone number at the bottom of the note.

Adalet has thought about visiting Nuray today, but as it is not visiting day and Mohammed has already been there, she decides to wait and go at the regular time. She is relieved that Nuray is better, and that Mohammed is visiting Nuray again. Nuray has told her about the visit when Mohammed informed Nuray that he would not be able to see her in prison. Adalet's distress at leaving Turkey with Nuray in prison is ever so slightly lightened by Mohammed's support. Adalet has not slept well worrying about Nuray. This is one of several reasons why she did not fly to New York with Mark.

Adalet determines that she will go to Avanos to deliver the papers to Ahmet and Bekir transferring the ownership of the building to them. She will not say goodbye to Nuray yet. She will do that the day prior to her actual departure, or as close to that as visiting day will allow. These are her remaining duties. Adalet cannot help but believe there ought to have been more. But her assessment of her of her life in Turkey now has proved to be correct. The death of her parents and the tragedy of the earthquake leading to her divorce and the loss of her baby, the closing of the deaf school, the death of Fatma, Mark settling back into life in New York due to the lack of opportunity for him in Turkey, and Meryem and Isha now working on getting their American citizenship, all of these facts have led her to believe that this is her best decision. And it is not as if she doesn't love Mark. She has loved him for years now. But he has always been in competition with her love for Turkey, her love for its people, her people, her language. This will be very hard.

Although it might have been easier for her to mail the papers to Fatma's two sons, Ahmet and Bekir—she has no desire to have to say goodbye to them in person—she does want to see Avanos and the pottery shop one more time before she leaves. She must visit Fatma's grave for what might be the very last time. If not for Fatma's loving support, she never would have moved back to Istanbul. She never would have met either Meryem or Mark.

Even with an American passport and American citizenship, even without any affiliation with the Hizmet people, she still has some concerns about ever returning to Turkey under this present government. She worries now that she should have gone to America with Mark. After all, Nuray has had no affiliation with them either, and just look where she is. Under these present conditions, it can be impossible to know what it is best to do.

Adalet spends the remainder of the day packing the things she will send to America. The wedding dress can be packed separately. She will wrap it in tissue paper and place it in a special box which she will mail directly to Mark. There is little need to carry much on the plane with her. This will make travel much easier.

Adalet decides to go to Avanos the next day, and so she calls Ahmet to let him know she is coming. She will only stay one night to be back in time to visit Nuray and to see about her wedding dress. Although he expresses his gratitude about the transfer of the property, Ahmet is as noncommittal as usual.

"Yes, of course, and we appreciate your generosity. But we will be busy in the factory and in the shop. Our wives are not so good in selling, not as good as my *anne* was, so we must take turns in supervising them. We must all take turns these days."

"I understand," Adalet tells him. "I will need just a few moments of your time, that's all. I understand that my old house is rented out now, so I will get a hotel."

"Yes, that would be best. We are overcrowded here, so I cannot offer you a room. I'm sorry."

"No worries, Ahmet. I am better on my own anyway. Please have no concerns."

"Thank you, Adalet. We will see you soon."

"*Inshallah*, Ahmet."

"Inshallah."

Adalet decides to rent a car and drive to Avanos. Since she no longer has her car there, she will need some way to get around. She cannot rely on Ahmet or Bekir, and as she has told Ahmet, she is better off on her own. She may wish to visit Temel and Emine, if there is time and it is possible. Temel was first her handyman, then he and Emine became her friends, and later Temel became the caretaker of her house when she moved to Istanbul. As Mark's wife, she no longer has any financial worries, so she books both a car and a good hotel. She might as well enjoy the journey. There is a lovely small tourist hotel near the caves where Fatma was born. It is actually dug into what used to be cave dwellings. She has often imagined staying there. As the tourist trade is so off due to the political tensions, she has no trouble in getting a room or a car. But as there are so few tourists now, she is a bit surprised at Ahmet's claims of being so busy in the pottery shop. She believes this is a way to insure that she will not overstay her welcome. Ahmet and Adalet have never been close, but she feels it would be Fatma's wish, under the circumstances, to return the building to the family.

Interestingly, Adalet reflects, she has no concerns at all that her marriage to Mark will end in divorce. As part of their marriage paperwork, he has already willed his entire estate to her. He wants her to feel secure, and she does. She has no fears that Mark will be unfaithful. This is just not in his character. She thinks at times that she should have some apprehension after her failed marriage with Yasar, but she and Yasar were both so young. She no longer blames him. In her eyes, they were both at fault. Mark is not Yasar, and he has proven himself to her. She loves him totally. Her only conflict is leaving her beloved country.

Well, she ponders, Mark has said there is a large Turkish community in New York. She has successfully looked for establishments and organizations on the Internet. Meryem will also be a tremendous help. She was so excited when Adalet told her about her decision to marry Mark. "It's about time," she said. "Now we can be together again."

Yes, this is all for the good. Well, mostly all for the good. Nothing is ever all good. Adalet smiles to herself. This is a lesson in life that she is still trying to learn. There is always some bad underlying whatever is all for the good.

CHAPTER 30

Nuray is out of the hospital and back in isolation only one day. The doctor has declared her well enough to leave the hospital but not well enough to be in the general population. At any other time, Nuray would object to this, but she honestly needs all the rest she can get right now. So she has no objections.

She has barely settled into her new surroundings when a guard comes to tell her that she should gather her things together. She is being released. The paperwork will take some time, but she should be ready. She is so shocked at this news that she blurts out, "Why? Do you know why I am being released?"

The guard looks hesitant, but she is someone who has been sympathetic to Nuray. "Please don't tell anyone how you know, but apparently you have a father who agreed to confess to some rather serious crimes on the condition of your release. I overheard this, so I'm not even supposed to have this knowledge."

"My father? He is involved in my release? How can that be? You have been so kind. I do appreciate everything you have done for me. I will get ready now. I really don't have very much to take with me, just the few things my friend brought."

The guard leaves Nuray to pack. Whatever can her father have done that the government is willing to take his confession as a bargain for her release? Had the police informed him of her arrest in order to get him to confess? Or perhaps that is why she was arrested in the first place, as bait. Is her *baba* the cause of all of her troubles now?

Nuray places her few belongings back into the bag Adalet used in order to bring them to her. She waits for about thirty minutes for the guard to return and walk with her to the release processing office. Nuray is still using a cane and moving slowly. She is not free from pain.

Nuray's mobile phone, her laptop, her purse and wallet with I.D. and a small amount of cash are all returned to her. She is asked to sign a paper stating that she has received them. This all feels surrealistic to Nuray. She has had no thoughts that she might be released from prison for some time now. She has been incarcerated for over four months without any definite charges being filed, and therefore, no trial or hint of a trial date in her future. She is freed without any pending charges. She could not have imagined this.

In the speed of her release, Nuray has not considered how she will get home. Adalet does not have a car, and she will not ask her to take public transportation to come just to help her get home, even though she knows Adalet would rush to her aid. She asks about transportation, and she is told the prison van will drive her to a bus or tram, or they can call a taxi for her. As weak as she is, Nuray has to consider her lack of funds, and so she has to take the bus or tram option as the most practical. As it turns out, she must take the van to the bus to the tram in order to get to her neighborhood. But as there is no one Nuray can call to pick her up, this is what she must do. Even in her current condition, it is a blessing to be free to be on public transportation. And so she takes in a long breath of fresh air before boarding the prison van. Soon she will be home. As soon as she can charge her phone, she will call Adalet and Mohammed to let them know. They will both be so relieved.

The trip home is exhausting for Nuray. By the time she is inside her apartment, all she can do is set down her bag, start charging her phone, and stumble to her bed. Although she would love to shower first, she knows she does not have the necessary energy. She falls on top of the covers and is almost instantly asleep.

When Nuray wakes up, it is dark outside and past 8:00 at night. This is the first sleep she has had without waking up in a cold sweat from night terrors she cannot recall or nightmares she can recall. She remembers that her phone is charging but not her laptop. Nuray forces herself up from the bed, grabs her cane and walks to the kitchen where her phone is plugged in and charged. She unplugs it and connects the laptop to its charger and plugs that into the outlet. This gives her a tiny sense of normalcy, but everything feels surrealistic. How can anything feel normal after all that has happened to her? Will anything ever feel normal again?

There is, of course, no food in Nuray's refrigerator. She is hungry but too tired to go downstairs, even to order take-out from the café. She dials Adalet's number and gets her voicemail. Nuray leaves a brief message just to let her know that she's at home, and then she dials Mohammed's number. He picks up.

"Nuray?" The shock is apparent in his voice.

"Yes, Mohammed, I have been released."

"*Mashallah!* That is incredible. You are at home now?"

"Yes, and very tired. I just wanted to let you know. Can we talk tomorrow?"

"Of course. Call me when you are ready, and I will come to see you."

"*Görüşürüz.* See you soon." Nuray closes the call before Mohamed can reply.

Nuray sits at the small table in her kitchen. What to do first, food or shower? She does not think she can manage the energy for a shower without some food first, but going downstairs also feels like quite a chore. She gets ups slowly and opens her cupboard. Yes, there is a can of soup. This will do. She opens the can, pours it into a pot on the stove, but then she must sit down to rest. Her lack of energy is frustrating. Her phone buzzes. She recognizes the caller to be Adalet.

"You're out? Is this really so?" Adalet sounds out of breath.

"Yes. I can hardly believe it myself. You sound funny."

"I'm driving to Avanos. I was coming to see you first, but so much has happened that my plans changed. I'll be back in a couple of days. I will come to see you then. How are you feeling? Why were you in the hospital anyway?"

"I'm fine now," Nuray says, stretching the truth. "I'll tell you when I see you. There's too much to talk about on the phone. And you are driving. Call me when you get home."

"As soon as I am home," Adalet promises. "I have so much to tell you, too."

"Good." Nuray forces herself up from her chair to turn off the now boiling soup. "I will see you soon."

"*Görüşürüz*," Adalet replies. The line goes dead.

She is on her way to Avanos, Nuray thinks. She is getting ready to leave. I wonder if I should think about leaving, too. But how would I go? And where would I go? I have no visa and no money.

As Nuray slowly sips her soup, she contemplates the severity of her circumstances. She has no income and little hope of finding any work. She is a marked figure, now that she has been arrested. Perhaps she could find menial labor work, if she were only physically able. But she is not. Who knows how long it will take her to regain her strength?

Fortunately, she does have some money stashed away. There isn't much, but enough to put food on the table a bit longer. There isn't enough to help her to travel anywhere. And then, there is the visa issue. She will not be able to get a visa as she is still under suspicion. Maybe Mohammed will have a suggestion. Perhaps Adalet would be willing to ask Mark's Turkish attorney. Could she live in another country? She may have no choice. This thought hits her like an avalanche sweeping down to cover and bury her.

Nuray finishes the soup and leaves the dirty pot and dish in the sink. This can wait until tomorrow. A shower will also wait until tomorrow. She stumbles to the bedroom, removes her outer clothing, and gets into bed in her underwear. There are too many problems to solve. She is in no frame of mind to consider them all now. She can only hope for sleep that does not terrorize her. That is the most she can wish for in this moment. In this moment, she is a free woman.

CHAPTER 31

Nuray awakens to sunshine streaming across her quilt and into her eyes, eyes not currently accustomed to such bright and cheerful morning greetings. She takes a moment to adjust to the most familiar and welcoming surroundings. As she sits up and reaches for her cane, a thought suddenly hits her. She must find her father, and not just to thank him for rescuing her. Of all the people she knows and can imagine, he is the one who might be able to guide her to a path out of the country. He has connections. On her way to the bathroom, Nuray sighs with some relief. She can finally urinate without pain, and at least she has a plan for something she might do next. She will find out where he is being held and visit him in prison.

Before Nuray can organize herself enough to shower, her buzzer sounds. She hesitates, not sure she wants anyone to know she is home. But then she realizes that it might be Adalet or Mohammed, and so she goes to the speaker and asks who it is.

"It's me, Adalet, and Mohammed is with me."

"Both of you at once?" Instantly Nuray realizes how unfriendly this sounds. "Oh, I'm sorry. Please forgive me. I'm not used to being around people. Please come in and come up." She buzzes them in the front door, wishing she had taken a shower and had some breakfast. She has no idea what time or day it is. She has been asleep and awake, up and down, for some time. If Adalet is here, it must be a couple of days. Well, shower or no shower, they will just have to accept her as she is.

When she opens the door, she is so surprised to see that each of them is burdened to the top of their noses carrying containers of food. Adalet is further encumbered by a large bouquet of a mixture of sunflowers and daisies.

"Oh, look at you two! Give me those flowers before you drop everything, Adalet. I don't know how you managed." Nuray leans her cane against a wall and takes the flowers from Adalet. "These are gorgeous. Should I assume they're for me?"

"No, of course not," Adalet chuckles. "They're for Mohammed. Of course, they're for you. I thought your unused apartment might need some cheering up, and a woman was selling these just a block away. How lucky, eh? And what's with the cane?"

"Oh, I had a fall. It's nothing." Nuray manages a smile.

"Move, please," Mohammed scolds Adalet, "before I drop all of this food and tea."

"Sorry." Adalet heads into the apartment, setting her bundles down on the dining table. "Put them here, Mohammed. Her kitchen table is too small. We do hope you are hungry, Nuray."

"Famished." Nuray grabs her cane and follows her friends into the dining room. "All I've eaten since yesterday afternoon is a can of minestrone soup."

"Well then, sit down and let us put out a banquet for you. Neither one of us knew the other was coming, and we ran into each other downstairs both carrying food. There could be duplicates." Mohammed actually looks concerned about this.

Nuray laughs. "I don't care what is in those packages. I will eat anything. I love you both for bringing food. I have none at all. I must warn you. I haven't showered since I got here."

Adalet is already in the kitchen pulling out plates, cups, glasses, napkins, and utensils. Mohammed looks over Nuray's clearly disheveled state. "You can shower after we eat, and for as long as you like. Then you can have a nice, long sleep. Have you discarded your headscarf? Is that a lapse or permanent?"

Nuray shakes her head at him, shoulder-length brown curls loose. She feigns annoyance. "I've had people telling me what I can or can't do for months now. I have not decided yet about the headscarf. I think it is off, but I'm not sure. Please, take it easy with me. I have been sleeping for two days. Go now and help poor Adalet. She is making a ruckus in there. I will let you both wait on me today. This will be a pleasure."

Nuray listens with happiness to her two friends sorting out dishes and bringing them to the dining table after clearing away enough books and papers to make that possible. This procedure is done with much laughter and many comments regarding Nuray's lack of housekeeping skills.

"Come on, you two. I haven't been here for months."

"And I suppose a genie visited while you were gone and left this mess for you to find as a prank." Adalet winks at her.

Mohammed sets a stack of paper napkins on the table. "Looks just like the office to me." Then he sees the expression on Nuray's face. "Sorry. I didn't meant to mention the office."

"Someone has to mention it sometime," Nuray says quickly. "No harm done. My goodness, did you two leave any food for the rest of Istanbul? This is quite a feast."

The table is covered with food: two plates of olives, green and black; a variety of dolmades stuffed with meat, rice, cabbage, parsley, and herbs; there are roasted chickpeas, a chickpea stew, a chickpea and potato dish with herbs; there is imam bayildi (eggplant casserole) and an eggplant salad; there are two stacks of Turkish flat bread.

Nuray looks at every dish. "What time is it, anyway?" she asks.

Mohammed checks his watch. "Just about 1:00 in the afternoon. But Nuray, please tell us how you were released. What happened?"

"Please, this is breakfast for me," Nuray announces. "Sit down, my dear friends. I am so ready to eat. I am not ready to talk about what happened."

And she does the food justice. Nuray does not normally eat meat, but she does on this occasion, consuming the meat-filled dolmades with as much gusto as the vegetarian.

Adalet looks surprised. "I didn't think you ate meat. Mohammed brought those."

"Good for Mohammed," Nuray says, taking another one and setting it on her plate. "I have not eaten decent food since the day I was incarcerated, and I'm pretty sure I've lost weight. I had very little protein in there, who knows what the meat was, so I didn't eat any. And I could hardly ask for protein substitutes. I did eat the beans whenever they were offered, but everything tasted pretty awful. There was no seasoning that I could detect."

The food disappears quickly, and when Mohammed and Adalet see that Nuray is hobbling around with a cane, they quickly say they will be back with groceries on the following day.

"You are not to go shopping on your own," Adalet tells her. "I know you don't like being told what to do, but you will need some help until you are ready to walk without the cane."

"And how do people with canes go shopping?" Nuray insists. "I am sure many of them have to do this on their own."

Mohammed does not hesitate. "Fortunately for you, you don't have to do it on your own. I am not working these days, and though I do have to be home in the afternoon by 4:00 to take care of the children, I am free during the day. And when Ayşegül has no meetings after school, she is home as well. But it is better if I am there to help her, as she has been with children all day long."

"How is her job?" Adalet asks. "Does she like it?"

"Hard to say. People are anxious and suspicious. So many have lost jobs and been in jail or prison, there is a lot of fear around saying or doing the wrong thing." Mohammed runs one hand nervously through his hair. "The children are very aware of the power they have. Ayşegül told me of an incident where a teacher criticized a child for bad behavior, and the child retaliated by spreading lies about what the teacher was supposed to have said about Erdoğan and his government. The teacher was dragged off to jail. She was ultimately released, but she was fired. She has not been able to find another job."

"That is terrible." Adalet gets up and begins to clear away the dishes and leftover food from the table. Nuray does not attempt to stop her. She is too tired and so grateful for her friends.

Mohammed looks at his watch and jumps up. "I must go. I have to pick up a few things for dinner before the children get home from school. Is there anything special you want from the store, Nuray?"

"Simple things are best right now. A few cans of soup, some rice, a few fruits and vegetables, bread. Not too much. I won't be eating like I did today. This food was too good to resist, especially after what I'd been eating."

"If you get the staples, Mohammed," Adalet adds, "I will bring some prepared foods that will make things easy for now."

"When do you leave for New York?" Nuray asks. She tries not to put any emotion into the question.

"Ah, so you have guessed my decision. I am not surprised. There just has not been a right time to tell you."

"You know I have wanted you to leave, and even though I will miss you terribly, I do think it is for the best. You have been torn between leaving Turkey and loving Mark for too long." Nuray is grateful to get this out of the way. She has no desire for Adalet to hang around out of pity for her.

"And I will miss you, too, dear friend. You can be assured of that. I have not set a specific date yet. I took care of getting the building papers to Ahmet and Bekir, so there is nothing of that nature holding me back now. I am sure I will leave within the month. Mark has been so patient."

"Yes, you must consider him, I believe."

Mohammed gestures with a shake of his hands. "Ladies, I must run. Thank you, Adalet. I will probably see you again before you go, but in case I don't, I want to wish you all the best in your marriage and in your new life in America."

"Thank you, Mohammed. And I thank you for all you do for Nuray. Once I leave, I will depend on you to look in on her."

"I can easily promise to do so. Take good care. Nuray, I will see you tomorrow. Please take things slowly and easily."

Nuray waves her cane at him. "Go, please. And don't worry. I will be fine. My big activity of the day will be a shower. I have enough food for dinner, so I promise not to even leave the apartment."

Mohammed grins, waves, and is out the door. Adalet sinks back into a chair next to Nuray. She takes Nuray's hands in hers. "Now," she says, "tell me everything."

Nuray is sorry to disappoint Adalet, but she is not about to tell her everything. Why should Adalet be burdened with the images that Nuray is forced to endure and must grapple with every day and night of her life now. Sharing will not lessen her trial. She is certain of this. She puts Adalet off.

"I am so tired, dear friend. I just want to have a hot shower and go back to rest for a while. The food has made me sleepy again. As you know, unfortunately for yourself, jail and prison are not easy. We will talk more, but not right now, please."

Nuray sees Adalet looking long and hard at her. She knows that Adalet is finding her evasion of disclosure difficult to accept. But she also knows that Adalet will accept the possibility that Nuray will never tell her what happened. Adalet does not want to upset her. She gently hugs Nuray, and Nuray hugs her back as best she can.

"Okay," Adalet tells her. "Get some rest now. We will speak more later."

As soon as Adalet is gone, Nuray turns on her laptop. She types in "Arman Demir-trial," and hopes for a news article that will give her details. She is disappointed to find nothing at all, only the same information she has already retrieved. She remembers that Mohammed used a contact of Zeynep's to find out information on the soldier. Guilt surges in Nuray. She has not been in touch with Zeynep or Alp since the raid on the magazine office. She knows they were released immediately, but what has become of them? Mohammed has not mentioned anything, but perhaps he does not know. She will wait until tomorrow to ask him. He has done enough for one day.

Nuray resigns herself to taking a shower. Clearly, prison has taught her little patience. She wants to get on with things, find her father and see if he can be of any more assistance. But she can only call on Mohammed so much. He has a wife and a family, and one more day is not going to make so much difference. Well, perhaps that is not so true in an autocracy, but that is something she can only discover with time.

CHAPTER 32

Adalet decides to stop at the dry cleaner/laundry to see about the wedding dress on her way back from Nuray's. She is exhausted, but she must continue packing, and so she must know the status of the dress. She decides to call for an Uber to take her back to Steep Street. She is too tired to get on the tram.

The Uber is only a few minutes away, and the driver, thankfully, does not try to engage her in conversation, and so she is able to reflect on the past couple of days. To get the news that Nuray was released just as Adalet was on her way to Avanos sent Adalet into a spin. She was torn during the entire trip, feeling the immediacy of wanting to be with Nuray, but needing to accomplish this final chapter of her life in Avanos. She felt in two places at once, and so she did not feel that she was ever totally in Avanos.

She was terribly disappointed to find no one at home at Temel's house. The children were in school, of course, and Temel may have been on a job somewhere, but what about Emine? So much for surprising people.

Ahmet and Bekir actually surprised her. They met her very formally in what was now Ahmet's dining room and used to be Fatma and Cengiz's dining room. The room was redecorated and refurnished. She did wonder at what had happened to Fatma's great grandfather's beautifully crafted table and benches which she and Cengiz had transported back to Avanos after her grandfather's death. Perhaps they had moved it to another section of the house.

Adalet was introduced to a short and very fat man who turned out to be their lawyer. Bekir seemed slightly embarrassed by the lawyer's presence, as he made a side remark to Adalet that "Ahmet just thought it would be a good idea to have him check over the paperwork." The lawyer left after the papers were read and signed by all the parties. As soon as he was gone, Ahmet asked his wife, never really introduced, to serve tea and cakes. She did not remain with them to partake of either. The whole process took no more than an hour and a half. Adalet could have sent the paperwork and been done with it.

With so much time on her hands left in Avanos, Adalet purchased a bouquet of flowers and went to the cemetery. She knelt by the stone, spread the flowers there, and spoke to the dead woman.

"I am leaving this country, Fatma, and so I don't know if I will ever stand on this ground again. If your dear Atatürk were alive now to see what is happening to this country, what is happening to this government, he would be very troubled, I think. Or maybe not. He lived through many changes from the Ottoman Empire to the Republic of Turkey and so many challenges to his own government. Anyway, I am going to live in America. Your dear Meryem is living there now. She is married to Isha—yes, they allow that in America— and I have married Mark. I so wanted to tell you that in person. I am terrified, Fatma, but I am also excited. I am all alone here in Turkey now, and life is very different from what it once was. To be honest, I believe you would have pushed me to do this much sooner, if only you had been here. I so miss you, my dear friend. You will be in my heart always. You and my beloved Turkey. Always and forever, as long as I have breath in my lungs, as long as my heart continues to beat."

The visit left her sad, but she was not sorry to have gone. Now, riding home in the Uber, she thinks, I did the right thing. Fatma would have wanted me to show Ahmet and Bekir the proper respect of turning the building over to them in person. She does think it was too bad that she missed seeing Emine and Temel, her old friends and helpers from the village, but she will write to them. Adalet wonders if Temel still drives the Fiat she left with him when she moved back to

Istanbul. She does not know what she would have done without Temel's expert help with the house in Avanos.

Adalet asks the driver to stop in front of the laundry. The shop is empty of customers, and the old man is sitting at his counter reading a newspaper. He quickly folds it up and puts it aside as Adalet enters. "Ah, Let me show you what I have done." He goes into the back to retrieve the dress. Adalet is curious and leans over the counter to see the newspaper he is reading. It is a pro-Erdoğan publication. She sighs, remembering when the discussion of politics took place everywhere. Now one does not speak in front of neighbors and even very often, in front of family members.

The wrinkled shopkeeper, in his same suit, emerges with the dress encased in a large plastic bag. He lays it on the counter and raises the plastic for Adalet to view. She is amazed. Other than a few hardly noticeable patches, the dirt has all been successfully removed.

"Wonderful," she says. She continues to unfold the layers of the dress to inspect it further, and she finds a few more discolored patches, but not enough to discard the dress. "I think I might actually be able to wear this," Adalet tells him.

"Of course," he says, unsmiling still, but clearly pleased with the results of his work. "What remains will hardly be seen. There was dirt but not stain, for the most part."

Adalet does not haggle over the price. Her new status as Mark's wife has freed her from financial worry, and the price the old man gives her seems quite reasonable. She pays him and takes the dress across both of her arms, carefully walking across the street. She wraps the dress around her back in order to bend down to open the front door, then places it across her arms again to negotiate the stairs. She fumbles with her door key, but manages to get the door open without dropping the dress. Once inside, Adalet takes the dress from the plastic and lays it across her bed. Her mother was right. The dress is stunning. She will send photos to Mark and see what he thinks.

Adalet pulls out some moving boxes she has gathered and decides to tackle the kitchen. She makes two piles, one to throw away and one to give away. Mark has a completely furnished kitchen, and if there are things she specifically wants, she can purchase them in New York. The only item she feels any strong attachment to is her *çaydanlık*, and she will leave that decision until the last minute. She is sure she will be able to find another one in New York, but the essence that lingers from old tea leaves, the whispering senses from significant tipping points in her life, the flickering heartbeats only settled with the drinking of *çay*, these can never be replaced. She presses the *çaydanlık* against her breasts, hugging it close before setting it aside on the counter. There are only a few things too precious to leave behind, but they are, unfortunately, bulky items.

Adalet wishes she had family photographs, but there are none. She has a faded wedding picture of her *anne* and *baba* that she rescued from a broken frame after the earthquake, but that is all. There were very few family photos to begin with, and the few her *anne* had were lost in the rubble by the time Adalet was in any condition to go back to retrieve them. The wedding dress was something of a miracle. The wedding dress, the photo of her parents, and the *çaydanlık* will have to be enough for her new life. She will carry Fatma and Turkey in her heart and in her soul.

What kind of kitchen utensils does Mark have, what sort of pots and pans? And what are his dishes like? Suppose he kept those fancy dishes of his mother's, the gold-rimmed ones? She will never be able to use them. For a moment, Adalet stops what she is doing and presses her hands against her face and sighs deeply. What is she thinking? What is she doing? Her whole life is changing. Can she do this? Is she prepared?

Adalet goes out and stands on the balcony to the room that once belonged to Fatma and her sister-in-law, Badia. Later this was Meryem's room, and finally, the room was shared by Meryem and Isha. Who will live here now? Nuray stayed in this room the night of the attempted coup, the night when so much began and so much ended. History is a funny concept, Adalet muses. We make up such a tiny piece of it for mere moments, and then it is completely erased by the history and the moments of others. But this house is now returned to the Celik family, and whatever transformations history will bring to its fine walls will be on their shoulders for a time, not mine. I must leave it to them. I have left it to them. She gazes up and down Steep Street, as if her eyes are a camera lens, and then steps back inside and shuts the door. This will not be her last look, but she knows that the last look is coming very soon.

Nuray is her final business here in Turkey, and she knows that she will have to leave this piece of business unresolved. There is only so much she can do to help Nuray.

CHAPTER 33

Nuray decides to wait until she can walk fairly easily without her cane before visiting her father. She has been able to locate him through Zeynep's friend whom she has never met but who was willing to help Mohammed. After her arrest, Zeynep vanished, and no one has heard from Alp. Nuray assumes he is staying close to home and to his mother.

After a week of practice, Nuray discards her cane, at least temporarily, and takes a tram to the bus that will take her to her father's prison. Nuray wonders what it cost him to get her out. Why did he even do this for her? How many names was he forced to give to get one person, his long-lost daughter, freed? Now that she has been in prison herself, even though she was never really officially charged or sentenced, she can well imagine what atrocities her father has experienced. Why now? Why come to her aid now after abandoning her for so many years? She must get some answers.

Nuray finds herself in a line with mostly other women and a few small children. They all carry packages for their loved ones. Too late, she realizes that she has nothing for her father, not even a *simit*. How thoughtless she has become.

Entering the prison is like being sucked into the bowels of an ancient reptilian dragon. The corridor is long and dank with dim, dirty yellow lighting. Nuray's instinct is to turn and run while she still can. She fears that when she states her name and who she wishes to see, they will immediately handcuff her and take her away, back to a prison cell. The guards are gruff with the people ahead of her in the line. She breathes in deeply, letting the stilted air out slowly in order to alleviate some of her anxiety. It is not just the prison that is creating so much angst. She has not seen this man in years, and she has no idea what to expect.

Once Nuray is past the guards, the body search, the indignity accompanying even a visit to a prison, she enters a long room encased in bars on the sides and the ceiling. She wonders that the small children do not seem to be more frightened. Perhaps they are used to this by now. Certainly, it is more severe than visiting in the women's prison where the room feels less closed in, and there is some air to breathe.

The cave-like room is lined with rows of booths enclosed in glass and facing one another. A phone receiver dangles from each booth. She sits in the booth indicated to her and waits. Well, she muses, this setup will eliminate any of her concerns over the awkwardness of physical contact. None is allowed here.

Fresh from her own recent experience, Nuray breathes in the fetor of human waste and unwashed bodies. The odor of damp iron and cement combine to pull her back to the cell she has been liberated from just a couple of weeks ago. The walls begin to close in, and she must look around her to stay in the present world.

In the booth next to Nuray is a young woman in *hijab* with two small children, a boy and a girl only about a year apart. They cling to their mother's cloak, one on each side of her, as there is only one chair provided. Nuray focuses on them to steady herself.

One of the guards leads a skeletal man with a scruffy beard towards them. He seems too old to be this woman's husband. Nuray is jolted when the man is seated opposite her. This man does not even resemble the photograph she saw online. This is a shadow of that man. His cheekbones protrude from his gaunt face. One eye seems discolored and slightly swollen, as if recovering from a graver bruise. He raises his phone receiver and motions to her to do the same. Slowly, Nuray lifts the receiver to her mouth and ear.

"*Baba*?" Nuray's voice sounds tentative to her.

"Nuray." Arman's voice also sounds tentative, and raspy, as though he has been smoking many cigarettes. Nuray instantly wishes that she had thought to bring him some.

"I never expected to see you again," the strange, skinny man tells her.

"It has been over twenty years. We never heard from you again— no letters, no calls, nothing." Nuray sees water is forming behind his eyes. She hopes he will not cry. She is incapable now of such emotion. She does not want him to embarrass himself. As if he can read her mind, his expression hardens, and the water recedes. Nuray returns to the point of her visit.

"I was told that it was because of you that I was released. I wanted to thank you."

"Of course, I did not want my only child to rot in prison if it could be helped. I am sure you did nothing." He scratches his head, and Nuray wonders if he has lice. The father she saw depicted online was so handsome, robust, well-manicured and well dressed. This is a completely different man. Is this reduced shell masquerading as her father? No, she recognizes certain aspects of his face. Even though Nuray lost fifteen pounds during her ordeal, this man is starving to death. She must bring him some food, if it is allowed. She will ask when she is leaving.

"What do they say you have done, *Baba*?"

"Ah, I am guilty by association. I am accused of being a putschist, but I had no part in the coup. Years ago, I did receive help from Hizmet. I met Gülen when he was still quite friendly with Erdoğan. There were some wealthy business people associated with Hizmet, and I did get some help from a few of them in setting up my import/export business. But that was the end of your mother and me."

"Why?" Nuray has never heard this story. Has all that she has believed been a lie? And why would her mother lie to her? Should she even believe him?

Her father sighs into the phone receiver. This is such an awkward way to communicate, Nuray agonizes. "She was afraid I was involving myself with gangsters, and that I would lose the money and never be able to pay them back. Your mother was a good woman, but she had no faith in me. When she found out the amount I had borrowed, she threw me out. She was afraid of what could happen to you."

"And did you pay them back?" Nuray asks.

"Every lira." Arman takes the receiver away from his mouth and ear for a moment, takes a breath, and brings it back. "I became more successful than even these fellows imagined, certainly much more successful than I ever imagined."

"So why didn't *Anne* have you back?"

"It was too late for us. She was too angry that I had gone and borrowed the money against her wishes, and I was too angry at her lack of belief in me. We met a couple of times—of course you never knew about this—but we knew it could never work."

"You helped us financially?" Nuray wants the answer to this question that has been plaguing her for some time.

"She told you?"

"No, I never thought about it as a child. But recently, thinking about it, I realized that we could never have afforded to live as we did without additional income, especially after she became so ill. I always thought that was why you left her." Nuray's voice drops at the shame she feels now in her confession.

"How could you know if no one told you?" Arman strokes what straggles remain of his beard. "Please don't blame your mother. We were young and both at fault. And it was sheer luck, my success. Suddenly Turkish carpets were all the rage, anything Turkish, kilim, plates, bowls, all sorts of trinkets. There was a huge boom in the economy, the tourists kept on coming, and I was a lucky man. And then everything changed, and look at me now. I am stuck in here for the rest of my days, and if they don't begin to feed me, those will not be many, and I have done none of the things of which I am accused." Arman shakes his head in despair and looks down at his hands. Then he quickly looks back up at Nuray. "Please, tell me how you are now? Are you okay?"

Nuray quickly revises how much to tell him. "Yes, *Baba*, I am okay right now. But I guess you know that I am a journalist with a women's magazine that the government has forced me to close. I can no longer work here."

Arman looks at Nuray, his eyes travel to the left and to the right, and Nuray knows he is concerned about what he says next. He whispers, "You have put yourself in danger by coming here to see me. They can hurt you to try to get more information from me. I am so happy to see you, please don't misunderstand me, but better you did not come. If you need some work, and you are not too fussy about what you do, my friend, Belgin Doğan, might be able to help you. I don't know." Arman looks down. "You can find her at the housekeeping services for the Topkapi Hotel. It is a hotel for poorer foreign tourists. She can give you something."

"Thank you, *Baba*. I will look into it." Although he is suggesting work, Nuray cannot help but think he is really talking about something else. This feeling comes from the way he is emphasizing his words.

Nuray is surprised at the anger that begins to surface from deep within her gut. Suddenly she feels all the empathy for her father seeping away. Her *anne* had not wanted to see him, but what about her? Why had he stayed away from her, even after her *anne's* death? Not all sympathy for this man is gone, as Nuray hesitates to ask her question. But then, she may never see her *baba* again.

"So why did you stay away from me? All these years, even after she was gone, you never tried to contact me. Why?"

Arman looks as if Nuray has slapped him across the face. In fact, he raises his hand to his face as if he has been attacked. He shakes his head and sighs deeply. "I have no excuse. When you were little, your mother asked me to keep away to not confuse you. She also had it in her head that I was connected with bad people. I could not convince her otherwise. The years passed, and it all became more confusing and complicated. I am sorry, but I guess that doesn't mean much now."

Nuray is torn between wanting to hurt him and wanting to protect him. She stares at the man she has avoided feeling the loss of all these years. A wound she has carefully sealed is now opening, and it is dangerously raw. She wants to break the glass that separates them, reach through the bars, and pull the hairs out of his scraggily beard. She wants to drive a knife through his heart to make him bleed. Nuray closes her eyes. She tries to regain a foothold on her sense of who she is. She has been a woman without a father. In fact, she almost believed herself that he was dead. In what feels like an instant, she is a woman with a living father, and a father who is living in prison.

When Nuray opens her eyes again, her father is staring at her. "I have been no kind of father to you. Can you forgive me?"

Nuray now looks down at her hands. "I don't know." She glares up at him, animosity glinting in her eyes. "How many names did you have to give them to get me out?"

Without any warning, Nuray feels as though she has stuck the knife in herself. She never meant to ask him this question, but his request for forgiveness has drawn this venom from her. She immediately regrets her words. "I'm sorry, *Baba*. I have no right to ask."

They look at one another, and then they look away. Nuray fights the impulse to get up and run. The desire to injure this man is as strong as the longing to hug him to her and never let him go. She knows little more than she did before she came, and she realizes that she will learn nothing more from this visit. Her father seems to read her mind.

"I will go now," he says. "I am grateful that you came."

"Is there anything I can bring you?" Nuray asks.

"No, but I thank you. We are not allowed to take anything in from the outside. The women come all the time with packages, as if the rules will change somehow, magically. Then they leave with their packages. I wish most for a book, but we are only allowed to take books from the prison library. I do thank you for your thoughtfulness." Arman motions to the guard that his visit is ending. Before he places the phone receiver back into its cradle he whispers, "Be well and be safe, *Inşallah*."

"*Inşallah*," Nuray whispers back, but too late. Arman has already returned the phone to its cradle, stood up, and is walking towards the guard and the inner door.

CHAPTER 34

The tables are turning on Safak Aksoy. He is ill prepared for this. When Altan takes him to "meet a few friends," Safak could not have anticipated what they would have in mind for him. He simply nods his head in agreement while they are in the tent. What else can he do? Is he allowed to defy them? Will they shoot him? Kill him for cowardice? Safak has no idea. Once again, Safak is befuddled by life. He is not only befuddled, he is trapped.

They leave the tent in a chorus of "*selams*" and "*Inshallahs.*" All has been agreed. When they are safely distanced from the tent, Altan grabs Safak to his breast. "My little brother, my hero. I never believed you would make me so proud."

Safak is speechless. He wants to tell Altan that he cannot do this. What they are asking of him is not possible. He will agree to almost anything else but this. But wait, he just agreed, didn't he? He drops away from his brother's hold, and their eyes meet. Altan picks up something in his brother's expression. Fright?

"I know this is not what you expected," Altan says in an attempt to encourage him. "This was not what I anticipated either. But we cannot second guess their decisions. We make a commitment to them without knowing what will be in store for us. This is an opportunity for you to be a hero, and you have accepted your destiny, as you should. I am proud of you. You do not disappoint me."

Altan's last statement is more of a command in Safak's ears than a statement. *You do not disappoint me.* What Safak hears is: Do not disappoint me. But Safak is not ready to die. He has not yet lived. He has come here to begin a new life, and now they are asking him to die. This is not something he has counted on, never in his wildest imaginings. He thought suicide bombers volunteer. He has not volunteered.

The sky above Safak darkens with his mood. There is nowhere to run. He is already a wanted man in his country, and he has no papers to be here in Syria. He is a man without a country. They will supply him with fake papers to get him to Ankara where the explosion is scheduled to happen, but will he have any opportunity to run? And again, where can he go? He has no money. Eventually, in Turkey, he would be picked up and then charged as a deserter, if not worse. Should they discover that he is a terrorist and that he has been sent as a suicide bomber, he is doomed. Safak looks around him. He is surrounded by sand and dirt, dilapidated tents, and derelict humans. There is no escape. There is nowhere to run and nowhere to hide.

Ambling along the dirt paths between and around the tented campsite, Safak tries to think. Is there any escape? What possible choices does he have? What are his alternatives? All Safak can see is more sand, more dirt, more stones on the pathways before him. He does not believe in the mythical virgins, try as he might. He wants to believe, but he just cannot get himself there. All he can see is oblivion.

Safak Aksoy determines that the only thing he can turn to now is his newly found faith. He does not need to believe in the virgins supposedly awaiting him. He does not expect faith to sustain him, but he has run out of options. Even his mother, if he were able to reach her, would not be able to rescue him from his fate. *Amor fati*, he thinks. He once saw that painted onto a tram wall. He looked it up and found that it was Latin for "love your fate." This is his only choice now. He will somehow become the martyr they expect him to be. He will embrace his faith and his fate and love it with all of his heart. He is positioned in front of a wall he cannot climb, cannot go around, and there is no turning back. Safak repeats to himself his new mantra, *amor fati*.

Later this day, Safak is taken to another tent where he is outfitted in a simulated explosives vest and shown how to detonate it. His cohort, Ali, a fellow of similar age but from a strict religious background, is instructed along with him. They will travel with senior members of ISIS who will outfit them at their destination. This is all preparatory and preliminary. Safak understands that their travel companions are there to keep them in tow and to ensure the meticulous outcome of this course of action.

Safak and Ali are now to stay with their caretakers. Nothing is said, but the caretakers have loaded weapons on them, and it is understood, if never uttered, that should they choose to run, it would mean instant death, a death of shame and cowardice. Not that Safak is particularly concerned with how he is seen after death. He just realizes that he can die a hero or die a coward; those are his choices. Since the inevitability of his death is undisputed, he might as well embrace martyrdom.

The men wait inside a tent that is set aside for them. There are several mattresses on the floor with pillows and blankets for them to rest, if they so wish. Food is brought to them, food of a better quality than Safak has seen in the camp thus far. There is a stew of some sort with chunks of lamb and vegetables that can actually be identified. This is served on rice with a large Syrian flatbread on the side. Safak is surprised by how hungry he is and how much he manages to eat. The two guards, as Safak has come to think of them, also eat heartily. Ali barely touches his food. No one makes any comment on this.

Time passes slowly for Safak. He wonders if he is somehow slowing down time to take in more breaths of air; or if he might wish to push time forward, to get this horrific deed over and completed. He is not a murderer. He is not even sure he is capable of killing someone in combat. He is better at beating and raping women than shooting another man. Blowing up total strangers, innocent human beings, is not the way Safak believes one should go about making a statement. Of course, Safak has no idea, and has given no thought, as to how he would make a statement. But killing people at random makes no sense to him. It makes about as much sense to him as killing himself.

One of the guards offers Safak a cigarette, and he accepts. The older man lights it for him, and Safak takes a deep drag. Ah, the rush of hot air, smoke, and nicotine coursing through his lungs. He could sit there for a year, after a hearty meal, allowing his body to relax and feel the soothing narcotic taking precedence. A raki or a beer would make this almost perfect, but there is no alcohol anywhere near this camp, as far as Safak is aware.

Since there is no conversation, Safak sits and wonders at death. He contemplates the lack of thought, the lack of consciousness, the lack of being. He cannot imagine such a state. There must be thought. How could one exist without it? Of course, that is what death is, non-existence, and that would mean the lack of thought. Safak struggles with trying to conceive of such a null actuality. He has never been able to slow his thoughts without a good deal of alcohol. Safak takes a long draw on the last of his cigarette. He slowly exhales the last smoke before crushing the butt in the dirt and discarding it in the filthy jar top being used as an ashtray. Will he be offered a last smoke? Does he have the courage to pretend to be a martyr? He does not know. And where is his brother? He has not seen Altan since he was given his mission.

The night is prolonged, interminable. The other three men are lost in their own thoughts. Safak is curious as to what Ali's feelings might be, but Ali is remote and removed, closeted within himself. Safak does not reveal his thoughts to any of them. The evening and night pass in a kind of silent torture. He nods off briefly, but is awake for most of the lingering hours, fidgeting, rolling back and forth in his bedding, craving a beer, and wanting another cigarette. Over and over, he asks himself the same question for which he has no suitable answer. How did he end up here?

There is no sunrise to see, as the morning is overcast with intermittent sprinkles of rain. The dirt is so dry that there is not enough liquid accumulated for mud. An acrid, bitter smell circulates in the tent.

The men wash. The men pray. Safak joins them in these morning ablutions. He utters the words. He performs the motions. Safak is a puppet on the strings of a master who is in complete control, and he is well beyond his own control. He complies. He submits. This is not in line with any of his former behavior. Safak is a rebel who defies orders and commands. He no longer knows himself. He is lost.

Breakfast is gruel and tea, but Safak no longer has any appetite, in any event. He experiences his very essence as a loaded bomb, waiting to be detonated. His two guards are indistinguishable to him, even though they do not resemble each other in any way. The older of the two is large, bulky, dark complected and covered with tattoos. He is called Malik. The other one, still older than Safak but younger than Malik, is light complected, muscular and wiry, also covered with tattoos. He is called Omar. Safak has trouble keeping their names straight and it is only when Ali refers to one of them that he can safely identify one from the other. Malik offers him a cigarette, and he gratefully accepts. He no longer has any of his own. When he informs Malik that he is out, Malik leaves the tent and returns with a pack of filtered American cigarettes, Marlboros, that he hands to Safak. Safak is grateful that he has retained half a book of matches. His lighter has been lost somewhere along the way.

Safak has barely finished smoking his cigarette when Malik announces that they should grab their belongings; it is time to go. They wind their way, encumbered only with light backpacks, on a narrow, gravel path through the tents to the outskirts of the encampment. A large dirty white van awaits them. There is a driver Safak has not seen before. They are not introduced. The four of them climb into the back, the doors are shut, no words are exchanged.

The ride is long and bumpy. There are no windows in the back, so Safak has no idea where they are or where they are heading. They bounce around on the soiled gray carpeting in silence. Safak thinks that Ali must be well resigned to his mission. He is outwardly so calm.

He even drifts off to sleep for a brief part of the drive. Safak wishes he could sleep. He would be most grateful for any escape, if only he could be assured of reawakening.

When the van finally comes to a halt, the men disembark in the midst of more stones, sand, and dirt. A worn four-door sedan, smudged with mud, a dent in one of the doors, and tires that could use some air, is the next assigned vehicle for their journey. Malik hands Safak and Ali passports and papers once they are assembled in the car. Malik is now driving. "We cross the border now," he says. "We are taking you to university. We are your uncles," Malik says as he points to Ali, "and you are his friend from school. You have been visiting with the family."

Safak panics. "What do I study there?"

"Shut up, and no one will ask you," Malik retorts. Then he considers. "Economics," he decides. "They won't have any questions about that subject, but they won't ask. This is the border between Syria and Turkey. They let us in all the time."

Malik is correct. The border guard who stops their car barely looks at their passports and papers. He gives them a quick glance, leans in to look into the backseat, and hands the papers back to Malik. "Okay" is all he says.

The next hours are interminable. Malik breaks for nothing but pit stops and two gas refills. He does not tire, has no need to stretch his legs. He smokes cigarette after cigarette, filling the car with stale smoke, only occasionally lowering his window to bring in fresh air when reminded. The back windows do not go down, and so Safak and Ali are at his mercy. Neither of them smoke in the car. Omar has one or two, his smoke barely detectable from Malik's.

Malik has made these runs before, Safak suspects. Light snacks are passed to them, bottles of water are stored in the trunk. Before the journey began, they were each handed several bottles. Safak is disappointed. He thought they would at least get to fly. He has never been on a plane. Instead, the endless road looms ahead. Safak cannot help but think such a sacrifice as he is expected to make should yield more than a mediocre lamb stew and a pack of American cigarettes.

This vehicle has clearly been in an accident that has somewhat dislodged the backseat. When Malik starts or stops the car, takes a sharp turn, or rides over a bump or impediment in the road, Safak and Ali are thrust forwards, backwards, or to the sides. There are no seatbelts to attempt to hold them in place. By the time they begin to see the closer buildings and city streets of Ankara, Safak is exhausted and indignant at how unceremoniously he is being treated.

Malik parks the car in a crooked street in front of a two-story older wooden building. He turns around, and when he sees the expression on Safak's face, he begins to laugh. "ISIS is not the Trump Towers, is it, my friend? We are not exactly flush with money right now, so we must make do with what we have. But we are here, and we can get you something good to eat soon." Safak grunts with annoyance in response, but Ali, compliant as ever, says nothing. Malik signals that they should get out of the car. They collect their backpacks from the trunk, and Malik leads them up the steps and into an unmarked building that looks just like the other residences on the block, other than possibly needing a bit of a spruce up on the splintering wood and peeling paint. Malik uses a key to enter, and there appear to be no other current occupants.

The house is more comfortably equipped than Safak would have anticipated. There are small but comfortable bedrooms, double beds in each outfitted with clean sheets and blankets. There are two large bathrooms with stacks of toilet paper, bath towels, soap, shampoo, and shaving supplies. There is a basket with disposable razors encased in plastic, cheap but perfectly usable. Safak is momentarily appeased at the thought of a long, hot shower. "Go ahead," Malik tells them. "Omar and I will wait. Anyway, we have business to get you ready."

Ready for death, Safak thinks, but he says nothing. The idea of a hot shower after the two enduring days in the tent and the stressful drive is extremely appealing. He instructs himself not to think, just to stand under the spray of water, which could be hotter and could be stronger, but is far better than nothing. When he returns to his room, a towel wrapped around him, he finds a clean set of sporting clothes awaiting him. They fit him loosely, perfectly. He lies down on the bed and is instantly dead to the world but very much alive in his disturbing dreams.

CHAPTER 35

Two days later, Nuray finds herself in the doorway of a miniature Topkapi Hotel, a much smaller version than the hotel she first tried, where there was no Belgin Doğan to be found. This tiny hotel, not very far from her old magazine office, has a broken sign and an intermittently tiled entryway. The cracks and crevices of dirt and gravel interlacing the tiles make Nuray's progress treacherous. This is not a hotel for even middle-class tourists. There is a buzzer at the empty desk which Nuray presses. A very fat man, short and unclean, ambles from the back.

"We're full," he informs Nuray. "No rooms." He begins to turn away.

"I'm not looking for a room," Nuray proceeds. "I'm looking for a Belgin Doğan."

"There is no one here by that name." He starts to walk away.

"My father sent me. He is Arman Demir."

He looks her over and then mutters, "Wait here." He disappears into the back.

Nuray is not feeling very strong yet. Once again, she is out without her cane, as she does not wish to appear weak to someone from whom she is seeking assistance. She leans against the counter, as there is no chair. She hopes not to have to wait too long.

After what seems to her like an hour but is in reality only about fifteen minutes, the door opens, and a woman she guesses to be around her father's age emerges. She clearly colors her hair to an ebony black to match her dark eyes and olive skin tone. She is tiny, especially so after the appearance of the fat man. She lifts the counter and motions for Nuray to follow her into the back. There is a small room with a table and chairs. The woman invites Nuray to sit which she gratefully does.

The woman offers her water, which Nuray accepts, and she holds out her hand. "I am Belgin, an old friend of your father's. How can I help you?"

"I have just been released from prison. I have been publishing a small women's magazine—"

Belgin cuts her off. "I know. I visited your father yesterday. He told me to expect you. I am familiar with your situation."

"Not the worst of it," Nuray continues. "I was beaten and raped in prison. I cannot go back there. I need to leave Turkey. I will go anywhere."

Belgin shakes her head. "That is a complicated request right now. I am so sorry for your terrible experience. I do understand, as a number of years ago, I was also raped in jail. You will overcome it to some degree with help. I can tell you that I have done so."

"I need to leave," Nuray repeats. "I don't believe they will leave me alone. I am too much leverage for my father. They will continue to use me to get to him."

"Does he know about the rape and beating?"

"Of course, I told him nothing. My face has healed. My body is still healing, but I am much better than I was."

Belgin sighs. There are deep wrinkles in her face, but Nuray can see that she was once a pretty woman. "Your request is not easy these days. You will need a new identity, and this will cost money. Bribes will need to be paid, and that will cost more money. Do you have any money?"

"Very little. The only thing I have really is my apartment."

"In the meantime, you will have to disappear. And you cannot disappear from this hotel. You will have to disappear from your home. I must tell you that your home is now dangerous for you. The police may show up at any time to rearrest you. I have seen it happen many times. Now that you have visited Arman, you are in even greater danger. You have shown a relationship with him that has been denied by you up until now."

Nuray is rattled, dismayed. "I felt I had to see him to thank him for getting me released. Oh, I probably should not have mentioned that he did that."

"Don't worry. I already knew that. Arman is very smart. He has done no harm except to send you here to me, and he had no choice. If the police have followed you here, they will suspect that you are seeking help from me, and they will arrest you again, so that you cannot leave the country." She reaches into a jacket pocket. "Take this. I will contact you on this phone. It is a disposable. Do not use it for your regular calls, and do not try to contact me again. You must leave now. Go to the next hotel down the street and ask for work there. They won't have any. Then go to a few other hotels and ask for work. No hotel will have any at this time. This might throw off the police. They are aware you have no work now."

Nuray hesitates.

"Come on. Go now. I will do everything I can. Go and charge the phone as soon as you can."

Nuray finally rises from her chair. "Thank you, Belgin."

"Don't thank me yet." Belgin finally manages a smile. "Thank me when I've done something. Better yet, you have no idea who I am. If anyone asks, your father merely thought I might have work for you at this hotel." Belgin rises and disappears into the bowels of the shabby building.

Nuray slips the phone into her bag. She forces herself up from her chair and back out into the street again. As much as she would prefer to get home to rest, she follows Belgin's instructions. Avoiding another arrest for herself is paramount. And if Belgin should be arrested, Nuray will have no one to help her. So she soldiers on to three other hotels asking for work. Nuray tries her best to appear enthusiastic, but she does suspect that even if there were work available, she is not representing herself as someone who anyone would wish to hire.

Once back in her apartment, she collapses on the couch. Then she remembers the phone, and pushes herself up long enough to begin the charging process. She would really like some tea, but she has no more strength. She returns to the couch, and is about to doze off again, when her own cell phone begins to vibrate from where she has placed it inside her sweater pocket. Adalet's number is displayed. Nuray answers reluctantly.

"*Merhaba*, Adalet."

"*Merhaba*, dear friend. How are you feeling?"

"Better than when you saw me last, but tired, too." Nuray thinks once again that she is blessed to have Adalet in her life.

"Why don't I pick up some food and bring it over? We can both have a nice meal together. You can rest until I get there. And I will make us some tea."

"Oh, that does sound absolutely perfect, Adalet. You are so good to me. I will not refuse your kind offer, most especially for the tea. I find I am too tired to make it myself."

"Hold on, then. I will see you very soon." Adalet disconnects the call.

Nuray sighs. She knows she will have to tell Adalet everything. And is that so terrible? Adalet deserves to know, and Nuray is beginning to feel that it will give her some relief to talk to somebody. She lies back down on the couch and allows herself to drift off into a light sleep, too light to summon her nightmarish demons.

Nuray is half awake and very hungry when the buzzer indicates that Adalet has arrived. When she opens the door, Adalet's arms are filled with packages. "I hope you're hungry," she says.

"Starving, and dying for a cup of tea." She removes some of Adalet's packages and closes the door behind her. They unload everything in the kitchen, and Adalet immediately reaches for the *çaydanlık*. The alluring aroma of kebab is too enticing for Nuray to wait. She opens a bag and pulls out a lamb kebab which she quickly devours.

Adalet laughs. "You really were starving."

Nuray puts down the now empty skewer and goes to Adalet. She hugs her close. "Thank you, Adalet. I would not eat without you. So much has happened and is happening to me that food is no longer a priority. I know it needs to be, but before I know, exhaustion overwhelms me, and I must sleep before I eat."

Adalet spoons the tea leaves into the smaller section of the *çaydanlık*. "I want to hear everything, but first, let's have some tea and some food. You need your energy." Adalet sets the prepared *çaydanlık* onto the fire and opens the packages. There is more kebab, rice *pilav* with almonds, there is cheese, fresh cut vegetables, a lentil stew, two types of bread, olives and *börek* with spinach and with potatoes.

"Another feast," Nuray tells Adalet.

"In these crazy times, food is a lift for the spirits," Adalet replies.

The water reaches a boil, and Adalet covers the tea leaves and sets the *çaydanlık* back onto the stove to allow the tea to steep. In the meantime, the women fill their plates and eat in a silence that is usually only comfortable between people who know each other well enough to make silence unworried and confident.

When the plates have been refilled and emptied again, Adalet rises to pour the tea. She places some Turkish biscotti with dried apricot and walnuts on the table between them.

"Oh, I adore these," Nuray laughs. "You are spoiling me."

"Just enjoy." Adalet's tone contains a note of sorrow.

"I know," Nuray sighs. "Soon you will be leaving. Do you have a flight yet?"

"Yes, in ten days." Adalet fingers her biscotti, turning it over and then over again in her plate.

"This is a secret, Adalet, you can say nothing to anyone, even Mohammed, but I may be leaving soon, too."

Adalet drops the biscotti she has finally lifted to her mouth back onto her plate. "Really, Nuray, where will you go?"

Nuray shrugs. "Wherever they can send me. I cannot go back to prison. I would rather die."

Adalet leaps from her chair and runs to embrace Nuray. She flings her arms around the now silent woman, pressing her to her breast. "It must have been horrible for you," Adalet whispers.

Nuray gently pushes Adalet away. "Yes, it was horrible. And if you want to hear my story, you must sit back down and refrain from comforting me, or I will never make it through it all. Please, Adalet. I am ready to speak, but you must promise me to contain yourself until I am finished."

Adalet smooths back her hair and studies Nuray's face. As if agreeing to something she is unsure she can provide, she backs up into her chair, takes a sip of tea and then says, "I promise to do my best."

"That is all I can ask." Nuray sips her tea and begins.

"When I was first taken to interrogation, during the first week, I was taken in handcuffs behind my back. I found it difficult to keep up with the nasty guard who was escorting me. He pushed me and pulled me, and as I remember it—and my memory since the hospital has been intermittent and vague—eventually I tripped on the stairs and bloodied my nose. At the time, I was afraid it was broken. It bled for some time, and they gave me nothing to stop the bleeding. I used my shirt. In this state, I was taken to see my interrogator."

Nuray pauses to take a sip of tea. "Could you please get me a glass of water? My throat is very dry."

"Of course," Adalet responds. She retrieves a tall glass of water and hands it to Nuray who drinks it down in two large gulps. Adalet refills the glass for her and then sits back down.

"This was just the beginning. I was not beaten in interrogation. I certainly was threatened, and they raised the question of my father. You may not remember, but the soldier also mentioned my father."

"Yes, I do," Adalet reflects. "I was curious about that."

"So was I. After all of these years, suddenly my father was being dropped into the conversation as if I knew things about him, and he had been in my life all this time. Of course, I denied any contact with him or knowledge about his activities. And to be honest, I still believe him to be innocent of any political involvement. He merely borrowed money from wealthy merchants who were involved with Gülen. He may have met Gülen on one or two occasions, but I don't believe him to be any more involved in the attempted coup than Gülen himself."

"So what has happened with your father?"

"He is in prison now. He has not been before the court yet. He has already bargained with them once to get me out, but they could take me back to use me against him again. That is why I must flee the country by any means I can, for my sake as well as for my father's. If he has any bargaining chips left, he must be able to use them for himself, not for me." Nuray pushes herself from her chair. "I must use the bathroom. Too much tea, but I will have another cup." She smiles at Adalet. Only the second smile Adalet has seen today. The first smile came after she devoured the first lamb kebab. And Nuray does not normally eat any meat.

Adalet watches Nuray navigate to the hallway and the single bathroom in the apartment. Her strong friend is feebler than she has ever known her to be. At the same time that Adalet longs to know what has happened to Nuray, she is equally afraid to acquire this knowledge. Whatever has occurred, Adalet knows it was violent to have left her friend in this state. She reheats the tea in a fog, fearing the next words her friend will utter.

Nuray sits for several minutes, sipping both her tea and her water. Finally, she clasps her hands together and continues.

"After that interrogation and the visit from Mohammed, they told me they were going to move me to another location. So I was unclear as to what was happening when a male guard came to collect me without my things. I was taken to a dark and filthy room without any furniture and told to wait there. I remember cringing in the corner, fearing a tortuous interrogation. I could tell them nothing, even to save my life. My worst crime was speaking out against autocracy and Erdoğan, but I had nothing to do with the coup. I had absolutely nothing to give them." Nuray pauses, taking more sips of tea, and then of water.

"I will be honest, Adalet. I was in terrible fear of being beaten. In my entire life, I had never been physically assaulted. Even the bloody nose was due to my tripping, not a punch to my face. I was more terrified sitting on that damp, dirty floor than I had ever been in my life. This experience, even now, I cannot completely recall. The feelings of dread and fear that were my only companions in those moments all have blended together like shadows on the wall. I became so small, so insignificant, and at the same time, too large, too significant, to disappear. I'm not sure any of this can make sense to you." Nuray hugs her now trembling body.

Adalet remembers her friend's words and dares not go to comfort her. She merely says, "I can only imagine. I felt my own fears during the short time I was there. I was completely immobilized by fear. What you say makes complete sense to me."

Nuray folds her hands and sets them on the table. She continues. "The door burst open, and soldiers entered. There were four or five of them. Now I cannot remember exactly. What I do remember is the cruelty, the savagery of their words and their actions. Through my work, through my readings, I always have known intellectually that men could be cruel, but in my experience, no. This was never in my experience.

"Adalet, I cannot give you details. Most have been mercifully erased from my memory. I was beaten, and yes, I was raped. I was brutally raped. I blacked out quickly, and so there is much that I do not remember. The horror for me is that I felt that I was not human to them. I was a thing that they could use however they liked. And the inhuman thing that they created, in order to use me in such a cold-blooded and barbaric way, has somehow inhabited me. I feel different in my own body." Nuray sees that silent tears are sliding slowly down Adalet's face.

"I am ashamed that I feared I would be raped. It happened to you and not to me. I feel so ashamed for my fears, and that this terrible thing happened to you." Adalet fights not to lose control.

Nuray softens at her friend's distress. "And how would it have helped anything if you had also been raped and beaten? You should never have been arrested in the first place." Nuray shakes her head in frustration. "None of this feels real. I had nothing to do with the coup. Neither did my father. I think there is some evil that resides silently in men, waiting for some excuse to surface and take over all reason and sanity. These men were no longer any more human than the inhuman creature they created of me." Nuray rests her head on her clasped hands, glad to have spoken the truth but exhausted by it as well. There are some truths she can speak aloud, Nuray thinks, but she cannot allow herself to travel back down into that tunnel of blackness to relay the details of her nightmare to Adalet.

"I am so sorry and sad that this happened to you." Adalet knows that her words are sincere, but they are of little comfort to the horrors her friend has endured.

Nuray lifts her head and looks at Adalet. "Thank you, dear friend. I know you speak from your heart. I also know there is little anyone can do to comfort me now. The woman my father sent me to for help was also raped in prison. She told me that she was able to overcome most of it eventually with time and help. I am hopeful hearing those words."

"Who is this woman? How can she help you?" Adalet asks, her eyes dried now, her sorrow replaced with concern and curiosity.

"I must leave Turkey," Nuray says again. "This woman may be able to help me get out. I'm afraid the police will put me in prison again, hoping to get information about others from my father. He gave them something, I don't know what, to get me out this time. He knows people who have been involved with Gülen and the Hizmet organization. They are who Erdoğan is blaming for everything. People from Hizmet helped my father to get started in his business. Funny, my mother always thought he was involved with organized crime. Instead, it was a group of people supporting religion, culture, and education. She was so convinced. I don't know why he didn't completely level with her from the beginning. I think he might have been afraid she would have thought he was becoming too religious. But that is purely guesswork on my part. I really don't understand it."

"I don't know much about Gülen or Hizmet. I have to confess that I am pretty ignorant. I don't understand why Erdoğan blames Gülen for the coup. He's been in the United States for years now."

"You aren't the only one who doesn't understand," Nuray tells her. "Many of the journalists I know see the coup as an opportunity for Erdoğan to permanently rid himself of Gülen. Best of friends once, now they are enemies. Although, I think he'll have to get rid of him through propaganda. He won't be able to get him back to Turkey now. At least, I don't think he will. Anyway, whatever happens, I must try to get away. I'm waiting for this woman to help me."

"Do you think she can? Maybe Mark's lawyer—"

"No, Adalet. I won't involve you in this. That is my last word on the subject. If not for me, you'd never have gone to jail, and you would never have been on their radar. And if not for my stupidity with that soldier, I might never have been on their radar. I may never be able to forgive myself." Nuray takes a long drink of water.

Adalet stares at her friend. "I hope you will be able to forgive yourself one day. None of this is your fault."

Nuray pushes herself up from the table. "My fault or not, it matters little now. I am willing to go wherever this woman can send me. Once I have papers and I am out of Turkey, I can figure things out from there."

"How will I know how to find you? I don't want to lose you." Adalet also rises from the table, knowing that her friend has revealed as much as she can.

"I will find you. Don't worry. I don't want to lose you either."

The two women finally embrace. They are entwined when the cell phone that Nuray has plugged in to charge begins to beep.

CHAPTER 36

Safak awakens to Malik's hand on his arm, shaking him back to consciousness.

"Time to eat," Malik says. He does not wait for Safak to respond.

Safak is hungry until he remembers where he is and why he is here. He reaches for a cigarette, lights it, takes a few drags and then extinguishes it for later.

When he reaches the dining area, an open extension from the small kitchen, the men have already filled their plates from the array of take-out parcels lining the kitchen counter. They are seated at the long, wooden dining table and appear to Safak to be deeply concentrated on eating. By the time Safak has filled his plate with assorted kebab, rice, salad, and bread, and has joined the others, Omar has already finished eating. He lights a cigarette. Malik looks up from his plate and glares at him, as if to scold him for doing so while he is still eating, but Malik says nothing. After filling the car with his own smoke for hours, his rebuke would carry little weight with anyone here.

The food is fresh and delicious. Ali goes back for a second helping. Safak is not really hungry any longer, but he wants to take as much advantage of everything offered as he possibly can. He rises and refills his plate. The silence at the table is thick with unspoken tension. Forks tapping against plates, knives scrape against cutlery, an occasional car passes by outside, and the brief sound of muffled voices comes from the street.

Omar finally breaks the quiet. "I'm going to make some Turkish coffee. Anyone else? There is a box of pastries for dessert."

The three other men nod or mumble yes to the coffee, and Omar goes into the kitchen to comply. Malik takes out his cigarettes and offers the pack first to Safak and then to Ali. Safak takes one, but Ali shakes his head no. Malik lights Safak's cigarette and then his own with what looks a lot to Safak like his missing lighter. But then he thinks it is likely a mere coincidence. Malik would not take his lighter and then light his cigarette with it, would he? Safak cannot decide. He has no read on who these men really are.

By the time the men finish their coffee and pastry, the hour is late. Safak is surprised at how long he was able to sleep before dinner. When he checks the time, it is 11:30 p.m.

"Everyone will need a good night's sleep," Malik tells them. "We have to be up very early. I will come to wake you. Please go to your rooms now. If you like, take some water with you."

Safak grabs a bottle from those stacked on the counter along with the food. The desire for a beer is so strong now that he almost asks before he checks himself. As he climbs the stairs to his room for the night, severely regretting the lack of alcohol, Safak again contemplates escape. He has no money. He has no passport or identity papers. Malik holds everything. If he runs, he is completely on his own without resources. His parents are the first place the military police will be searching, and it is a long way from Ankara back to Istanbul, although he could hitchhike. But what would he do once he got there? And although his mother has probably forgiven him for stealing money from her, that is another risk he must consider. Safak examines these obstacles while seated on his bed. He comes up with no answers. But the problem resolves itself when he hears the lock being turned on his bedroom door. When he goes to the door, he hears the lock being turned to Ali's bedroom door as well. Clearly, he is not the first nominated martyr to entertain flight. Not until now does it occur to him that there are no windows in his bedroom. He is sealed in for the night.

Unless he can break the lock, Safak thinks. He actually might be able to do that. Would he make too much noise in his attempt? Possibly, he could get away with it, but then, what does he do from there? For all he knows, either Malik or Omar could be guarding the outside door. These questions plague him for minutes, then hours. He briefly considers trying to lose himself in prayer, and he even makes an effort, but he is unable to hold his concentration for more than a few minutes. *Amor fati*, he reminds himself. There is no way out.

And it is in this manner of recycled thought that Safak spends his night and early morning. He has once again arrived at accepting his fate, when Malik unlocks the door. He enters with an electric razor and scissors in his hand. When he sees that Safak is wide awake, he places the razor and the scissors on his nightstand. "You will shave your head and beard. It is the state of a martyr. Allah be praised. Then you will come downstairs and join us. Ali is already prepared."

Safak stands in front of the medicine cabinet mirror. His hair has become quite long. He holds a thick lock of it between his fingers, sensing the life of it before taking the scissors and setting it free. Yes, this is how he will see all of this, as setting himself free. No more worries. No more cares. Perhaps there really is an Allah awaiting his martyred acts of righteousness. He grabs another chunk of hair and then another, and cuts away until there is little left. He grabs the razor before he can think anything and shaves his head until it is smooth. He rubs his pate, trying to recognize the face he sees in the mirror. Now his beard seems out of place.

Safak cuts and shaves his beard until his chin feels smooth to his touch. His image looks like that of a child to him, not like a man in his twenties. He stares at himself for a time, wondering still if any of this is real. Is this man in the mirror the same man who is about to die? Is this really Safak Aksoy or an imposter? Or is he wandering through a dream state of his, or even of someone else's creation?

Slowly and methodically, Safak cleans up the hair from the sink and the floor and deposits it in the bathroom trash can. Pieces and parts of himself. Will there be any pieces and parts of himself left for anyone to claim? Will his brother claim him? He sincerely doubts this. Will his mother? His father? If, of course, there is anything left of him to claim.

The horror of the fact of the explosion itself is too much for Safak to contemplate. He truly does not have the faith for this, but alas, it is his fate. He takes some deep breaths, leaves the bathroom, and manages to climb down the stairs.

The three men are drinking tea, and Malik and Omar are smoking. Ali also appears even younger without his hair and beard. A large tray of *simit* and assorted buns is centered between them.

They all praise Allah and say their greetings. Malik motions for Omar to pour Safak some tea. Omar puts out his stub of a cigarette and retrieves the hot tea for Safak. Safak takes the tea and drinks deeply. He takes a *simit* and a bun filled with honey and pistachios off the tray. He is certain that both are fresh and well made, but he is unable to taste anything. When he sees that his hand is trembling, Safak realizes that he is frightened.

Malik leans over and places what he hopes to be a reassuring hand on Safak's shoulder. "This is normal. What you are about to do is not easy. Faith has not come naturally to you. You are still struggling with it. He is different." Malik gestures to Ali who has seemed to not have a moment's doubt throughout the days and nights they have spent together. "Praying soothes him. He is ready. He will help you."

Ali looks over at Safak. He speaks directly to Safak for the first time. "Prayer brings me to a state of complete peace. I know this does not work for everybody. This took me some time before I could achieve this state of mind. Allah will be with us. I know this. You must trust me. We carry out Allah's words and mission. We are so lucky to have this privilege. We have been chosen." His large eyes focus on Safak. He does not break his gaze. Finally Safak looks away.

"I will help you," Ali tells him. "We will carry out this mission together. This is God's will. You will not be alone. I promise you, my brother." Ali gets up from his chair and walks over to Safak. He leans over and hugs him. Safak folds into him and begins to sob.

"No worries, my brother. I am here for you, to take care of you. This is my task from Allah."

And although Safak knows in his mind that this is no assignment from Allah, that Malik and Omar have given this task to Ali, the comfort of Ali's arms and the words "brother" and "take care of you" take hold of Safak's heart. Has he not been searching for a brother, a father, a male figure to love him, accept him and help him to fulfill his purpose on this earth? This peaceful man, this man grounded in prayer, has offered to help him get through this impossible feat. A sudden calm comes over Safak. He rises from his chair and grasps Ali's hands in his. "I accept your help, brother. Thank you. I need it."

"Good," Ali says, "then let us pray together before we go. Let us pray for our release from this world and our peaceful journey to the next." He releases himself from Safak's grasp, but takes one of his hands and leads him into the next room where there are prayer rugs laid out on the floor. "Come," Ali tells Safak. "Let us kneel and pray."

CHAPTER 37

"Aren't you going to answer that?" Adalet asks Nuray, as the cell phone continues to buzz.

"I'm afraid," Nuray admits.

"Here," Adalet picks up the phone and places it in Nuray's hand. "You know you must."

Nuray takes the vibrating instrument and slides her finger across the green light. "*Salem*," she says.

The voice on the other end is male and not Belgin. "I am calling for Belgin. You must leave right now. Take only essentials, a very small pack. No more than five minutes, please. Go around the corner and wait for a black Fiat with a driver named Eymen. Quickly, go now!!" The line disconnects, and Nuray stands there, staring at the phone.

"What did they say?" Adalet asks.

"Get out of here now!" Nuray yells. "You must leave immediately. I must, too. But you must get out of here right now. Go!" She runs to the door and opens it. "Go—now!"

Adalet grabs her bag and is halfway out the door, when she stops to look back at Nuray. She so wants to hug her, hold her friend.

But Nuray is adamant. She will not be responsible for her friend being jailed again. "Get the hell out of here now!" she shouts again. "Take the stairs," she yells to Adalet's back before she slams the door. Adalet runs from the elevator to the door to the stairs and does as her friend commands. She races down the three flights of stairs to the street and darts out the front door and around the corner, just in time to miss the police van pulling up in front of Nuray's building.

Nuray grabs some papers on which she has been journaling and writing ideas, a sweater and a jacket, a couple of changes of underwear, a toothbrush. She finds it hard to breathe. Is there anything truly important that she is forgetting? She throws these things into a small backpack. Why didn't she plan ahead for this? Will she ever come back to this apartment? What is she forgetting? There must be something. She throws another pair of pants into the bag, presses down to zip it closed, and she runs to the door. A bra. She never packed another bra. She throws down the bag, races back into the bedroom and pulls a bra from her underwear drawer. She unzips the bag, stuffs the bra inside, and rezips the bag. She takes a deep breath and opens the door. Three large man are standing outside.

One of the men steps forward. "Nuray Demir?" he asks, holding a police identification card out for her to see.

Nuray's heart takes a dive into her gut. She starts to fall forward, but one of the other men steps up and secures her by grabbing her arm. He takes the bag from her other arm and tosses it back inside the apartment. "Going somewhere?' he smirks. "You won't need anything where you are going." The first man shuts the door to Nuray's apartment, and the three men escort her into the elevator.

Only seconds too late, Nuray thinks. If only I had left with Adalet. I didn't need to take anything. Oh Allah, where are you now? Seconds, only seconds. She shudders, and one of the men pulls up on her arm. He is kinder than the others. "Are you okay?" he asks, as if that would even be a possibility now. What seems almost comical to Nuray is that they do not handcuff her until they reach the van and have her seated in the back. She is glad that she is cuffed in front and not behind her back.

.   .   .

Adalet, now somewhat recovered from the shock of the call and Nuray throwing her out of the apartment, has backtracked and from behind a parked vehicle, she watches the police putting Nuray into the van. Tears stream down her face, and she breaks into open sobs. Now that she knows what her friend has suffered in the hands of these awful men, the thought of her having to face this nightmare again is unbearable. But what can she possibly do? Is there anything? She can contact Mark's lawyer. Once the police van has pulled away, Adalet pulls out her cell phone and calls an Uber. While she is waiting, she swipes WhatsApp to call Mark, even though it is late in the evening there now. Mark is not asleep.

"Hi my darling," he says. "Do you have flight plans yet?"

"No, but I'm on my way home now, and I will make them today. I have to get out of here."

"Has something happened?" Mark asks. He is clearly concerned.

"Nuray has been arrested again. It was awful. I was there seconds before it happened. She got a phone call and practically threw me out of the apartment. She knew they were coming. I barely made it out of there myself."

"Oh, Adalet, thank goodness she made you leave! They might have arrested you with her again. Please make the flight arrangements as soon as you get home, and then call me to let me know when you are arriving. I want to be there to pick you up, of course." Mark's voice is concerned but also excited. Adalet knows he will not rest now until he has her in his arms.

"I promise you. I will do it as soon as I get back home. But please text me your attorney's name and number here. I want to ask her to help Nuray. You cannot imagine how Nuray has suffered. I never thought my own people—Oh, Mark, why are some men so cruel? Why are women so vulnerable to these atrocities? What happens to simple humanity and honor?"

"Adalet, listen to me. Go home right now and make your reservations—"

"Okay, the Uber is here. Text me the attorney info. I'll call you and text you my plane flights. I love you."

"I love you, too." Adalet knows that Mark has refrained from asking her anymore about Nuray. There will be plenty of time later to tell him. He just wants her to get out of there while she still can.

Adalet does not believe the police will come to arrest her. If they had caught her there at the apartment, they might have taken her with Nuray, but there is no logical reason for them to come after her. At the same time, she knows many people have been arrested without any judicious explanation, and the fact remains that she has visited Nuray in prison. Perhaps Mark is right to be so concerned. Guilty by association is certainly not out of the province of the current rationale for detainment.

When the Uber reaches Steep Street, Adalet pays the driver quickly with her credit card and runs up the stairs to her apartment. She copies down the information that Mark has texted and immediately phones the attorney. She gets a secretary who takes the message. "Please," Adalet insists, "she knows my husband, Mark Aronson. This is an emergency."

The secretary grunts. "Every call is an emergency these days. I will have her call as soon as she gets back to the office. She is at the prison right now."

"Thank you," Adalet tells her. "I'm leaving the country in the next couple of days, so I need to speak to her quickly."

"I will let her know."

Adalet pulls out her laptop and immediately looks for flights. She finds a direct flight on Turkish Air that leaves Sunday evening. She immediately books a single one-way ticket in business class. She might as well depart in style and comfort. Once she is confirmed, she texts the information to Mark. She wants to keep the line open in case the attorney calls her back. Adalet keeps herself busy checking all around the apartment to make sure she has not neglected to pack anything she wishes to bring with her to America. She has done this twice before her cellphone beeps.

"*Merhaba,*" Adalet says, hoping that this is the attorney.

"*Merhaba,*" the voice on the other end responds. "I am Afet Can. I am Mark Aronson's lawyer. Is this Adalet Aronson, Mark's wife? Are you the person I arranged the marriage for?"

"Yes, yes. I am that Adalet. Thank you so much for returning my call."

"How can I help you now? Are you having any trouble leaving?" Her voice expresses some concern.

"No, I don't think so. I should be leaving Sunday evening. I have my flight scheduled, and I am packed and ready to go. Mark will be meeting me at the airport in New York." Adalet takes a breath and is about to explain why she is calling, but Afet Can begins to speak again before Adalet can say anything.

"This is good news. I wanted you to leave with Mark, but I am glad your flight is booked, and you are going now. Things are getting more complicated every day. But you are married now, and so you should have no problems. I know Mark will be thrilled to see you."

"Yes," Adalet agrees, "but that isn't why I'm calling. I want you to help my friend, Nuray Demir. She has been detained twice now, and she has nothing to do with the attempted coup. If you go to see her, she will give you all the details."

"Do you know where they have taken her?" Afet Can asks.

"Not this time. They just took her earlier today." Adalet does not comment on her own narrow escape. She does not wish to divert the attorney's attention from Nuray.

"That is okay," Afet Can tells her. "I have her name now. I will ask you for a few personal details now that might help me to locate her more quickly, if that is all right with you."

"Of course," Adalet replies.

Adalet supplies the lawyer with Nuray's date of birth, her address, the details she knows about the magazine, and several descriptive physical details. She explains to the lawyer that she and Mark wish to remain involved in Nuray's case, and if there are fees involved that Nuray is unable to pay, that she and Mark will be happy to help in any way they are able. She is careful about agreeing to pay for everything because she is unsure how Mark will feel. She knows that he is generous, but this is not something they have fully discussed.

Once off the call with Afet Can, Adalet calls Mark. Mark's response is as Adalet hopes it to be. "Of course, we will help her in whatever ways we can. But please, my darling, get on that plane on Sunday. Don't let anything change your mind."

"Don't worry," Adalet tries to assure him, "I will be there. I promise."

Three days, Adalet worries. Only three days before she leaves her country behind. Now that she and Mark are married, she does not believe she will ever return to live in Turkey. She supposes that circumstances could always change, but in this moment it seems highly unlikely. She looks around the apartment. Fatma has shared stories with her about how her grandfather purchased the apartment after his boss died and left the fish restaurant to him. He and his new wife sold both of their homes in order to buy it. Later, as Fatma's grandfather became more successful, he managed to buy the whole building. This was a source of great pride for him and for Fatma. Adalet had been shocked to learn that Fatma had left the building to her in her will. She had wanted to ensure Adalet's future would be secure.

So much for security, Adalet thinks, her eyes traversing the living room. One can plot and plan, but the universe operates in its own sphere, predictably unpredictable. And in some ways, human nature being what it is, terribly predictable. Just a few years back, Turkey was well on its way to becoming a democracy. Human rights, women's rights, LBGQ rights, religious freedom, everything was on the table. Turkey wanted into the European Union, and it seemed remotely possible. Now there is no chance. Four steps forward and five back. We never quite make it over the hump, Adalet muses. Fatma could not have predicted any of this, although she was never a fan of Erdoğan.

"Give him an inch and he'll take five miles," Fatma would say. "He'll bring back the veil and say any woman not wearing one is a prostitute. He'll overturn everything Atatürk did to bring us into the 20th century. Don't trust him, Adalet."

Fatma need not have worried. Adalet has never trusted any politician. Now she knows how precarious life can be. She learned this in the earthquake that nearly took her life, took the life of her unborn child, killed both of her parents, and left her with terrible leg burns. This is not the first time that Adalet has known upheaval and life change. She thinks about the recent presidential election in America and wonders what that will portend for her future with Mark in America. Mark said Trump would never be elected, but he was. Mark was devastated.

"I can't believe it," he'd almost shouted into the phone. "What has gone wrong with this country?"

"But you have checks and balances," Adalet had reassured him. "How much harm can he do?"

"I don't know. Let's hope the checks and balances hold. I guess we're about to find out. Sorry, my darling. You're leaving one country in turmoil to come into another one possibly going into turmoil. At least we will be together."

That seemed to have satisfied Mark, but for Adalet, it was less than comforting. She knew from experience that being together would not solve everything.

Alone now, in the apartment she will be forsaking in just a few days, conceivably never to return, Adalet tries to take in every feature of her Turkish home. She pulls out her phone and wanders into all the rooms, photographing everything. She goes out onto the balcony and photographs the street below, the same scenes she has been taking in every day for so many years now. She pauses on the balcony, breathing the street smells in deeply, and wondering what it will feel like to wake up in a new bed, in a new home, with completely new sounds and smells. She has taken all of this for granted, and soon it will all be gone.

Adalet places the phone down on her bedroom nightstand, and then picks it up again. She needs to talk to someone who might understand. She starts to call Nuray before she startles into the realization that she cannot speak to Nuray. Nuray is back in police custody, and Adalet may never see her friend again.

Frantically, Adalet scans her phone to see if she has any photos of Nuray. In all these years has she never taken a single photograph? She runs to her laptop and pulls up all her photographs. She scans through them all. Her life flashes by. Ah, at last, yes, there is one old photo from some years ago when they were in university together. It is a group picture that someone else has taken. Nuray is one of five women and blends into the background. But she is there. That is what is important. There is some physical evidence that Nuray has existed, still exists, and will always exist, in the mind and heart and eyes of Adalet.

CHAPTER 38

On Sunday morning, Adalet awakens to the morning call to prayer. She savors the tinny, recorded version, as she knows she will no longer be hearing these calls five times a day. Even though it is not the real voice she heard many years ago in Duzçe, the village in which she grew up, she has grown accustomed to this one. A heaviness forms in her belly. Out of habit, Adalet heads to the kitchen to start the *çaydanlık*. Then she remembers that she has wrapped the teapot in bubble wrap and placed it in her carryon case. She will get *çay* on the way to the Sunday market. Her plane does not leave until late afternoon, and she has planned to make this last trip before heading off to the airport.

All that remains are her bathroom necessities, one bag of clothing and her carryon, stuffed with her computer, a few valuables and the *çaydanlık*. Mark assured her that they could buy a new one, but Adalet cannot imagine leaving Turkey without it. And if Yetim had not left this world when she did, Adalet does not know if she would even be boarding this plane today. Ah, she thinks, Of course, I would merely have taken Yetim with me. She and Mark have talked about getting a kitten together, and perhaps, even a puppy. She smiles at this aspect of her new life.

Adalet takes a quick shower, throws on the loose light blue silk pants, white silk blouse and dark blue jacket she will wear on the trip, and quickly packs her toiletries. She makes one last walk through the apartment to make sure she has left nothing behind.

Adalet hesitates before opening the door to put on her shoes. What if Yetim had not developed cancer and died? Was it unthinkable that she would have decided to remain in Turkey because of her cat? Many would find this ridiculous. Nuray certainly did. When Adalet visited Nuray in prison, finally allowed to see her, Nuray encouraged Adalet to leave. "Get the hell out of here while you still can," she'd admonished Adalet. "Go to New York and marry Mark. You can have a good life."

"But what will become of Yetim?" Adalet argued.

"You're not going to go because of a cat? Adalet, what is wrong with you? Can't you see what is happening to this country? If you dare to defy Erdoğan and defend democracy, you go to prison for the rest of your life. Don't be a fool."

Adalet saw the truth in what Nuray was saying, but still she had hoped there might be some way she could manage to avoid the politics, manage the long-distance relationship with Mark, and continue her life in Istanbul. Now she knows that she was living in a dream, a fantasy.

Adalet puts on her shoes outside the door and takes the winding staircase down to the street. The heavy door screeches behind her. She hesitates a moment to stare up at the building, her balcony, and then looks around at the familiar signs and sights of Steep Street. The tailor and laundry vendor across the street is sweeping in front of his store in the same worn-out jacket and pants she has seen him wearing all these years. She smiles. She wonders if the pants and jacket have ever made their way into his laundry.

The Sunday market is a good twenty-minute walk, but Adalet decides she can do without the çay on the way. She will get some at the market. There is precious little time, and she wants as much of it as possible to wander the marketplace. She will find nothing like it in the United States, or so she believes.

It is a beautiful December morning. The air is crisp but mild. The streets are not yet as busy as they soon will be. Shopkeepers are setting up for the day, opening awnings and sweeping the sidewalks out in front. Gulls and pigeons squawk at one another, flying low and threatening their wingspans over bread crusts on the pavement. This is a day like so many Adalet has known. And yet, in this moment Adalet is supremely happy. She will revel in the hours that remain to her in her mother country.

Adalet purchases a çay at a tiny stand at the edge of the market. A child serves her, as her aging grandmother looks on. Adalet slips the girl an extra coin, and the girl smiles shyly at her. Adalet stands there for a few moments sipping her tea and looking around at the market. The tea is quickly tepid, and Adalet takes one last sip before tossing the paper cup in a nearby trash receptacle. Tea is never good from a paper cup, she muses.

Vendors are still setting up their stalls. She gazes at the two dark-skinned young Kurdish men hanging ladies' braziers and panties from hooks surrounding their tented stall. Their boss, their father or grandfather perhaps, looks on, puffing strenuously on a cigarette. No, she thinks, there is nothing like this in America. Where will she find these open stalls selling eggplants and underwear side by side? Where will deep purple, bright pink and red flash their wares under the open sky?

Adalet begins to stroll along the street between the stalls. A stall a bit farther down is displaying large tables covered with bright red peppers. Adalet moves in closer and takes several photos with her phone. The vendor, a stout mustached man in his fifties wearing a cap over thick black hair, stops to grin and pose for her. Just to be affable, Adalet clicks his picture among the peppers. He gestures to the peppers and to his mouth. "Please try, if you like," he says.

Adalet is not quite ready for red pepper at this hour of the morning, but she feels obligated. She picks up a pepper close to her and bites off the end, hoping to avoid the miniscule but volatile seeds. And this one is filled with the dangerous missiles. They stream along her tongue like the little grains of coated sugar that burst forth from the candies that her mother used to give her when she was just a child. But these are not coated granules of sugar, and her tongue is a raging fire. Tears fill her eyes and mucus runs down her nose and her chin. Adalet blindly reaches into her pocket for a handkerchief, but there is nothing.

The vendor gives Adalet a malicious twist of his mouth, too ironic to be considered a smile. He hands her a tissue. "So, they are good, no?" He points to the small cardboard pricing sign listing the number of lira required for different weights.

Adalet cannot breathe, let alone speak. Her taste buds are singed. Her sense of smell is gone. She blows hard into the tissue and wipes her nose and face as best she can. The vendor holds up another tissue. Adalet shakes her head no.

"Thank you," Adalet chokes, "but I am leaving today. I am traveling. I am not able to buy any peppers."

"That's okay," the vendor replies good naturedly. "When you come back, you will remember my peppers."

"If I come back," Adalet manages to tell him, "I will most certainly remember your peppers. I don't think I will be able to forget them."

The vendor shrugs and turns away to attract the attention of those wishing to actually make a purchase. Adalet strolls along, taking in the smells of the fruits and vegetables, tables arrayed with deep purple eggplants, bright red tomatoes, persimmons and pomegranates, onions, and garlic, all without imperfections of any visible kind. She remembers the flawed fruits and vegetables she observed in the small markets in New York City. The vendors there seemed to have no pride. She hopes she just did not have the time to locate the better markets.

Adalet wanders to the end of this particular path in the market where there is a closed tent without any designating signs. A whisp of smoke rises from the slightly open flap. Curiosity gets the better of her, and she approaches to see what is being sold inside. Not without a bit of apprehension, she folds back a slight portion of the tent flap. Inside it is dark with the exception of several kerosine lamps set on the ground in the corners. A group of elderly men, bearded and accoutered in colorful long robes, are sitting cross-legged on the worn carpeted floor in a semicircle. Facing them is an ancient man, the only one dressed all in white, with a beard so long that it is close to touching the carpet beneath him. They are passing a hookah, taking turns smoking, while chanting a Sufi incantation that feels somehow familiar to Adalet. In the very rear of the tent, a *çaydanlık* is simmering on a small portable stove. Adalet is quite still, not wishing to make her presence known, afraid they will ask her to leave. There is something comforting as well as alluring in this medieval ceremony.

The Sufi, who looks to be the youngest member in this group, rises and raises the *çaydanlık* from the tiny stove. He fills dainty glass cups with the liquid and sets them on a tray with a bowl filled with little cubes of sugar. He carefully carries the tray around, serving the Ancient first, and then each of the others. Adalet notices that there is an empty cup remaining.

The chanting increases in intensity as the men somehow manage to sip their tea in between breaths of chants. Four of the men pick up instruments from the rear of the tent and begin to play. A tall, large man in a silver and green robe plays the *ney,* an end-blown flute used for centuries in classic Sufi ritual. A much smaller man dressed in a red and purple robe commences on the *armudi kemençe*, a pear-shaped bowed fiddle. The oldest man, or to Adalet he appears that way, seated next to the Ancient, begins to strum a *tambur*, a fretted string instrument. He is dressed in black with orange embroidery. Next to him, a whisp of a gentleman also wearing black, but with red embroidery, gently taps on the *kudüm* drum. The result is exhilarating.

Adalet does not believe that anyone is aware of her presence, but the Ancient beckons a gnarled index finger toward her, gesturing that she should enter the tent. With only a brief shudder of hesitation, Adalet complies.

Adalet has not noticed until now the incense tray behind the Ancient, creating some of the thin-layered smoke she first observed. The strong whiffs of sandalwood are intoxicating. The Ancient taps the carpet next to him, indicating that Adalet should sit. So intensely drawn by whatever this ceremony is creating, Adalet can do nothing but obey.

The Ancient himself fills the remaining glass cup with çay. He hands Adalet the cup and the bowl of sugar cubes, and then he motions with one hand for her to take the sugar and to drink. As if she is the star in a silent film she has never seen, Adalet does as the Ancient instructs. The music, the incense, and the chanting all begin to pleasantly hypnotize her.

As if all has been prearranged, the Sufi who are not playing instruments slowly rise. They begin to spin and twirl. The Ancient takes Adalet's hand and pulls her to her feet. He fixes his eyes on her as he whirls with a dexterity that Adalet could never have imagined. The size of the tent magically seems to expand so that the dancers are not impeded. The Ancient's eyes on her lead Adalet into a revolving motion, very slow at first. Before she can think about what is happening, her speed picks up and her whirling thrusts her into a dream state of consciousness she has never experienced. She is completely at one with this dance. She could whirl forever without stopping.

The weight of her pending departure lifts. Her anxieties, her fears, her misgivings, all leave her mind and her body. She transcends her body and becomes a seagull soaring over the Bosphorus, sailing on the shifting winds. There is no Turkey. There is no America. There is no Erdoğan. There is nothing but the surrounding air and the water below. Adalet twirls and twirls, no longer aware of time or the men twirling around her.

Gradually the music fades. Wherever they have been drifting, the men return calmly and slow their movements, lowering the hands raised to heaven and lifting the hands lowered to the earth. Adalet, too, comes back into her surroundings, collapsing onto the carpet next to the Ancient. For the first time he expresses any emotion. He smiles warmly at Adalet, but he says nothing. Then he turns away, back to his ineffable stance, motionless, unknowable.

Some moments later, when Adalet feels sufficiently recovered, she rises, nods her thanks to the silent group, and backs out of the tent. She stumbles back into the marketplace, still recovering from this somewhat uneasy but strangely reassuring experience. She leaves the market, wandering for a bit towards the small park next to the Bosphorus. She sits on a bench and watches the gulls soaring and chattering amongst themselves.

Adalet does not question what has just happened. She believes in signs and ceremonies. She is as superstitious as any Turkish girl raised in a village. More than anything, Adalet is grateful. Whatever has just taken place has freed her. She can leave Istanbul. She can depart Turkey. Turkey is now lodged within her soul. She can take her beloved country with her.

CHAPTER 39

Safak Aksoy is resigned to terror. His terror is not the radically focused terror of an assassin, but it is more definitely tied to the prospect of his own demise. *Amor fati* be damned, he does not want to die. His partner in crime and his handlers are well aware of this, as his fear is ubiquitous. No other emotion, no other passion, no other sentiment, emerges from his being. Safak's panic is palpable enough to frighten away the birds from the trees. They scatter frantically as the four men leave the house to enter the car.

Safak's dread has increased steadily since Malik and Omar fastened explosive vests around him and around Ali. Safak is soaked in sweat, and even he can smell his fear. The giant water bug that stares up at him from the gutter, as he waits for Malik to unlock the car, quivers its tentacles, and scurries quickly in the other direction. Ali remains as undisturbed as the windless day.

The four men climb into the airless vehicle. Safak and Ali sit in the back, two dummies stuffed with explosive sausages wound around their bodies. Safak thinks for a moment that he could detonate right here and now, saving some lives, but certainly not his own. Does he even wish to save lives? He is unsure about this, as he is unsure about his entire life.

Again he asks himself, how the hell did I end up here? If I had not denounced that damned Nuray Demir, and then my commander had not been so pissed off at me because her friends were all worthless arrests, would I have gone off to find Altan? My brother has tossed me to the wolves. He's dumped me like I'm a piece of bulky baggage. I'll bet he looks good to his superiors, giving up his own brother. What kind of sacrifice was that for him anyway? If I never meant anything to him, where is the loss? I'm a fool, a complete idiot. Why did I ever think he would embrace me, make me his friend? He's thrown me out like rotting garbage. These thoughts send him to an even deeper layer of despair. His body sinks, as much as it is able with his vest of death, extending downwards into the ragged upholstery.

Amor fati, he repeats to himself. This is my fate. *Amor fati*. This is my fate. Safak repeats these words over and over in his mind. He is now dripping with sweat. Ali looks over at him, concerned.

"How is it going, Brother? Are you going to be okay?" He says this too quietly for Malik and Omar to hear.

"I don't know. I don't know if I can do this when the time comes," Safak reluctantly confesses.

"That's okay. We have anticipated, so we will do this a bit differently." Ali leans a bit forward and calls out, "Malik. We will go to Plan B."

"Are you sure?" Malik calls back.

"As sure as I can be."

"Okay," Malik responds. "That's good enough for me. We'll do bigger and better in one location."

"What does that mean?" Safak asks Ali.

"Don't worry. We will do it together. One big bang in one location, and I will pull the triggers for both of us. You won't have to do it. I will do it for you. You won't have to move. We'll take the car with us."

"What about them?" Safak indicates Malik and Omar.

"It's not their time. They have more deliveries to make. Just me and you, my friend. We will travel to martyrdom together. We are so lucky. We won't go alone. Allah will be twice as happy to receive us."

Now all hope abandons Safak. He will never leave this car. He will not be allowed to do so. They are well prepared for him. His panic and fear have been foreseen and programmed into the plot. He has never fooled anyone. They never fully believed he could pull the cord. Did they believe him to be so useless that getting rid of him was always the plan? Of course, he reminds himself, he is not totally useless. By his own hand, or by the hand of the man sitting next to him, he will kill many people. Is this what Allah wants? Safak has always had a question about even the existence of an Allah, never mind knowing what that Allah might want. But just in case, he finds himself silently praying. The other men in the car are also mute.

The drive is not so long before Malik pulls over to the side of the road and parks the car. Safak sees that they are in a bustling public market in the busy morning rush. "We're here," Malik announces. "Ready?" he asks Ali.

"I am ready." Ali responds confidently.

Both Malik and Omar turn around to face the two murderer/martyrs in the backseat. They both say, "Allah be with you."

"And Allah be with you," Ali replies. Safak is unable to say anything.

The two men get out of the car. Safak thinks to open his door and make a run for it, but he hears the doors lock behind them. They have expected him to try to escape.

When Malik and Omar are at a safe distance, Ali says, "Open your jacket." He moves in closer to Safak. Safak does as he is told. "Now close your eyes and pray to Allah." Safak feels Ali's hand on his detonation cord.

With one hand, Ali pulls the cord on his own device, as he pulls the cord on Safak's vest. The explosion is huge, but Safak does not hear a thing. He does not feel a thing. And he will never hear or feel or see or speak—or hurt another human being again.

CHAPTER 40

Guards transport Nuray to Bakırköy Women's Prison in Istanbul. Nuray knows they jail many women journalists there. She is processed and taken directly to a large cell, referred to as a pod, with a group of about twenty women. It is a huge relief for her not to be alone. Nuray immediately recognizes two of the women as journalists she only knew peripherally through organizational meetings over the years. But they greet her as if they have always been friends.

One of the women is named Ezma. She is somewhere around Nuray's age. She is Kurdish, a tiny woman with very dark features. She just misses being pretty, her nose and mouth, each a little too large for her face. She wears her long, thick hair in a bun at the base of her neck. The other woman Nuray recognizes is called Sera, and she is also Kurdish. Sera is a tall, large-boned woman with cropped curly, dirty blond hair, and piercing green eyes. She looks to be in her late twenties. Now Nuray begins to wonder if the Kurdish side of her, her father's side, is what is getting her into all of this trouble. In the Republic of Turkey, the Kurds are always to blame for everything. Well, perhaps having Kurdish family has contributed to her current difficulties, she thinks, but she cannot pin the blame totally on her genetics. Safak Aksoy is the real reason she was targeted and arrested. If not for Aksoy, the police might never have found her or connected her to her father.

The pod, as it is called, is a large area with metal bunk beds stacked together. There is one that remains vacant on the bottom level. Both fortunately, and unfortunately, it is closest to the toilet and sink closet inside the pod. She guesses that the odor of vinegar and sulfur she already detects emanates from that closet, and that is the reason the lower bunk next to it is the only available bunk. Nuray decides to look on the bright side. It will be easy access in the middle of the night.

The pod reminds Nuray of gray concrete blocks she has seen at construction building sites that homeless people have tried to make homey. The women have attached thin strings across the beds over which they hang underwear and small items like t-shirts to dry. There are a few posters and photos of family and loved ones taped to the walls and the ends of the beds. The posters depict country scenes and flowers. There is a creased Monet Water Lilies with tattered edges and another of sunflowers on a country road by an unknown artist. The women have made weak attempts to make the place their hopefully temporary but more agreeable home.

Once Nuray has placed her few belongings in the small cubbyhole next to her bed, Ezma says, "So, I am guessing that you haven't been to trial, since we are all just detained here. None of us has had a trial or been convicted."

"That's right," Nuray tells her. "No one has said anything about a trial yet. I'm not even sure of my charges. The one who interrogated me initially said I'd be charged with terrorism and insurrection, but I don't see how."

Sera laughs, but she stops herself when she sees the expression on Nuray's face. "I'm so sorry," she tells Nuray, "but none of us can see how. I know they say that everyone in prison is innocent, but in this case, it is mostly the truth."

"Not completely," says an older woman.

"Well, most of us are guilty of saying something negative about Erdoğan and the government, even protesting," Ezma responds, "but I will bet money that no one here actually had anything to do with the coup."

"Attempted coup," a young woman in a head scarf corrects. "The coup did not succeed."

Sera laughs again. "If the coup had succeeded, none of us would be here now."

"Yes," the young woman in the head scarf replies. "That is true. If the coup had succeeded, Erdoğan would be the one in a cell. Clearly, he is too smart for that." The woman adjusts her scarf, and Nuray can see that she is very pretty and probably not more than twenty-five years old. Her fingers are long and slender, a pianist's fingers. But the nails are badly bitten, the cuticles chewed away.

Sera shakes her head. "That would be great, wouldn't it? But we should be careful." She lowers her voice. "They are probably recording everything we say."

"What is your name?" Nuray asks the young woman.

"Aysun," she replies. "And you are?"

"Nuray."

"And how did you end up here, Nuray?" Aysun asks.

"I ran a magazine called *Turkey's New Woman*. It was a small publication I took over from a journalist named Badia Celik when she died. I had written a couple of articles condemning Erdoğan which might never have gotten me into trouble, but there was a soldier out to get me because I refused to sleep with him."

"Ah, sex," Aysun says with a large grimace, "the source of so much evil." She lowers her voice to a whisper. "What they accuse me of is mostly true. I had nothing to do with the attempted coup itself, but I have been an activist since I was fifteen years old."

"It's almost funny, " Ezma says. "No one in here was actually involved with the attempted coup, but everyone in here is accused of it, myself included. So where are the people who are guilty?"

"We'll never find them," the older woman laughs. "Probably, neither will they. But we'll pay for it anyway."

"Why are you here?" Nuray asks the old woman.

The woman's eyes crinkle, the dark shadows of the prison lighting play on her grin, and turn her sharp features into something seeming almost sinister, demonic. But her long, dark skirt, and her tattered t-shirt displaying the scientific symbol for "woman" work to defy this initial impression.

"My name is Yıldız Kaya."

Nuray breaks into a wide smile. "Ah, of course. Now I recognize you from your photos in the newspapers."

"Not terribly flattering, eh? Always being arrested. I've spent more time in these cages than anyone here, or anyone I know, for that matter. Although there are some men who have spent as much time or more. I probably hold the record for a woman." The pride in Yıldız's voice is unquestionable.

"I don't doubt that this is true. I've been reading about your crusade for women's rights for years. I've admired you for so long, and I've attended a few of your protests and marches. It's an honor to meet you."

"I am pleased to meet you, too, Nuray. But we all wish it could be under different circumstances." The old woman reaches out and takes Nuray's hand in hers. Nuray feels the gnarled knuckles and cracked, dry skin. The woman's hand is like unused sandpaper. But Nuray is relieved to be in such good company.

A small boy slides down from an upper bunk. Nuray has not noticed him until now. He is a wisp of a thing, all eyes, very dark ones, and a mop of thick black hair.

"And who might you be?" Nuray asks.

"I am Arslan."

"He's my son." Sera smiles widely and proudly. "He's five years old."

"Five and a half," Arslan corrects his *anne*.

"Hi there, Arslan. I'm Nuray."

Time loses meaning here. The days pass much like one would expect, slowly, often uneventfully. Eventful days are not always positive. There is the morning body count. Outdoor courtyard exercise is daily but dependent on the weather. Meals come around on large trays. They are barely essential and usually unappetizing. Everyone loses weight. Since the women in this pod are all detained, they do not work. The days are long and boring. Their detained status prevents them from having the few amenities of sentenced inmates. They are all in limbo.

Mohammed visits and brings Nuray her requested copy of *The Forty Rules of Love* by Elif Şafak. Some of the other women have books and magazines, and so they trade them to read. There are cards, a chess set, a few other games, and some basic art supplies for the child. Somehow they manage the days, and for a few of them, a small family is formed. Nuray finds herself a bit friendlier than in her past. Prior to coming to Bakırköy, Nuray was isolated in prison, and being with these women provides a feeling of safety, however false, that is comforting.

Although Arslan can sometimes prove irritating because he is understandably bored, enough of the women pamper and attend to him that he leaves Nuray alone. He senses her reluctance. He is a bright little boy, and the women take turns giving him school lessons. He draws and paints on the walls, and his creative and talented creations are quite whimsical. Even Nuray finds herself watching him with delight.

Nuray receives a letter from Adalet. It bears a New York postmark. Adalet writes that she flew to New York the Sunday after Nuray was arrested. She is safely with Mark now. Her letter is carefully worded, giving very few details. Adalet knows her mail will be censored. She gives Nuray the name Afet Can. *She will be visiting you. She is the attorney who will be handling your case.* Adalet includes her address in New York. I am so lucky, Nuray thinks. Adalet will not abandon me. She has no obligation to help me, and yet I know she will do everything she can. I should have been a better friend to her. As soon as I meet with Afet Can, I will write to let her know.

Although Nuray feels more secure in the pod than she did in a solitary cell, the nightmares continue to plague her. Rough hands and arms reach out to grab her, and she wakes up in a sweat. One night she awakens to Arslan shaking her. "I have those, too, sometimes. Do you want me to sleep with you? When I sleep with my *anne*, it helps me."

"Won't your *anne* mind?" Nuray asks.

"No, it's happened with some of the others before."

"Okay," Nuray decides impulsively. Why not, she thinks. I can use a new friend. She pulls up the covers, and Arslan crawls in beside her. Soon the two are fast asleep.

CHAPTER 41

"I'm sorry, Nuray. They can detain you for a long time without a trial. They are doing this to so many people. I can push and protest, and I will, but there is only so much I can do. I promise you that I will fight to get you to trial, but that might not have the outcome you would like." Afet Can pushes a pen around on the table in the conference room used for these visits. It is clear to Nuray that she wishes she could bring her better news. "Everything has changed, and yet, everything remains the same." Afet Can picks up her pen and takes a legal pad from her briefcase. "And now you must tell me everything about the course of events. And I do mean everything. Please do not omit any detail, no matter how insignificant it might seem. I need to know everything."

For some inexplicable reason, Nuray feels completely comfortable with Afet Can. Her eyes convey an enormous intelligence. She is an unassuming woman of average height, slender, simply and modestly dressed in a matching jacket and calf-length navy blue skirt. Her brown leather shoes boast only a tiny heel. Her hair is dark with streaks of gray in the front, short and thick, stylishly cut, and again, modestly combed back from her face. Tiny gold stud earrings and a functional leather watch are her only jewelry. At the same time, she is empathic and all business. This is an attitude that Nuray can trust.

The hour they are allotted passes quickly. Nuray begins to tell Afet Can about the soldier, about her father, and how she came to be in this mess. Afet Can listens quietly, sometimes jotting down notes on her legal pad.

When Nuray finishes speaking, Afet Can explains that she will not be able to return to finish the interview for another week. This is according to regulations and not by her choice. She also tells Nuray to call her Afet. "There is enough formality here. There are enough rules and regulations. Our relationship is both highly personal and highly professional. I think we are both capable of understanding the complexity involved in this kind of association. If either one of us feels that the other is crossing a line, we need to confront the other and be completely honest. Honesty is so crucial to our success."

"I will do my best," Nuray replies. "But if I am to be completely honest, trust does not come easily to me. Adalet and Mohammed, as I've told you already, are my only two friends in this world. But I do have a gut feeling that I can trust you, that you will do whatever you can to help me, and that for me is an excellent beginning."

"Good," Afet says. "We will start there. I will see you next week."

Nuray goes back to the pod with a welcomed sense of relief. Just having someone who might be able to alter the course of her predicament, as slim as that possibility is, gives Nuray the tiny glimmer of hope that she needs so badly now. She is slowly healing physically, but the psychological scars plague her every time she has a moment to think, and there are too many of these emotional intrusions into her present circumstances.

When Nuray is released back into the pod after her visit with Afet, several of the women, including Ezma and Sera, are huddled around a newspaper.

"Ah, Nuray, look at this," Sera says as she motions her. "Terrible stuff. There has been a terrorist bombing in Ankara in the marketplace. Look."

Nuray does not bother to ask how they came to have this newspaper, as she knows the women have their ways of obtaining news other than the controlled news of the television programming they are allowed to view.

But as Nuray reads the article and sees the photos, Ezma notes the change in her expression. "What is it, Nuray? Do you know someone who might have been killed or hurt there? Do you have family or friends in Ankara?"

Nuray shakes her head no. "This is unbelievable." She waves the paper in front of Ezma. "He is dead. He killed all of these people, and now he is dead. I had no idea that he was capable of something like this."

"You know the terrorists?" Sera asks.

"Only one of them. But he seemed so incompetent, even though he is the reason I'm here." She looks again at the photos. "No, it is definitely him. There is his name." Nuray jabs the newspaper with her finger. "This is unimaginable."

"This is the soldier who wanted to sleep with you? He's just a kid." Ezma takes the paper from Nuray to look again at the small photo of Safak Aksoy. It is a photo taken from the military, and he is dressed in his uniform.

"It says here that he defected from the army and joined ISIS. They claimed responsibility for the attack." Ezma reads to herself and says aloud, "He did it with this other guy, Ali Aydem. He looks like a kid, too. Nice name for a terrible man." She shows the photo to the other women.

"I didn't know him," Nuray mutters. "I really didn't know Aksoy either. I took a photo of him and some other soldiers harassing protestors on the night of the coup, and he smashed my camera. When I showed him my press card, he grabbed it and kept it. I know it was stupid of me, but I never thought it would lead to so much trouble. Well, I'm not sorry he's dead, but I'm sorry that he took so many people out with him. What a tragic shame."

"I can't believe it," Aysun joins them. "This is the guy who gave you so much trouble? Wow."

"I really misjudged him." Nuray takes the newspaper back from Ezma to have another look. Aysun leans over her shoulder. "I would never have thought him capable of joining ISIS. I didn't think he was capable of very much."

"Well," Aysun says, taking the newspaper from Nuray and gazing at the photo, "he was certainly capable of getting you locked in here. And as for ISIS, who can know who is susceptible. I have a cousin who ran off to join them. No one knows what happened to him. These are strange and unpredictable times."

Aysun hands the newspaper back to Nuray who now reads the article closely after the initial shock. "Aha," she says, nodding her head, "now that makes more sense. They ignited their explosives together. He wasn't on his own. The coward probably never pulled his own cord."

Aysun smiles the smile of one who knows better. "It isn't ever possible to know. These people come from all sorts of backgrounds, and some of them believe as strongly in their cause as we do in ours."

Nuray shakes her hand dismissively. "I don't think Aksoy believed in anything. But I suppose I could be wrong." She stares at the photos again. "No, I don't think I'm wrong. This Ali looks like he could manage it all." Ali is depicted with a group of ISIS men in the back of a truck, his head circled for the purpose of identifying him in the newspaper. "He looks determined here." Nuray shows Aysun the photo again, her finger illustrating Ali's face.

"You will never know," Aysun says. "We can never know what makes these people do what they do. I walk around and hold up signs. We can see how much good that has done and how far it's gotten me. But I could never resort to violence. I will never believe in that."

"Good," Sera says. "I am relieved to hear it."

Nuray hands the paper back to Ezma. "Enough of him. I hope not to think of him again. I am sure my lawyer will want to know about all of this. I will tell her when I meet with her next week. Now that she has his name, though, she may know about it already."

"You have met with a lawyer?" asks Aysun.

"Yes." Nuray smiles. "My friend Adalet arranged it all. The lawyer seems very competent and honest. She will not give me false hopes."

"False hope is sometimes all we have," Yıldız chimes in from the other end of the pod. "Please don't knock false hope."

Nuray goes to her bunk and lies down. Even though the encounter with Afet Can was brief, the meeting took a lot out of her. And then to come back and find her nemesis gone, and with such a disastrous outcome, it all feels too much at once.

Arslan, who was quietly engaged with lessons when she returned, is now racing around the pod to work off his endless energy. He mimics a train and makes the accompanying sound effects. Nuray stops herself from screaming at him to shut up. None of this is his fault, and he is only five years old. She has to remember that he is behaving as a normal child in wholly abnormal circumstances. Nuray lies back and places her pillow over her head. Ear plugs might be nice right now. She will ask Mohammed to get her some.

Nuray is just about to drop off to sleep when the pod is opened and five guards enter, three women and two men. One of the women, a guard Nuray has seen before, yells harshly, "Inspection. Count and step outside! Quickly now. Move, move." She waves her truncheon in the air.

The women line up quickly, say their names and count their numbers in the line. Nuray is number fourteen. Two male guards wait outside to keep the women lined up and obedient. "No talking," one of them orders. Even Arslan knows better than to open his mouth. Nuray has heard about these searches for unauthorized goods, but this is her first experience. She hears the banging noise of mattresses being overturned, cubbies being emptied, personal belongings torn apart. She hopes *The Forty Rules of Love* will remain intact. She has nothing else there that she values.

"Whose is this?" One of the guards waves the newspaper in the air. When no one responds, she rips it in half, not pushing the ownership issue any further. She thrusts it into a container to be confiscated. The newspaper is run by two Kurdish men who have absconded to Germany after their newspaper was shut down by Erdoğan. They continue to run their paper in exile. This publication is not allowed in Turkey, never mind in this prison. Fortunately, the guard chooses not to press the point on who owns it and how it got there.

This time around, the newspaper is the only item confiscated. But now the women, after standing silently in the corridor for close to forty-five minutes, must return and clean up the ransacked pod.

Once they are back inside, Nuray asks Ezma, "How often does this happen?"

"As often as they like," Ezma tells her. "There are rules, but they don't follow them. When the mood hits them, and perhaps they're bored, they decide to harass us. You learn to live with it. Never happily, but what can we do?"

Nuray is relieved to find that her book has not been damaged. Obviously, someone rustled through the pages, as her bookmark is lying on the floor. Well, she has read this book several times, so losing her place is not terrible. She will find it again quickly.

"Just look at this!" Aysun holds up a jacket. "They ripped open the lining. Now I will have to ask for sewing tools to stitch it back together."

"I have a small sewing kit," Yıldız says. "You will have to ask them for a sewing needle, though." She hands Aysun the tiny kit containing thread and a thimble. "They took the needles away."

"Like you could kill someone with a sewing needle. Ridiculous." Aysun is upset that the lining of her jacket has been torn open. "I don't even know if I can repair this. I might have to just rip out the lining." She waves the jacket in the air, her anger and hopelessness apparent.

For a moment, the room is silent. The women share Aysun's frustration. They allow themselves to participate in a morose moment of gloom. But then Arslan, forced to be silent far too long, yells to his Anne, "Let's clean up now."

Sera laughs which lightens the mood. "I'd better take advantage of this while I can."

And so the women turn back the mattresses, remake their beds, put their belongings back into their cupboards, and put into order what is now the disorder of their lives.

CHAPTER 42

Adalet is overcome by delight to be in the presence of Mark, Meryem, and Isha all at once. Leaving Turkey, the layover in Frankfurt, Germany, and then going through customs in New York, this has all been more bureaucracy than Adalet has ever experienced. The Turkish authorities held her for questioning for so long that Adalet almost missed her plane. She was about to call Afet Can, Mark's attorney, when they finally allowed her to pass through to her flight. When she got to her seat, her sigh of relief was loud enough to attract the attention of the woman seated next to her. "Flying isn't so easy these days, is it?" The woman attempted to console her. But it was not the flight itself that worried Adalet. It was getting out of the country.

During the two flights, though, and for the duration of the three-hour layover in Frankfurt, Adalet wondered if she would ever visit her country again. Would she ever be able to see Nuray? The melancholia that enveloped her occupied her to the degree that she barely experienced flying at all. She had been alone the first time she went to New York to visit Mark after September 11th, and so traveling alone did not cause her any distress. The woman sitting next to her on the flight from Istanbul to Frankfurt quickly went to sleep, and the man on the flight from Frankfurt to New York buried himself in his laptop. Adalet was thus released from the burden of making conversation.

Although Adalet and Meryem had seen each other on Skype, and once in a while Isha had joined them, Adalet is surprised by them in person. Meryem is even more energetic than Adalet remembers. She hugs Adalet to her tightly, and it is only with Mark's nudging that she finally relinquishes her to Mark's embrace. Adalet does feel a sense of coming home, just feeling Mark's loving arms again. Hugs from Meryem and Isha certainly help to give her hope about her new home.

The trip from the airport out to Northport, Long Island, Mark's relatively new home, is over an hour's drive, possibly even more with traffic. Meryem and Isha have taken the day off to welcome Adalet, and so they will take their rental car to meet them there. Adalet is grateful for the time alone with her new husband.

As they make their way through the airport terminal to the parking lot, Adalet glimpses newspaper headlines plastered with photo images of the newly elected President Trump. His tinted orange hair is swept up in cartoon-like fashion, more fodder for the comedians, Adalet considers. What is she walking into, she has to wonder. Leaping from the frying pan into the fire. There doesn't seem to be much security in fleeing from Erdoğan to Trump. No matter how reassuring Mark has sounded with words like "checks and balances," and "our constitution," Adalet has been a witness to the vagaries of a republic. She knows firsthand how quickly freedom can disintegrate, overnight, in fact. At least she is now with those she loves, with one haunting exception. Nuray's fate weighs heavily on her, even in these moments of reunion and joy.

Mark's car is a new Subaru Forrester, a bright red. "Easier to find in crowded parking lots," he tells her, a bit sheepishly. "Actually, I would have had to wait too long for the silver color I wanted. Living out there without a car is impossible, you'll see."

Adalet immediately pictures Steep Street, the walk to the marketplace, the tram, the buzzing street life she has been living. She will have to get a New York driver's license. More bureaucracy, she thinks. More paperwork. Mark will help her through all of this.

Mark is on the highway almost immediately. Adalet can catch sight of the Manhattan skyline for mere minutes as they head from JFK Airport out to I-495. Adalet has never before seen so many cars traveling at the same time on both sides of any highway. On her last trip to New York, she never left Manhattan. She decides not to focus on this too much, but she is curious about Mark's commute to NYU where he is teaching art history and art appreciation.

"Do you have to deal with this whenever you teach?" she asks, pointing out the window to the steady stream of traffic.

"I only go in two days a week, and I leave the car at the Long Island Railroad and take the train into the City. We'll get a second car for you as soon as you get your license."

Adalet looks out of the window, skeptical of wanting to drive in this herd of vehicles.

Mark smiles at her. "You'll get used to it. You'd be surprised at how normal it becomes."

"I'm used to a lot of traffic in cities," Adalet responds, "but not at these speeds."

"Yes," Mark tells her, "but there's only so fast they can go when there are so many of them. Give everything time, Sweetheart. I had to adjust, too, after living so long in Turkey."

But you were not born and raised there, Adalet thinks, but does not say.

More rapidly than Adalet would have imagined, the landscape changes from concrete gray to dirt brown with a few last vestiges of green. Large trees, now mostly vacant of their leaves, due to the time of year, line the road on both sides. Adalet can imagine that come spring, they will be fully decked in all of their foliage and very pretty. She leans back and relaxes a bit.

"This must be beautiful in the spring," she remarks.

"Yes, it is," Mark says. "This is not the best time of year to appreciate how beautiful New York State can be, but if it snows, well, you will see a winter wonderland for the first time."

A small rental car passes them on the left, honking their horn rapidly.

"Meryem and Isha," Mark laughs. "Meryem is quite the city driver. She'll get there before we do."

Adalet grins. Meryem has always been so quick to adjust to everything. She will help Adalet in ways that Mark cannot. Mark is her husband, but Meryem is a Turkish woman. This knowledge temporarily sets her mind at ease. Fatma sent Adalet to Istanbul to be Meryem's guardian, but Adalet often thinks Meryem was the one to instruct her. And there is Isha who has lived in India, Istanbul, and now New York. Why is it, Adalet ponders, that it is always the women we feel we can rely upon? As unusually understanding a man as Mark is, from Adalet's meager experience of men, it is still the women in her life she is most likely to turn to for help. She has sometimes speculated that these feelings emanate from the ancient traditions of the harem, a tradition Adalet sees as often misunderstood by Westerners and misrepresented in fiction and film. She likes to think so, anyway. She has always seen Turkish women work together in groups. Once again, she will become part of the Meryem, Isha, Adalet harem. A much calmer Adalet gazes out the window at the increasing numbers of trees.

"Are you okay?" Mark asks.

"Yes, I'm feeling less anxious. I can't wait to see the house."

"I hope you will love it there. If you don't, we'll sell it and buy another one." His face takes on a pathetic expression that makes Adalet laugh out loud.

"If you haven't doctored the photographs, or gone somewhere else when we've been on Skype, I can't imagine not loving this place." Adalet takes Mark's hand from the steering wheel and squeezes it. Mark breathes a loud sigh of relief. Adalet realizes that this is the first sign she has given him, other than their initial embrace, that they are now a married team.

Why is all of this so difficult for me? Adalet wonders. Many women might envy her position. She is the wife of a wealthy and handsome American professor who has rescued her from an authoritarian government. She loves him dearly; that is not even a question. And yet, even so, Adalet cannot dismiss the slight sense of nausea that has been resting in her gut since her plane took off in Istanbul. Relief mixed with nausea is a strange combination, she reflects. This is a sensation she does not believe she has ever experienced.

Mark turns off the highway at the exit to Northport, and they drive through the village to get to the house. "Oh, this is so pretty, Mark." Adalet is charmed. She pictures herself strolling through the town and stopping at the bakery to buy fresh bread. They pass a little tea shop with tiny iron tables and chairs. Colorfully decorated boxes of tea are displayed in the two front windows.

"Look over there, Mark. There's a tea shop." Adalet points to illustrate.

"Yes, I know," he says. "I can assure you that they don't have Turkish tea."

"That's okay," Adalet reassures him." I've brought my *çaydanlık*."

They pass quickly through the village, past lovely cottages and manicured lawns with rock formations and a variety of small fountains and lawn art deco. Adalet marvels at the individually decorated mailboxes topped with birds, deer, dogs, horses, and even a bear. The large trees are varied, strong, majestic. "This is straight out of a child's storybook," she says admiringly.

"You ain't seen nothing yet," Mark replies chuckling.

At the edge of the village, Mark turns onto a narrow and curvy road. The landscape changes to flat and sandy with tall grasses dancing to a mild wind. The road stretches onward enveloped by a dark blue winter sky with only a few puffy clouds to transform it.

Although it feels to Adalet that this painted scene might never change, abruptly, without warning, they reach the water's edge.

"The ocean?" Adalet asks.

"The Sound," Mark tells her. "The Long Island Sound is a tidal estuary of the Atlantic Ocean. We have a mixture of fresh water from river tributaries and salt water from the sea, a bit of everything, the best of all worlds."

Large, interspersed homes begin to block the waterfront view. Adalet feels her body almost lifting from her seat in her curiosity to see her new home. As she is about to lose all patience, Mark pulls through a gate which he somehow opens automatically from the car. Meryem and Isha's rental car sits in front of a large garage which is all Adalet can see from where she is sitting.

Mark pulls the car into the garage, huge and spotless. "I'll come back for your luggage. It's cold. Let's get you inside."

Mark is not exaggerating. A chilling wind hits Adalet as soon as she leaves the car. Meryem and Isha are waiting outside. They climb a long winding flagstone path up to the house.

"Wow!" Adalet exclaims. "This is amazing. Mark, is this really ours?"

"Every inch. All 6,000 square feet." She can tell he is proud that he has created such a response from her. She knows that is exactly what he has been anticipating since he bought the place.

Adalet steps into an alcove and a hallway leading into a large living room bounded on the far wall by floor to ceiling windows and overlooking a sandy beach, waves pulsing against the shore. Sea gulls prance on the edge and soar above, diving for food and chasing one another. Adalet notes there is a good-sized wooden deck that appears to go around the seaside front of the house.

"Isn't it wonderful?" Meryem cries.

"I could not have imagined." Adalet passes a large stone fireplace on her way to the windows. She finds a sliding door and steps out on to the deck, undeterred by the biting air. Isha follows her.

"This is my favorite place in this house," Isha says. "I could sleep out here in the summer."

"And so you shall, if you desire." Adalet leans over the edge of the deck wall, and quickly jumps back again. "But I think it is a bit nippy for that now. Let's go inside."

Isha follows Adalet back in where Meryem and Mark are busy building a fire.

Without warning, Adalet fumbles in a funnel of fatigue. She sits down on the couch, afraid of fainting. "I'm sorry," she announces, "I think I might have to lie down for a bit. I am suddenly so tired."

Mark abandons the logs he is about to set in the fireplace. "Let me show you to the bedroom, Sweetheart. We'll all still be here after you've had some good rest."

Adalet barely notices the walk to the bedroom or its magnificent décor and views. She lies down on a plush king-sized bed, not bothering to remove the spread or the pillows, and is immediately fast asleep.

CHAPTER 43

After ten days together, it is Yıldız who first notices and comments on Nuray's shaking hand. "What is that?" She points to Nuray's twitching fingers, as the women are finishing up their bland breakfast cereal and weak tea.

"Nothing," Nuray responds, quickly grabbing the offending left hand with her right and shoving it into her lap.

"That does not look like nothing to me," Yıldız insists. "Why don't you have the infirmary have a look at it? Could just be a bit of PTSD, but then don't you want to know if it's something else?" The women join in to agree that Nuray should have a doctor's opinion. Nuray is not convinced.

"I'm pretty sure it's just nerves, some sort of Post Traumatic Stress Disorder. I never had this before the night of the attempted coup. It all started with that damned soldier."

"But why not just check it out?" Ezma encourages. She is unsuccessfully trying to get Arslan to finish his breakfast, but he is filled with the rambunctious morning energy of his five years. He struggles to disentangle himself from his *anne* and the meager breakfast tray in front of him. She relinquishes her hold on him and sighs, as he scampers off eagerly to his art supplies. "It's getting harder and harder on him to be in here, or maybe it's just getting harder and harder for me." She turns back to Nuray. "Maybe I could go with you? If you can see Dr. Aydem, she is the best one here."

"Thank you for offering, but I will ask to go today. I doubt they'd let you go with me, anyway. Kind of you to think of it, though." Nuray does not want company. If there is anything physically wrong with her, she would prefer to maintain the option to inform the others of this, or to keep it to herself. The women all appear to be very nice, but she has learned from her reading and from the experiences she has gleaned from others that prison relationships are not always to be trusted. And there is her father to consider. Intimacy can be used as collateral, a get-out-of-jail ticket for any useful information. No, she must keep up some level of defense.

Nuray's request for a visit to the infirmary is not granted for several days. Somehow a shaking hand does not convince the first guard she asks that she is in any medical difficulty. And since her hand does not shake on cue, but when she least suspects it, the mere explanation of her condition is not enough to warrant an infirmary visit. But when a new guard comes on duty, a young woman none of the women have seen before, Aysun nudges Nuray.

"This one is new and inexperienced. Just ask her. Can't hurt, right?"

The guard immediately grants her request. She does not question Nuray. She fills out a paper and hollers for another guard to accompany Nuray to the infirmary. Just like that. Nuray is handcuffed, in front this time, and escorted by a minivan to the building where the infirmary is located. There is momentary fresh air. There is momentary relief from the confinement of the cell. This is something different from the monotony of daily life. Even if it brings no results, Nuray is glad to be doing this. She ignores the guard conveying her, except to obey her short, guttural instructions: Get on the van; Get off the van; Move; Stop; Sit! Nuray obliges. She is a mere dog to this woman, not a human being, and she knows this.

Nuray sits on a bench lined with ten other women. Her left hand is steady as a rock right now. Of course, it is, she thinks. The doctor will probably think she is faking.

But Nuray is pleasantly surprised by Dr. Aydem when she finally meets her after a two-hour wait. She is an attractive enough looking woman in her fifties, Nuray guesses, gray hairs died black, and strong features that convey business. The doctor is short and plump, softening her no-nonsense demeaner a bit. Her white medical jacket covers a simple blouse and trousers. There is no fuss about her. She holds a file in her hand when she greets Nuray.

"*Merhaba.* I am Dr. Aydem. You are Nuray Demir?"

"*Merhaba,* yes." Nuray notes that the doctor greets her by name and not by prison number.

"What brings you to see me? I see from your record that you suffered a severe attack. The file says the medical problems have been resolved. Is that true?"

Nuray is startled that Dr. Aydem refers to the "attack." So even though her rape was not recorded as such, Dr. Aydem seems aware of what occurred.

"Yes, I do think the medical problems have been resolved, although I'm not sure."

Dr. Aydem motions to the guard, who has accompanied Nuray into the examining room, to remove her cuffs. "Please leave us," she tells the guard. "I'll call for you when we're finished here." The guard does not look happy, but apparently Dr. Aydem carries some weight in this place. The guard unfastens the cuffs from Nuray's wrists and then shoots a hostile glare her way. Reluctantly, she leaves and shuts the door behind her. Nuray guesses that she has been instructed by those in charge not to leave her alone with the doctor. They will want to know everything she has to say.

"Now," Dr. Aydem says, plopping down on a stool and shifting more towards Nuray, "sit and tell me what is bothering you."

The only place to sit is on the examining table, and Nuray feels reluctant to be there so soon, but she places herself on the edge and rubs her hands from the assault of the handcuffs.

"I'm not sure about this," Nuray begins slowly. "It's a long story, and I'm not even sure if the long story is related."

"Tell me everything, and I will make that determination." Dr. Aydem is simple and direct. Nuray likes her already. She has to wonder why she is working in this prison, but perhaps she has a misguided sense of altruism. In any event, it is lucky for Nuray that she is here.

In stops and starts, with some short interruptions by Dr. Aydem for clarifications and questions, Nuray tells the doctor all that has occurred to her since the night of the attempted coup. For the first time since she spoke to Adalet, and in greater detail than she shared with Adalet, she tells another human being of the attack and rape in the jail.

"But the shaking of your hand, as far as you can remember, started with the threats of this soldier?" Dr. Aydem listens intently, taking no notes at all.

"Yes. And so I do think it is possible that it is just trauma, a nervous reaction to the combination of the threats and then all the changes that came with the coup. I lost my magazine, the work that has been so important to me."

"I understand how awful this has been." Dr. Aydem looks directly into Nuray's eyes, and Nuray can believe that Dr. Aydem does in fact understand. "You are not alone, you know. Although, that might not bring you much comfort. The amount of rape and physical abuse for women in custody is very high. When I came here, I wanted to start a group for women who have gone through this, but the authorities do not want to even acknowledge that it happens, never mind deal with it. And women are afraid to come forward. I am grateful that you have been able to be honest with me."

Nuray starts to sob. Her whole body begins to shake. And then, so does her hand. She holds it out to Dr. Aydem. "See, there it is," she chokes in between sobs. "Now you can see what I'm talking about." The sudden cooperation of her hand calms Nuray, her purpose being accomplished.

Dr. Aydem takes Nuray's hand, and slowly, it stops shaking. She examines the hand for a moment, rises from her stool, and Nuray can see that Dr. Aydem is considering carefully.

"I tend to agree with you that you are suffering from Post Traumatic Stress Disorder. Even if there is another physical explanation for the shaking of your hand, it would be a miracle if you did not have PTSD after what you have been through. However, having said that, I think it would be wise to draw some blood and do some lab tests to rule out other possibilities. Do you agree?"

Nuray is momentarily floored. No one has questioned her agreement to anything in some time. She slowly nods her head yes. "I do agree. Thank you, Dr. Aydem."

Dr. Aydem calls on her nurse to take Nuray for a blood draw. Nuray, once again accompanied by the guard, follows the nurse, the guard trailing behind her. The guard holds the cuffs in her hands, and stands slightly outside of the doorway, one foot in and one foot out, as if Nuray might decide suddenly to bolt. Where does she think I could go? Nuray wonders. The guard stares vacantly off into the hallway as the nurse draws the blood from Nuray's vein. Nuray has to smile. Is the guard squeamish at the sight of blood? How did she ever end up working in a prison? The nurse informs Nuray that she will have another meeting with Dr. Aydem once the test results are back from the laboratory.

The guard is more relaxed on the way back to the pod. Nuray is still handcuffed, but the guard does not speak to her so harshly. When they arrive, there is a noticeable pall over the pod. Something has changed in Nuray's absence. No one is speaking. No one asks her how her appointment went. The silence is so profound that Nuray is afraid to break it with a question. Then she sees Sera lying on her bunk, facing the wall. There is no sign of Arslan.

Nuray starts to go to Sera, but Ezma stops her by grabbing ahold of her arm. She pulls Nuray over to a corner. In a low voice, she says, "They came for Arslan while you were away. Her ex-husband has been trying to get custody of him for some time now, and the judge finally ruled in his favor."

"They just came and took him away?" Nuray is stunned. As surprising as it is to have a child in her prison cell, and as much as she might expect such a thing to happen, it shocks Nuray that he could be so easily removed so quickly. "Can they really do that?"

Ezma looks at Nuray as if she is about to scold an ignorant child. "Don't you know by now? They can do whatever they like. They can take away everything from us. When you end up in here, you lose all power. You have no rights. This is the hard truth."

Nuray goes to her bunk and lies down on her back, not speaking to anyone on her way there. She folds her arms behind her head and ponders what Ezma has just said. Is this true? And if it is true, what is there left to be taken away from her? Her mother's apartment? The contents of her mother's apartment? Old and worn furniture? A few worthless pictures on the walls? Books and more books? Lots of paper? None of it is worth very much. None of it is worth anything, except to her. And what is my value now? Nuray asks herself. I am a number, a number that must be fed and housed by the State. That is all.

The few moments of fresh air, the brief but hopeful encounter with Dr. Aydem, all of this is swept away by the merciless and monumental wave of truth. *Abandon hope, all ye who enter here.* Nuray cannot drift beyond this thought.

CHAPTER 44

Adalet is awakened by a hand on her shoulder. "Hey, Sleeping Beauty, time to wake up. You're in the prince's castle, and it's time to eat." Meryem's hand is firm, even though Adalet's instinct is to close her eyes again and return to the deep sleep brought about by jet lag and enormous change. She could lie here forever.

"Come on, Adalet. You can sleep after Isha and I leave. You've slept all day. It's time to eat now." Meryem shakes her shoulder again, and this time, Adalet responds.

"Okay, I'm coming." She rolls over to face Meryem and sits up. "Have I really slept all day?"

"Yes. But that's okay. Now we have the rest of our lives together. I can't believe that you're really here and married to Mark." Meryem brushes back a wave of Adalet's hair that has fallen across her face in sleep. "We're both married ladies now. All the way from Steep Street in Istanbul to New York in America. Unbelievable, eh? What would Fatma say?"

Adalet pushes herself up from the bed. "Fatma would say, I'm hungry. Let's eat."

Meryem laughs. "That's exactly what Fatma would say." Meryem leads Adalet down some stairs and into the dining room. The room is bright and airy, made of wood and glass, not bound by walls, and open to the large kitchen behind it. Adalet thinks, this is so beautiful, but it is too grand for me. I feel like Cinderella in the prince's palace, except that the shoe doesn't quite fit. She immediately tries to shake this feeling off. Of course it fits, she scolds herself. I can be the princess. Why not?

Adalet is relieved to see that the food is simple fare.

"Food from the local Jewish deli," Mark explains. "I hope that's okay."

"It's perfect," Adalet says grinning. "I was beginning to feel like I'd woken up in a fairy tale that was a bit too strange. Bagels and lox and egg salad make everything feel more real."

Isha scans the food and looks a bit forlorn. "Not when you're Indian." She sighs. But she sits down and begins to dish out some of the take-out onto her plate. And when she does, Adalet looks at Isha's hand and gasps.

"Your ring, Isha! Let me see it. Oh, it's beautiful. I don't think I've ever seen it before." Isha holds out her hand to Adalet so that Adalet can examine the ring more closely. "Is that new?" Adalet asks. She runs her finger across a row of green emeralds, so shiny it's as if the sun has chosen to shoot its golden rays of light through them. The emeralds are surrounded by smaller diamonds.

"You haven't seen it before?" Meryem asks. She sounds surprised.

"No. It's so beautiful. I would have remembered it, I'm sure."

"It was Fatma's," Meryem explains. "The ring came from her grandmother, her *anneanne*. Fatma never wore it. She said she was always working with her hands, and it was too big and too much for her. She stashed it away, and when she died, it came to me. It felt too big for me, too much to wear, so I gave it to Isha as a wedding gift. Perfect for her, eh?" Meryem smiles and looks glowingly at Isha.

"Yes," Adalet tells her. "It could not have found a better home. Fatma would be so happy that Isha is wearing it now."

"I found it wrapped up in my grandmother's things," Meryem goes on to say. "There was a note attached in Arabic from her mother, I guess. Uncle Ahmet translated it for me. It just said that she would have wanted her to give it to her daughter someday, if she had a daughter. Something like that. But of course, my mother died, so the ring came to me."

"Let me see your rings, Adalet. I haven't seen them closely." Isha leans forward to examine Adalet's engagement and wedding bands. They are white gold encased with diamonds. The engagement ring has a larger single diamond.

"I put them together from my mother's jewelry," Mark says with a tone of pride. "So the jewels of the mothers are passed on to the daughters." He smiles lovingly at Adalet.

"Elegant, Mark. Nice job." Meryem winks at him. "We're two old married ladies from Istanbul! What do you think, Adalet?"

Adalet gazes at the rings on her finger, a bit in wonder at how things have turned out. "Life is full of surprises. I could not have expected anything like this."

" I could not have expected bagels, cream cheese, and lox," Isha bemoans. "Thank goodness you got some egg and tuna salad, Mark. Otherwise, I'd be starving to death."

"Whitefish salad?" Marks holds up the container to Isha.

Isha wrinkles her nose in distaste. "No, thank you."

"I'll have some of that," Meryem says as she holds out her hand to take the container. "I love this stuff. I think I'm part Jewish."

"Only the stomach." Mark laughs and hands the whitefish salad to her.

Meryem dumps a large portion from the plastic container onto her plate and takes another bagel. She spreads the salad on both halves of the bagel and bites into it vigorously. Mark watches her in amusement.

"You can see for yourself," he says to Adalet, "Meryem's voracious appetite has not changed."

"Thank goodness." Adalet looks around the room. "So much else has changed. I have to get my bearings." She takes a forkful of egg salad and tries to eat. The food feels difficult to manage. Swallowing is strenuous. The food does not want to go down. She almost chokes, but takes a breath, and then manages to get the egg salad down her throat. She forces herself to swallow. Adalet puts down her fork on her plate.

"I think I really need to get my bearings here." She gets up from the table and walks over to the large kitchen windows. She can see the neighboring house, but it is too far away to get much of a sense of it. At least there are neighbors, she thinks. Everything is so large and spacious. Even now, just the short walk from the dining room table to the kitchen window has put distance between her and the others. She takes this moment to think.

A small bird flutters on the branch of a rather large tree that is somehow growing in the front of the house. The kitchen faces away from the water, Adalet now realizes, while the living room with the fireplace, and the surrounding deck outside of it, face the water. This house is still a maze to Adalet. Once again, she is overcome by a desire to sleep. She feels Mark coming up behind her.

"This must be overwhelming," he says, putting one arm around her shoulders. "One minute you're packing up a lifetime on Steep Street, and in the next minute, you're eating Jewish deli food in a strange house that now belongs to you."

"Everything does feel very strange," Adalet confesses. "I just want to sleep. My eyelids get so heavy, and I am just figuring out where I am in this house."

"It must feel a lot more difficult than it really is. It's just a simple rectangle, a box, really." He points out the window. "Straight ahead is how we drove in. If you look out of the window to the right of this kitchen, you can see the doors to the garage. The door to the side of the laundry facilities leads into the garage. We came in through the front door because I wanted to impress you." Mark grins and swings Adalet around in the opposite direction. "If we were to walk straight ahead through the dining area, we'd end up in the living room. There is a library on one side and a study on the other. Come, I will show you. It's really very simple." Mark squeezes her shoulder and extends his hand. "The food will keep," he assures her. Mark glances over to Meryem and Isha. "They won't mind."

As they walk back into the dining room, Mark informs Meryem and Isha, "I'm going to show Adalet the house now."

"Good idea," Meryem responds, through another bite of bagel and whitefish salad.

The house is perfect. Adalet could not have done a better job if she had spent months designing the place herself. The floors are a simple stone and tile downstairs, easy to clean and maintain. The upper floors are wooden, draped with the Turkish carpets Mark brought with him from the apartment in Istanbul. Adalet sees many items from the apartment Mark was forced to sell, or to risk losing completely with the change of events in Turkey. Adalet was unhappy to learn that the apartment had gone to someone high up in the Erdoğan government circle.

"Who else could afford to buy it?" Mark told her on Skype at the time of the sale. "I sold it through an agent, and what else could I expect? To be honest, I was very lucky to be able to sell. It was in the family name and not in mine, so there were some maneuverings that had to take place that were not entirely legal. I was just happy to have it taken off my hands."

"But now we will have absolutely no home in Turkey anymore," Adalet said. "If I give up my building, we will have no home to come back to here."

Mark was silent. His face over the Skype connection gave nothing away. And perhaps if Nuray had not been arrested, and the attempted coup had not failed, Adalet would not have acted as quickly as she had.

Adalet runs her fingers across an antique carpet from southern Turkey that Mark has carefully hung on the wall behind their bed. The colors have been so beautifully preserved. He has made sure to hang it where direct sunlight will not damage it over time, but there is enough light to appreciate its splendor of shape and form.

"Do you like it here?" Mark asks.

"It's perfect." Adalet goes to Mark and puts her arms around him. "You have done an incredible job, my darling. I could never have done it better. I don't have your sense of design—and in such a big house."

"It's really not so big. Do you really like it? We can make any changes you want." He runs a finger across her cheek.

Adalet holds him closer. "I cannot imagine a single change. And such big closets. I don't have that many clothes."

"If you're going to become a Long Island, American wife, we'll have to get you more."

Adalet grasps onto Mark tightly. Until this moment, this very moment, she has not truly faced the truth. Even though all the facts have been staring her in the face, she has refused to see them. She no longer has an actual written address that she can say is her home in Turkey. This new, strange place, this large, cold, strange place she doesn't yet know, this building with no smells she can recognize, no oil splattered into the kitchen walls, no hints of spice in the air, no foreseeable plumbing problems in the many bathrooms, this emptiness of recollection is her only home. There is no going back. Her bridges are burned. Turkey is a memory, far across an ocean, a distant dream in what is becoming her past. Adalet has no words. She clings tightly to Mark. He misinterprets.

"I'm so relieved that you like it here. I know what a huge change this is for you." He holds her close until he feels her pulling away from him.

"Tell me what is wrong, Adalet. Don't hide anything from me. I want to know."

Adalet sits on a loveseat placed by a window on the side of the bed. She looks off into the estuary. She can see gulls circling over the water, positioning themselves to dive for more fish. They cry out to one another in their language, a language that seems to translate more easily from the Bosphorus to the Long Island Sound than the human language Adalet possesses.

"To put it as simply as I can," Adalet tries her best, "I have lost my country. And even though I know well that others have lost their countries and come to nothing, not even a home, never mind one like this, I cannot help feeling bereft." Adalet bursts into tears. "I'm so sorry, Mark." She chokes on her tears. "Everything is so beautiful…" Adalet walks over to the window and stares out at the sunset, red and gold disappearing into dark clouds.

Mark quietly comes and stands behind her. "I don't pretend to know what you are going through, but I am here for you always, Adalet. I love you more than my life. I have loved you since the day I met you in my horrible office at the university, when I thought Meryem was going to be a royal pain in the ass. All I wanted to do was to get rid of her so that I could be alone with you."

Adalet has to laugh, hearing Meryem's voice below, emphasizing a point she wants to make to Isha. "You know I'm right," she tells her.

"We may have to do something about the soundproofing here," Adalet says, changing her own mood abruptly.

"There's not a thing we can do. I've tried. When the walls are all this open, the sound just travels."

Adalet turns around and into Mark. "I love you, too, Mark. I know that I have for a long time. I will never be an American woman. I am a Turkish woman. But I will love you with all my heart. That much I can promise."

Mark holds her closely and whispers into her ear, "And that is more than enough."

CHAPTER 45

At last, Nuray is on her way to meet with Afet Can. The week since her last visit has seemed much longer. The mood in the pod has been subdued since Arslan was taken away. Ezma sleeps most of the day and barely speaks to anyone while she is awake. Although Nuray is sad for Ezma, if Nuray is completely honest with herself, she does not miss the frenetic energy and noise that coexisted with Arslan's presence in the pod. Even though she grew fond of the boy, and she misses his cuddling up with her, there is no denying the fact that Nuray has been feeling calmer and more at peace since his departure.

The visitor's area is fairly busy when Nuray arrives. This time is reserved for detainees and prisoners to meet with their lawyers, and so, although there are quite a few people in the room, it is fairly quiet and well contained amongst the parties. Afet Can is seated at a table waiting for Nuray.

Nuray has a wave of envy when she sees Afet. Afet wears a simple, navy-blue pantsuit, a blue and gray striped turtleneck, low black leather shoes. She wears the same gold stud earrings and her utilitarian watch. The envy, Nuray feels in her gut, comes from the ability that Afet can choose what she wears. Nuray has never cared that much about her clothing, but since she is forced to wear the prison garb, she feels a terrible sense of the loss of her individuality. Afet Can is able pick out what she will wear every day. Nuray has lost this right, this privilege. This hurts.

"*Merhaba, günaydın*. Hello, good morning." Afet Can greets Nuray warmly.

"*Günaydın*." Nuray takes the hand that Afet holds out to her.

"How are you doing?" Afet asks her.

"Everything is as expected. The pod has been quiet. The little boy of one of the women has been taken away. Her ex-husband won custody. She's hardly spoken since that happened."

Afet shakes her head while getting a legal pad from her briefcase. "Life is so much harder inside for mothers. But the fact that these women are raising children doesn't seem to soften the judges any. Believe me, I have tried. But the truth of the matter is that prison is no place for a child. As sorry as I do feel for mothers being separated from their children, I don't feel keeping them in prison together is an answer. And please don't ask me for the answer. All I can say is that some of these mothers don't belong in prison at all. These are crimes against women."

"I don't have a child," Nuray says, suddenly feeling angry at Afet's sympathy for mothers. "And I could be the next one spirited away. Do you think I belong in here?"

"Of course not. Nothing I have seen gives them any right to hold you in prison, but things have changed since the attempted coup. Erdoğan is on a warpath, and all of his henchmen are staying right in line. So I need to know every detail of every conversation you have had so far with any authority and also, more about the conversation with your father. Did you know that his friend, Belgin Doğan, has been arrested?"

"No, I didn't know. Is she here?" Nuray finds this news upsetting. This is a direct link to her father. She was afraid this might happen.

"Yes, but she has been charged with aiding and abetting terrorists, so she is being held in a different location. She is in an individual cell." Afet sets her legal pad on the table and scribbles down the date with her pen.

"Are you her lawyer as well?" Nuray is now concerned. "Is that a conflict?"

"No, it's not a conflict. I've defended Belgin before. This is not her first arrest. But we do need to go over your visit to her. You must tell me everything, as damaging as you feel it might be to your case. I have to be prepared."

"I was trying to leave the country. But Belgin told me to pretend I was looking for work. They took all of my papers when I was arrested, so I could not leave on my own or even find work on my own."

"Yes, this is standard practice," Afet Can tells her.

" If my father and I were being recorded," Nuray continues, "I don't think we said anything damaging. I was to contact Belgin for work only. But if she and I were recorded—"

Afet stops Nuray mid-sentence. "Let's start from the beginning with each conversation. Please tell me everything, every single word you remember, every detail of what happened. Try not to leave anything out. I will only interrupt if I have an important question. I'll try to hold the questions until the end."

And so the hour passes quickly, with Nuray repeating, as completely as she can, each of the incidents Afet has requested. When she feels she can no longer continue, or she will explode in frustration and anger, she stops. "I'm sorry, Afet, but I feel I need to say some things to you."

Afet stops writing and puts down her pen. "Of course. I know this is hard work and very tedious. I'm sorry that we have to do this. I would not insist unless it was absolutely necessary."

"Please help me to understand, Afet, because I am finding it hard to comprehend. How did I end up in here? Why am I even here? I had absolutely nothing to do with the attempted coup. I have had nothing to do with my father for so many years. I didn't even know if he was dead or alive. If I did anything wrong, it was being stupid. I shot a photo of that idiot soldier at Taksim Square, and then I refused to sleep with him. Is that where everything went wrong for me? Is it because of this idiot that I now know is responsible for blowing up people in Ankara?"

"What? You didn't tell me this. This is the same guy?"

"I just found out. It was in a newspaper I saw in the pod, one we were not supposed to have, by the way. He blew himself up. Well, the other guy might have blown them both up. There was another guy with him, and my guess is he pulled the plug for both of them. Aksoy didn't have the balls for something like that. He was a sleezy coward."

"A sleezy coward who has ruined your life." Afet says this looking directly into Nuray's eyes.

"Yes, it is the one thing the bastard succeeded in doing on his own."

"But you did write the articles on your own," Afet reminds Nuray.

"I did." Nuray's left hand begins to shake again. She reins it in with her other hand. "But people were not being arrested for their opinions when I wrote those articles. There were only a couple of them."

"You are a journalist in Turkey, a female journalist in Turkey. People have always been arrested for expressing their opinions. You are not the first, and you won't be the last. I'm sorry, Nuray, but you had to know the risks you were taking when you wrote those articles about Erdoğan. If Aksoy had not had it in for you, you probably would never have been arrested in the first place. It would not have come to anyone's attention. But it did. Unfortunately for you, it did."

"So because of a random, stupid, soldier I didn't even know and refused to sleep with, I am in prison, after being brutally raped by guards, and now I am accused of being a terrorist who participated in the attempted coup." Nuray's face is contorted with outrage. She breathes in deeply and expels a loud burst of air.

"Whoa, you haven't been charged yet. We don't really know what you are being accused of, so let's not jump to any conclusions." Afet takes in and then exhales a deep breath of air. "Please, Nuray, I can't even begin to imagine how difficult this has been for you. I won't pretend to presume—but please, let's try to stay with the facts. We don't know the charges, and there may end up not being any. That would be the best case scenario. Let's not make up charges when there aren't any."

"But here I sit." Nuray is feeling the full force of her indignation. "You get to come and go, so how can you possibly understand? I was raped, Afet, raped by the authorities, the very people who were supposed to be guarding me." Nuray bangs her fist on the table. "Five of them, Afet! Five of them beat and raped me. And will they go to prison? No, of course not. If I even accuse them, I'll end up with charges for having the nerve to insult the Turkish State! What kind of justice can I expect?"

Afet rolls her pen across her legal pad. "Life is not easy for women here."

"Not easy?" Nuray stares at her lawyer. "Not easy? Are you kidding me? Life is impossible for women here. If I were a man, none of this would have happened to me." Nuray lets out a growl of frustration that turns the heads of several others engrossed in deep consultation.

"Sorry, sorry," Nuray tells them. She turns back to Afet. "I'm just so angry at all of this, and I have no place to put my rage. So that's why I'm giving it all to you. You are the lucky recipient."

Afet stares back at Nuray. "I cannot begin to think about how furious I would be if I were in your situation."

"I'm infuriated. Funny, I did not realize how incensed I am until now. I want to beat the walls until my fists bleed. How did this happen to me? Why me?" Nuray grabs at her hair, pulling on fistfuls. When she looks at Afet again, Nuray can see that she has frightened her attorney, and she has to smile. "Perhaps the question I should be asking is, why not me?"

With this, along with Nuray's smile, Afet regains her composure. "Yes, I think you're right. These days, and in these circumstances, that is the better question, I'm sorry to say."

"Do you ever worry," Nuray asks, "that helping us will get you into trouble?"

Afet shakes her head from side to side. "You know, I suppose it could happen, but I never think about that possibility. I wouldn't be able to work effectively if I did. I am a woman, too." Afet picks up her pen again. "We need to keep working at this if we're going to have a defense. I might be able to use the fact that you wrote these articles before there was a law about speaking out against the government. You haven't written anything like that recently, and it might be an argument, but they can use the articles as motive for your participation in terrorism or even in the coup. "

"But that is ridiculous," Nuray cries out.

"Let's keep working," Afet encourages. "However ridiculous it feels or sounds, this is where we are now." Nuray sees that Afet is determined to get the information she feels she needs. There will be no dodging around the facts. "Now," she says firmly, "Tell me all about your conversation with Begin."

CHAPTER 46

Christmas is coming to New York. Adalet is learning that Christmas in New York is an inevitable occurrence for everyone. Whether one is Muslim or Jewish or Hindu, the holiday is impossible to avoid. Nativity images and displays sit in the windows of homes and establishments not even owned or run by Christians. She is told that Jewish people have what they call "Hanukkah bushes," which are in truth, Christmas trees. Adalet is confused by this behavior. In fact, Adalet is becoming aware that the birth of Christ for many is a mere side event to the actual celebration.

Oddly enough, Adalet discovers, Mark has always had a Christmas Eve dinner somewhere. When his mother was living, they sometimes dined together early in the evening, and then Mark would go to visit friends. As a single man, he only had the dinner in his apartment once, but now that he has a house, he would like to have dinner in his own home. "Just a few friends from the university, and Meryem and Isha, of course."

"Will Meryem and Isha want to celebrate Christmas?" Adalet asks. She has no idea what Meryem and Isha do about the Christmas holidays.

"It's not so much about Christmas," Mark explains. "It's the time of year. Everyone gets into a holiday mode, and I want to celebrate your being here. We'll wait until the weather is warm to have the wedding party outdoors, but I'd like you to meet a few of my friends.

We can make it simple. We'll cater in all of the food and just serve it buffet style. You won't have to do a thing."

"I can make some Turkish meze dishes, too. I'd like to do that, if we can find the ingredients."

"That would be wonderful. And I know just where we can go to find them."

Adalet is surprised at her own enthusiasm. She has now been in the Unites States for one and a half weeks, and she has barely left the house. Mark is on leave for the winter semester break from the university, so he has been at home with her, and they have just been enjoying being together after so much time apart. Although these have been valuable hours for Adalet, she increasingly has been groping with the sense of being in some sort of a time warp, a vacuum, a void. She feels like an unused garment, waiting to be taken from the closet, out of the garment bag, and pulled from the hanger. What will she do with herself? Adalet has no idea.

"Do you plan to have Christmas decorations in the house?" Adalet asks Mark.

"Why, do you want them? I didn't think you would want them." Mark is balancing a tray of fresh fruit on his arm. It is late morning, and they are having a light brunch in the enclosed sitting room off the living room and by the deck.

"Not really," Adalet tells him, taking a few slices of cantaloupe melon from the tray and putting them on her plate. "I just wondered if that is something you normally do here."

Mark laughs. "No, I do draw the line there. No gifts either. Hanukkah is in reality a very minor Jewish holiday, but because of the time of year, Jews end up getting roped into the whole Christmas craziness. I've never had a tree, or decorations, or even lights. And I gave up lighting the menorah when my mother died."

"We could light a menorah, if you would like," Adalet offers.

"I don't have any need, Sweetheart, but thank you. I always participated in that for my mother. She always had the menorah, and I went for the first and last nights to be with her. Being Jewish is more of an identity for me, a tradition. I haven't followed a religion since my bar mitzvah."

"Why did you give it up?" Adalet sips her tea, Turkish tea she has made for herself. Mark is drinking coffee.

Mark runs his fingers around his coffee mug. "I don't think I ever really had religion, so it wasn't actually something I gave up. My parents wanted me to attend Hebrew school, and I never felt I had much of a choice about a bar mitzvah. I'm glad I did it, but again, for me it was a tradition, something that I needed to fulfill, an obligation to my heritage. I know I have told you this before, Adalet. I don't believe in God." He looks up at her from his coffee.

Adalet wonders if Mark is waiting for a criticism from her. She has never felt any. Nor has she ever felt any need for him to leave his religion and embrace hers. "You are a good and kind man, my love. In my own world of religious belief, Allah accepts you as you are. I know that many might not agree with me, but that is how I see things."

Mark puts down his coffee cup and comes around to give Adalet a long and loving embrace and kiss. "How you see things is what matters the most to me."

They are interrupted by a sound Adalet is not yet used to hearing, the melody of the doorbell. They look at each other. Who could it possibly be?

Mark jumps up. "I'll see who it is." He disappears down the hallway through the kitchen and to the front door. There is a brief pause before he calls, "Adalet, it's a package for you. You need to sign for it."

Adalet runs to get her passport for identification. She finds Mark waiting in the doorway with a young, skinny, pockmarked fellow in full post office uniform. He is holding a large package.

"I'm Adalet Aronson," Adalet tells the young man. She shows him her passport.

"Oh, but this package is addressed to Adalet Ulusoy." He holds tightly onto the package.

"Oh, dear, that is from habit. We had just gotten married, and I wasn't used to using my married name. Hold on, I still have some identification with Ulusoy, if you need it."

The young man considers, and then seems to decide that he is not dealing with criminals here. "That won't be necessary. Just please sign with both names here." He hands her a sheet and a pen to sign. He drives off in his little post office truck, as Adalet and Mark go back into the house.

"What is it?" Mark asks.

Adalet smiles. "It's my mother's wedding dress, the one I rescued from the earthquake."

"Wow, yes, the one you sent me a picture of from Istanbul. Let's open it. I want to see."

Adalet carries the package into the dining room and sets it on the table. After the letdown she had experienced over this dress with Yasar, her first husband, Adalet is nervous about showing the dress to Mark. Her *anne* had been so disappointed when she'd had to tell her that she would not be wearing the dress in her wedding, and that Yasar's mother had helped her to pick out a "modern" suit to wear instead. But Mark is not Yasar, she reminds herself, and so she picks up a knife and carefully undoes the packaging. Slowly she unfolds the tissue paper surrounding the dress and pulls it from the box. She holds it up in front of her.

"My God," Mark blurts out, "that is amazing. Wow! Did your mother make that?"

"No, her Italian friend made it for her wedding to my father. Do you like it?"

"I love it!" Mark's enthusiasm is too genuine for Adalet to question.

"Should I wear it to our wedding party here, or do you think it's too much?"

"It won't be too much with my tux! No, Sweetheart, it's perfect. You are so beautiful, and the dress, well, it has found the perfect woman to show it off. Now I can't wait for the wedding party." Mark runs his fingers over the silk. "This is exquisite workmanship. I do see a bit of soiling in the very ends here that he wasn't able to get out, but it's barely visible and doesn't matter."

"That is exactly how I felt." Adalet is thrilled by Mark's response. If only her *anne* could have known Mark. But on second thought, Adalet wonders if her *anne* would have given Mark half a chance. A Jewish man? My daughter marrying a Jewish man? Perhaps not, she thinks.

Adalet takes the dress upstairs to their bedroom, finds a good wooden hanger, and places the dress inside her almost empty giant wardrobe closet. At least I don't have to squash it, she thinks, smiling at her lack of clothing and the rows of vacant hangers. Mark wants to take her shopping, but Adalet has other plans. She imagines that Meryem and Isha might be better shopping guides for her, as they know her taste and conservative dress habits. They will know where to take her to shop, Adalet hopes.

When Adalet joins Mark downstairs, he has just picked up the mail that the regular postman has slipped into the mail slot. "This must be your day. There is a letter for you, and there is one for both of us." Mark hands Adalet a thin airmail letter envelope with the return address of the prison where Nuray is being held. He also hold out a larger envelope addressed to both of them from Afet Can's office.

"I hope there is some good news." Mark opens the envelope addressed to both of them.

"Any news at all would be good," Adalet says frowning. "They just hold her there without any charges. I had no idea our judicial system was so bad." She holds onto Nuray's letter, waiting to find out what the attorney has to say first.

Mark looks up at her from the envelope he is opening. "Ours is often not so good, either. When people can't afford bail, they spend months, and years sometimes, in prison before their cases go to court. We have more people sitting in jails and prisons here than anywhere in the world."

Adalet shakes her head, disgusted. "What is wrong with this world?"

"Plenty." Mark pulls out a letter, as well as what appears to be a contract from Afet's firm. "But there is plenty right with this world, too, my dear. We have to try to remember that."

"I know." Adalet sighs, fingering the letter from Nuray. "Is that Afet's contract? She did mention that she would be sending something. She has to make sure she's paid. Nuray can't pay her."

"Yes, and there is also a letter from Afet. She's seen Nuray a couple of times now. Afet just wants to keep us informed and let us know of any progress she's made. I'll get a retainer check off to her this week."

"Are you sure you don't mind doing this?" Adalet wishes she didn't have to turn to Mark to help Nuray, but the building on Steep Street had been her only asset, and she relinquished that to come to the United States. Since the building came to her in Fatma's will, she could not have imagined selling it back to Fatma's sons. She had simply turned the property over to them.

"Of course not." Mark sets the letter and contract down on the table and reaches for Adalet. "She is your oldest friend. And if we weren't helping her, I don't know if you would have consented to leave Turkey. I hardly know Nuray, but she is important to you. And so she is important to me." He holds her close.

"I will never be able to thank you for this."

"Every day you live with me is thank you enough." Mark reaches for the letter. "Do you want to see this before I write the check and file it away?"

"Yes." Adalet takes the letter and the contract. She looks it over and sighs again. "This is a lot of money. Do you think she can get Nuray out of prison?"

"That is doubtful, but maybe she can get her a lesser sentence. Without a lawyer, she's helpless. Anything we can do is better than nothing. Let me know what Nuray has to say."

"I will." Adalet retrieves the thin paper from its envelope. The paper feels so fragile in her hand, as fragile as she imagines Nuray to be after so many months in and out of prison. A few lines have been redacted, but for the most part, the letter is intact.

My dear Adalet,

The days here are all the same and very long. You will be glad to know that I have been to see a doctor about my hand. She had some blood drawn for tests, and it seems that I do not show anything significant. The conclusion is that the hand shaking is a result of tension, nerves, and PTSD. The prison does have a psychiatrist who visits, but there is not really any medication that works well for PTSD, and I would rather not take any medication anyway. I am guessing that you are thinking I should have some therapy for this, and maybe when I get out, I will do that.

As far as my case goes, I know that Afet Can is keeping you informed. Please tell Mark how grateful I am to him for paying her fees. I could never do it myself. If this goes on much longer, or I am sentenced, I will ask Afet to see about selling my mother's apartment in order to raise some funds. She knows someone who could take care of that for me.

The women in the pod are kind and look out for one another. This is much better than being alone, but I have no way to know how long I will be here. I will let you know if anything changes, as long as I am able to write to you. ——————————————————————— (redacted)

I hope you are finding life in New York good and kind. I know you must be thrilled to finally be with Mark. And now you have Meryem and Isha as well! I miss your visits, but I am truly happy for you. You did the right thing, and what I encouraged you to do for so long.

I send love and hugs to you and Mark. Oh, and Mohammed sends his best. He visits me whenever he can.

Nuray

Adalet hands the slender slip of paper to Mark. "Here, you can read it yourself." She bursts into tears. "My poor friend. Why is her life so hard and mine is so easy? Why?"

Mark pulls Adalet to him again. "Life is not always so kind, and your life has not always been so easy. Just think of all you lost in the earthquake. Your husband was having an affair that you knew nothing about; you lost your baby, and you suffered burns all over your legs. You had to have multiple surgeries, and you were left in such pain. Your husband's family forced you to move away. Your life was not always so easy. We can only hope that with time, and with our help, things might improve for Nuray. It's not your fault that she is where she is."

Mark reads Nuray's letter and hands it back to Adalet. Adalet folds it gently back into the envelope. She knows it isn't her fault that Nuray is in prison, but for no logical reason she can explain to herself, she is overcome with guilt. "I'll write to her later today."

Mark tweaks a strand of Adalet's hair. "What do you say we go shopping today? Dare we get into the insane Christmas shopping crowd? It might be fun for you to see how nuts people are at this time of year. What do you think?"

Adalet smiles. "I was saving that for Meryem and Isha after Christmas. But you might be right. Even if we don't buy anything, getting out might be good."

"Let's do it then." Mark starts up the stairs. "I'll just shower and change."

"Me, too." Adalet heads up the stairs behind him, clutching the letter from Nuray in her hand.

CHAPTER 47

Nuray sits in the holding cell, unable to think. What has just happened to her is unfathomable. This is a nightmare from which there is no awakening. She sits on a single bench that is chained to the wall, resisting an urge she has had now for some minutes to urinate. But in order to do so, she must ask the guard to accompany her to a toilet, something she has no desire to do. She replays the scene she has just lived through.

Afet Can is with her in the courtroom. Courtroom? This is a joke, Nuray reflects. If only it were funny. She is taken to a large building that appears to be more of an office building than a courthouse. The guards take her up a large wide staircase to the third floor. Three men sit behind a large table in a stuffy room. This comprises the courtroom. There are rows of chairs lined up across from them, as if a real courtroom was what someone had originally had in mind, but the room is empty, other than a clerk, the three judges, Nuray, and Afet Can. This is the trial of Nuray Demir.

The chief judge, a man in his sixties, short, fat, and bald, is perched in the middle of the other two. Nuray cannot recall in this moment what they even looked like. The chief judge impatiently asks Afet Can if she has a statement. While Afet Can makes her statement, the judges yawn, play with their fingernails, scratch their pens across what appears to Nuray to be blank paper, and most regularly examine their watches. The clerk stands at attention.

Once Afet Can has completed her statement, the three men whisper together for about three minutes. The chief judge then asks Nuray to stand. She rises and stands with her attorney.

The chief judge speaks instantly, as though waiting another minute will throw the entire system into a scheduling crisis.

"Nuray Demir, this court finds you guilty of the charges of insulting the Turkish government, participating in a terrorist organization, and participating in an attempt with that terrorist organization to overthrow the Turkish government. For these crimes, the court sentences you to a term of imprisonment of ten years, including the time served, with the possibility of early release for good behavior." He bangs a gavel on the table. He motions to the clerk. "Call for the guard to escort the prisoner, please."

And it is over, just like that. The guard is waiting just outside the door, handcuffs at the ready. Afet Can leans over to Nuray and says, reassuringly, "This isn't over, Nuray. We'll fight the verdict, get it reduced. This is just the beginning."

The beginning of what? Nuray asks this question, alone in the holding cell, wondering how long she can wait before requesting a visit to the toilet. Such a natural occurrence, the need to urinate, and yet, she has to obtain permission for even this call of nature. There is nothing anymore that remains solely within her control. There is an explosion brewing inside her chest, inside her head, rage pushing itself up and outward. She wants to wrap her arms around her body to ward these dangerous emotions off, but her handcuffs prevent her from even exerting that much control.

Nuray waits and waits. When she can bear it no longer, she yells for a guard. Again she waits and waits. Again she yells. Just as she feels she can no longer suppress the pressure on her bladder, the guard calls into the cell, "What's wrong?"

"I need the toilet." Nuray can hear the anger in her voice. The submissive state she has forced herself to carry thus far is gone. The verdict has pushed her into another state of being, dangerously without hope.

The lock on the cell door turns, too slowly. Nuray knows she must remain on the bench until the guard enters and tells her to stand. Her urgency has no influence on the guard. The guards operate on their own time, at their own will, with a very few exceptions.

"Get up and come with me," the guard tells Nuray. She pushes Nuray along a dimly lit hallway to an unmarked door. She opens the door and motions Nuray inside. There are a set of four toilets that are enclosed just halfway down. The guard unlocks Nuray's handcuffs and ushers her inside one of them. The guard waits just outside the stall.

Nuray pulls down her pants and sits tentatively on the seat. Her time in jail and prison has accustomed her to a lack of cleanliness that she would once have never been able to tolerate. But now she has been holding her urine back for so long that she cannot release it. She pushes and pushes, and nothing happens. She feels the impatience of the guard, whether real or imagined, and this frustrates her further. Her urine will not come out.

Nuray tries to breathe. Rage is boiling inside of her. She forces air to go in and out, then more deeply, in and out. She sits there breathing like this for some moments before there is finally a trickle, and then, with another breath, her liquid rushes out in full force. Relief. Several flickers of Nuray's outrage pass along with it.

Nuray washes her hands vigorously in the single sink before the guard secures them back into the handcuffs. The guard does not utter a single word. Nuray would like to know how long she can expect to wait in the bare holding cell by herself. Where will she be going next? Will she be able to retrieve her things from the pod? Will she be allowed to say good-bye to the women in the pod? And what if she has to use the toilet again before they move her? Will she have to holler for someone to come and take her again? These are all questions Nuray would love to ask, but she knows the guard will not answer any of them. She has experience with asking these sorts of questions. So she shuffles back along the dark corridor, enters the holding cell, and sits back down on the bench. Nuray hears the lock fall into place as the guard leaves her.

There is no clock. There is no time. Ten years. Ten years of this is unfathomable. What will she do with all of this time? How can she possibly survive hours, days, weeks, months, years of this life? Come on, Nuray, she scolds herself, others have done it. So can you. Write a book. That's what you can do with your time. Write about your experience. Or even better, write a novel that will take you away from these walls. But I'll be an old lady by the time I get out of here. No, don't be ridiculous, you'll be middle aged, in your late forties. You won't be so old. And if you were out there struggling, you would never find the time to write a novel. And there is Afet Can. Maybe there really is something she can do. She will appeal.

Write, Nuray thinks. I am a journalist. I know how to write. But in my heart, I have always wanted to write fiction. I have always complained about the constraints of fact and form, and I have always complained about the lack of time in my life. Now I have all the time in the world. I can bring another woman to life in my mind. I can create a Kurdish woman with completely different problems to solve.

Nuray begins to create a woman in her mind. This woman is young and intelligent. She is Kurdish. Her name is Ezo. Her mother cleans apartments for Turkish people who can afford a housekeeper. Ezo's father was killed in a skirmish with Turkish soldiers in their primarily Kurdish village in southern Turkey. Ezo's mother immigrates to Istanbul now that she must support her only child. When the story begins, Ezo is sixteen years old.

Nuray feels her inner energy shifting. There is a softness of light inside where there was only a black darkness. She is giving birth to something, someone. She is discovering meaning, hope. She will ask Mohammed to bring her notebooks. She will give herself life through Ezo.

Nuray hears the cylinder on the cell door lock shifting. The door creaks open, and a different guard enters. "You're being relocated," the guard tells Nuray. "Let's go. Your things will be collected for you and sent to your new location."

Well, Nuray thinks, that is that. I do not get to say good-bye. Like Arslan, I have been removed. They will understand. They are used to this. But now her mind and her brain are focused on Ezo. Nuray is glad she kept herself from getting too involved with the women in the pod. She is sad to lose them without a farewell, but she never allowed herself to become too attached. Since it was a matter of a couple of months and not years, she was able to maintain her distance.

The guard leads her down a different corridor to an exit from the building. There is a van waiting outside. Nuray is buckled into the rear seat, and the guard jumps into the front seat with the driver. Outdoors again. A moment of fresh air from the building to the vehicle. That unprocessed air is so precious. Nuray gulps in as much as she can tolerate before the door is shut next to her. The van drives past a few buildings, and in a matter of minutes, the driver stops in front of a large, gray building. My new home, Nuray considers, looks like a prison. It would be difficult for it to pass for anything else. What can I expect? Better not to expect anything.

Once again, Nuray feels a brief moment of fresh air in between her exit from the vehicle and the guard ushering her inside the building. Nuray finds herself in a small processing area. Once more she must take off her clothing. A guard examines her orifices and her hair. She is given a new set of garments. These have a number inscribed on the back of the shirt: 743329.

"You are now Prisoner 743329," the guard explains to Nuray. "When you are called for any reason, that is how you will be identified. You must learn to respond to this number. Please memorize your number and respond to it when it is called."

Nuray is dressed in her new, tan outfit. She is wearing the same underwear, socks, and sneakers that she wore into the building, but her name has been replaced by a number: Nuray Demir is now Prisoner 743329. The justice system has taken away her clothing and her name. She has no name and no rights, except the rights the justice system decides to allow her.

There is no mirror in the processing area for Nuray to contemplate her new appearance, should she even wish to do so. She does not wish to do so. She has begun to live through Ezo. As Nuray is handcuffed and led out into another hallway, Ezo rides the tram from her secondary school to the bus she has to take to the apartment where she lives with her mother. The tram is a twenty-minute ride to the bus which is a half-hour ride to the Kurdish neighborhood of their apartment building outside of Istanbul.

As Nuray is escorted along the dim hallways to her new prison home, she disembarks from the bus with Ezo and follows her into a cheaply crafted building. She rides the elevator to the fourth floor. She observes Ezo pull a set of keys from her school backpack and open the apartment door. What does Ezo look like? Nuray will decide once Mohammed brings her notebooks, but she has a figure in mind. Nuray pictures Adalet as she was in university, a very young and beautiful Adalet. Yes, that will be Ezo, with perhaps more Kurdish features.

The guard stops in front of a cell-like structure. She searches for the right key. They walk inside a small hallway where there is a second door. She raps on this door before she enters. The door opens into a small area with a table and chairs. There is a young woman, Nuray gauges to be in her early to mid-twenties, sitting at the table reading a book. She is wearing a headscarf, and Nuray sees that the book she is reading is the *Quran*.

"Where is Defne?" the guard asks the woman.

"She is using the toilet." The woman closes the book and stares at Nuray.

"This is Nuray Demir, Prisoner 743329. She will be living here with you in the empty cell upstairs." The guard removes Nuray's handcuffs. "Your box of belongings will be here later. There is bedding in your cell upstairs. This is Asmin. Asmin and Defne will show you everything." The guard takes the handcuffs and goes back out the entryway to the outside door. Nuray hears the cylinder click as the guard secures the lock.

A rather tall, slender woman, loose, dark curls gracing her shoulders, emerges from the toilet closet. She might be about Nuray's age. Her angular features and deeply set eyes gaze at Nuray standing by the door, rubbing her wrists from the handcuffs.

"Should I say welcome to our hell hole? I am Defne. I see you've already met Asmin. Do not suppose we are friends. We have been thrown together here by our glorious justice system, and so we make the best of it. You will learn to live with us."

Nuray stares back at the two women. "I will certainly do my best to learn to live with you. And I hope you will do your best to learn to live with me."

"Of course," Defne laughs. "Come on. I'll show you your cell. We have this common area, but we are locked in separate cells overnight. The bathroom is down here, so we have to use a pan to pee overnight and dump it in the morning. Best not to drink too much tea before bed." She starts up a staircase that Nuray did not see when she first entered the common area. It is off to the opposite side of the room from the toilet. At the top of the stairs is a small hallway with three heavy metal doors. Defne opens the middle one.

"All yours," she says, motioning inside.

Nuray walks into a tiny room, barely big enough to hold the cot inside. There is a small wooden chair and a table with one drawer. There is also a large box sitting at the end of the bed.

Defne motions to the box. "For your stuff, whenever it gets here. Do you need to use the toilet?"

"Not just yet," Nuray replies, wondering what Asmin's story is, since she has not yet said one word to her.

"Well then, make your bed, and then I will show you our elegant facility. There is a toilet and a sink, but they take us to showers about every few days, unless they are in a bad mood, and then it can be once a week. At least we can wash up somewhat in here." Defne is out the door and back down the stairs.

Nuray goes over to the cot and surveys the spotted, worn, grimy-looking sheets, the pillow without a pillowcase, and the rough army blanket provided. The thin, shabby mattress is stained. Nuray places the sheet onto the mattress, realizing then that there is only a bottom sheet, and there is nothing to separate her body from the abrasive texture of the blanket. Regardless, she places the blanket over the sheet. The cells will doubtless be cold at night, and no matter how coarse the material, she will need it for warmth. If they ever bring her things, she has long johns that Adalet brought for her before she left for America. Under the bed is a bedpan of sorts for overnight emergencies.

Nuray pulls the chair over to the small table. She opens the drawer. Just big enough for a couple of writing notebooks and a pen, she thinks. If I can write here, I can survive. I won't allow myself to think about the ten years. I will force myself to live only one day at a time.

Taking in a deep breath and letting it out, Nuray climbs back down the stairs. Both women look up at her.

"I am sorry I did not greet you," Asmin says, still gripping her *Quran*, "but I was in the middle of reading and praying when you were brought in. The guards have no respect for interrupting us, no matter what we are doing. As Defne says, welcome to hell."

Defne gets up and takes Nuray by the arm. "The toilet is over here." She opens the door to a small water closet. There are several shelves containing deodorant, shampoo, combs and brushes, toothbrushes, and toothpaste, soaps, washcloths and hand towels, and assorted items. Defne points to one that the women have cleared for her. "This one is yours. Toilet paper is under here in this cupboard. Please use it sparingly, as they don't always bring it on time."

The sink is small, but at least there is running water, and at least she won't have to holler for a guard every time she needs to use the toilet. Nuray thanks Defne. "Are you both religious?" she asks.

Defne grins. "I'm not at all religious. Asmin is very religious. She prays five times a day, and she spends much of the rest of the day reading the *Quran*. What about you?"

Nuray shakes her head, no. "I'm not at all religious either. I wore hijab for a time. As a single woman, it made my life easier, but I have discarded that as well. Once I was arrested—well, that is a story for another day."

"Come," Defne says, "Let's join Asmin. The toilet is not the best place to talk."

The women orient Nuray to her new surroundings. They keep some snacks in a cupboard, some to be shared and some in bags with their names written across them and not to be shared unless asked. Meals are delivered to them three times a day, just as they were in the pod. There is a door to an outside courtyard that is opened for an hour a day. When dinner arrives, Nuray discovers that it is the same food she has been receiving in detention. The women eat together at the one table in the common area. Asmin prays before she eats. Nuray and Defne wait respectfully until she is finished before they begin to eat.

Nuray's belongings do arrive before bedtime, and so she is able to sort her few things in the bathroom and in her cell. As of yet, she has no snacks to share. At 11:00 p.m., the women are locked into their individual cells for the evening, and the lights are eliminated. Nuray has one writing pad and a pen. She will ask Mohammed to bring her more paper and another pen, and possibly, some sort of battery-operated light she can use to write by at night.

Now she lies in her long johns on the single bed sheet, her head on the naked pillow, the coarse army blanket pulled up to her chin, and she dreams of Ezo. Ezo, the sixteen-year-old daughter of a Kurdish cleaning woman who looks so much like the youthful Adalet. Nuray wonders, what does Ezo want from her life? Does she sometimes dream about the boy she sees kicking around a football with several other boys in the courtyard? What is his name? Has she heard one of the other boys call him Salih?

Nuray drifts off to sleep with images of Ezo and the life she is creating for her. The nightly noises of the prison, water running through pipes and metal clanking, the intermittent voices of prisoners and guards, all slowly recede into Nuray's imaginary world of Ezo.

CHAPTER 48

Six months have passed since Adalet stepped off the airplane in New York. Her first spring in the Unites States is lush and green, flowers pop up everywhere, birds capture and carry small fish and insects to bring back to the young they have just hatched. In a nest just outside their home, house finch parents travel to and fro to plop food into the mouths of their three hungry offspring.

And Adalet has just discovered that she is nine weeks pregnant. When the doctors told her after the earthquake that she would not be able to have another child, they had been wrong. She is elated and terrified. Mark is ecstatic, the happiest she has seen him since she agreed to marry him and move to the United States. The obstetrician she has seen has told her that she is perfectly healthy, in spite of the traumatic leg burns inflicted by the earthquake. Yes, she is in her late thirties, but women deliver perfectly healthy babies in their early forties, and Dr. Julia Epstein sees no reason why Adalet should have any difficulties. Dr. Epstein is a neighbor, and owns a home not too far from them in Huntington. Adalet is glad to have an OBGYN close to home.

Mark has undertaken the task of setting up a nursery. Since they will not know the gender until after the prenatal ultrasound, he plays with neutral colors. He goes online to explore all sorts of designs for nurseries. In the one week they have known for certain, he has not waned in these endeavors.

In contrast, Adalet feels a lethargy that the good doctor did not help her to explain. She has just been able to connect with a Turkish organization in Manhattan, Raindrop Foundation. She attends one lecture there, a lecture concerning the politics and future of Turkey under Erdoğan, and she connects with two of the women there. At first, she feels a bit shy. The women in this organization all appear to be devout. They welcome Adalet warmly, seemingly without prejudice or any expectations from her. She has let them know that she would like to become a participant and to help them as a volunteer in some of their activities. When they discover her background in education, they are quite enthusiastic.

"Raindrop Foundation is committed to education," Azra tells her. "We have schools all over the country, all over the world, as a matter of fact. Of course, you will have to get a teaching certificate here."

"Everything is still very new for me, but that may be something I might want to pursue. But are you Hizmet, the organization that Erdoğan accuses of starting the coup?"

Azra smiles. "Because he accuses us does not mean we are guilty. And although we do follow many of the teachings of Fethullah Gülen, we are our own organization. Hizmet is a civil society movement, and we believe in what they propose. But it is true that Erdoğan accuses us, and many of us have been arrested and imprisoned in Turkey."

Adalet looks around the lecture room. The women are all in hijab, with a few exceptions. They serve a Turkish brunch, delicious varieties of *börek*, *menemen*, and Turkish tea, smiling and gracious, every one of them. Adalet is thrilled to speak her native language once again. Nothing in the speaker's lecture has felt dangerous to her here. He has only spoken the truth, as Adalet understands it.

Azra is married to the current director, Ahmet. They have two children, a boy aged eight, and a newborn girl, just six months. Azra introduces Adalet to Zehra, an older woman with a pregnant daughter, Miray, who has helped with the baking and cooking and serving. Adalet wonders if she will be able to help them as her pregnancy develops.

"I am not religious, although I do read the *Quran* and pray" Adalet explains to Azra. "My husband is Jewish, although he is also not religious. But I would still love to help out here, if I would be accepted."

"Of course," Azra tells her. "We are happy to have you here."

Now Adalet looks back on this day, and realizes that she wishes for more of this kind of experience and interaction. She is lonely for Turkish anything. Adalet desires more of a Turkish world, whatever form this might take. At the Turkish House, there are Turkish mothers who might see a world that is more compatible to her own. Meryem and Isha, although Adalet is sure they will be incredibly loving aunts, neither one of them has any real infant experience. And they both appear to have assimilated so easily to American culture. These women at The Turkish House all have children, and they are devoted to perpetuating their culture here in America. There are only two obstacles that Adalet can foresee. One isn't really much of an obstacle, and that is the distance she has to travel into Manhattan. This trip is nothing for Mark, so he insists, but Adalet does find the thought of the long trip into Manhattan does keep her at home more often than she would like. The second possible obstacle is Mark. How will he respond to these people whose purpose is to extend their culture here in America? They are devout Muslims, and Mark is a man who does not believe in God. Adalet has no idea. Although Mark has assured Adalet, time and again, that he has the greatest respect for her culture, she has a sense that he wishes she would assimilate as quickly as Meryem has done.

Now that Adalet has obtained a driver's license, she must wait for her car to arrive at the dealership. She chose a new Honda Accord , but they had to order in the silver color she wants. In the meantime, when she decides to go anywhere, she drives Mark's car, first dropping him off, and then picking him up from the train station. When she is simply in the mood to experience and experiment, she takes the train into Manhattan. She likes to pick out people and fantasize about what their lives might be like. She creates stories about them in her mind.

Adalet daydreams of writing a book, especially since Nuray has written to her that she is doing exactly that.

On Adalet's most recent trip into the city, she found herself following a woman and her little girl from Central Park to a small bakery on Columbus Avenue in the eighties. She sat at a small table near them and ordered a chocolate croissant and tea. As she watched them, Adalet imagined sitting there with her own daughter, hoping that her baby will turn out to be a girl. Mark has expressed that he also wishes for a girl.

But now it is early morning, and Adalet feels a bit lazy. Mark is already gone for the day, and she must decide how she will spend her time. She wants to call Afet Can, but it is evening in Istanbul. She vacillates, picks up her phone and sets it down again. She has Afet's cell phone number, but since she is well aware of the long hours Afet puts in every day, she is hesitant to disturb her when she is away from the office. But these days, Afet is often away from her office, or there only in the evenings when she catches up on writing briefs or making deferred phone calls. This might, after all, be the best time to reach her, Adalet reasons. The phone only rings twice before Afet answers.

"Adalet, *iyi akşamlar*, good evening. You must be clairvoyant. I was just about to call you."

"Oh, do you have some news?" Adalet asks, pleased that she has made the right decision.

"Well, it's not exactly news yet, but I am hopeful."

"Please tell me, whatever it is, I want to know." Adalet can hear soft music playing in the background. Afet has a strong affection for classical Turkish music. The notes of the *zurna* leave Adalet wistful for home.

"Apparently, Nuray's father is seeking to make a deal with the authorities to get Nuray an earlier release."

"Oh, but that is wonderful. How did you find out? Did Nuray tell you this?"

Adalet can hear Afet clearing her throat. "Heavens no. Nuray will be the last person to know anything. If she finds out, she'll try to stop her father from helping her. She's too afraid of what they can do to him. He's probably going to be in prison for the rest of his life. Please, do not say a word to her. We cannot have this information leaking. And I am certainly not able to tell you how I found out."

"Of course," Adalet agrees, "I understand. I won't say a word to anyone but Mark."

"Good. It's extremely important, or it might never happen. Even so, I don't know if it will ever happen. I am just trying to be as optimistic about this as I can be. Arman Demir, Nuray's father, has been through an awful lot. He must love her a great deal to even attempt this. I know he has been absent for many years of her life, but this has to be of great sacrifice to himself."

"And she has always thought of him as the bad guy," Adalet reflects.

"He is not perfect," Afet says, "but he is trying now. This is more than many would dare to do. Anyway, when I have more information, I will let you know. Oh, and please thank Mark for the bank transfer. The money really helps."

Adalet smiles. "I will tell him, Afet. Oh, Afet, some good news here."

"What? Tell me."

"I am pregnant."

"*Tebrikler!*" Congratulations! I am so happy for you."

"I have written to Nuray, so please, don't tell her."

"She will tell me when she gets your letter. I won't let on that I already know."

"Thank you, Afet."

"Okay, we'll talk again soon."

"Yes, be careful, Afet."

"Take good care, Adalet. There are two of you now."

The line is disengaged. Adalet places the phone inside her jacket pocket. Sunshine radiates through the windows. Balmy breezes caress the leaves on the tree outside the window. Adalet decides she will not miss this beautiful June day. She will go for a walk, maybe even as far as the village tea shop. There might even be some kind of adventure close by.

CHAPTER 49

Ezo is a living and breathing entity for Nuray. Days and evenings pass, and although she interacts pleasantly with Defne and Asmin, Nuray is more connected to Ezo and the life she is creating through her.

Like Adalet, Ezo lives through the earthquake that kills her *anne*. But Ezo escapes without the burns to her legs. Other than a mild concussion, Ezo eludes the devastation of the quake physically unscathed. Emotionally, though, Ezo is devastated. Her *anne* and their building are both gone. If Ezo had not spent the night at her friend's home, she would also be gone. Now she is motherless and homeless, and there are times she wishes to be with her *anne* and free from the pain of her losses.

Nuray projects all of her pain onto Ezo, and only because of this, Nuray can finally sleep through a good portion of the night. Mohammed comes to visit her, and he brings her writing materials. In just a few months, she has gone through several notebooks. There are days that Nuray goes back through what she has written, crossing much of it out, scribbling over it, wishing she could use a computer instead. Ah, for the delete function, she groans. But no matter, she forges on ahead.

There are days she even prays with Asmin. Once in a while, Defne will join them. The women are kind to one another. They are very different people, thrown together by an unjust lottery that extends them no mercy. So they make the best of things and learn how to live together without friction. There is enough of this outside the small world they inhabit. They adapt to one another's customs and preferences silently. Thus, a quiet respect for each other begins to develop and grow amongst the three women.

Asmin does not speak of the circumstances behind her incarceration. Defne tells Nuray that Asmin says she was framed for a crime her employer committed. Apparently, Asmin was close to her employer, and so this was a traumatic betrayal. Asmin has never disclosed the details to Defne. Whatever the crime was that the employer committed, Asmin received a sentence of twenty years.

Defne believes she is incarcerated as a bargaining deal to bring her brother out of hiding. Defne knows little about her brother's involvement, if there even was any, in the attempted coup, but he was politically active and spoke out against the Erdoğan government. Her brother went into hiding right after the attempted coup, and Defne has no idea where he is. She was charged as a co-conspirator to her brother's crimes in a similar courtroom scene to Nuray's. She is sentenced to ten years. Nuray was afraid she would be locked up with genuine criminals, but it is painfully clear to her that none of them belong in prison.

Since Ezo has entered Nuray's creative life, she has not had an episode of her hand shaking. Although Dr. Aydem has told Nuray that the posttraumatic symptoms might return under stress, she is much relieved to learn that she does not have any neurological or physical disorder. She is grateful to the women in the pod for encouraging her to see the doctor.

On this particular Thursday morning, Nuray is preparing for a meeting with Afet Can. They have only met once since Nuray's trial, although they have spoken by telephone. Nuray is curious as to why Afet has scheduled this meeting. Afet did not indicate during their brief telephone conversation.

Nuray spends a few additional moments in the toilet combing her hair, attempting to look a bit more presentable. She has allowed her hair to grow out quite long. She first ties it back with an elastic hair band, gives a quick look into the small, cracked mirror, and then pulls the elastic band off again, letting her dark curls embrace her neck and her face.

Nuray makes the handcuffed journey to the visiting area, slightly annoyed to have been taken away from her writing. She has made much mental adjustment to her sentence and circumstances in order to be able to get through each day, and she does not have much faith that anything will lead her from her ten-year sentence. Although she likes Afet and is extremely grateful to Adalet and Mark for financing Afet's services, Nuray does not believe this will lead anywhere to her advantage.

Afet is already seated at a table when Nuray is led into the visitor's room.

"*Günaydın*, Nuray," Afet greets her. She does not get up, as they are not allowed to have any physical contact.

"*Günaydın*, Afet." The guard removes Nuray's handcuffs. Nuray sits down, and the guard leaves them, standing just outside the door.

"What a boring day these guards lead. Waiting and waiting. I would not want their job." Nuray first grimaces, then smiles at Afet.

"Yes, most of the time, I imagine it is quite boring. I would not like to guard people, in any event," Afet goes on to say. "My job is to get people out of here."

"And sometimes that job is impossible." Nuray looks directly at Afet, still rubbing her wrists from the handcuffed trip to the visitors' room.

"Maybe not," Afet retorts.

"What do you mean?" Nuray asks, resting her elbows on the table, her head in her hands.

"We have an appeal date, two weeks from today." Afet looks genuinely triumphant.

"An appeal? How can that be? And what does it even mean? They can reject it, turn it down, no?" Nuray refuses to let her hopes rise.

"Yes, that is possible. However, I don't believe they will this time." Afet appears confident, and now Nuray becomes suspicious.

"And why is that?" she insists.

Afet hesitates. She has prepared for this question, but she is not good at altering the facts. "Well, these days, they aren't even hearing appeals unless there are good grounds for them. I don't think we would have been granted the appeal unless they plan to do something. I have no way to know that, but it is my firm feeling."

Nuray moves back from the table. She brushes her hair back from her face and gazes into Afet's eyes. "This is my father, isn't it?"

Nuray's directness throws Afet's determination not to let on to Nuray that her father has had anything to do with this completely out the window.

"I'm not a good liar, even for an attorney." Afet does not smile when she says this. "But yes, I have been in contact with him."

"I didn't want this." Nuray looks away. She already feels the guilt she has wished to avoid.

"I know you didn't want this," Afet quickly responds. "And I have had nothing to do with it except to submit the appeal when the time was right. You can fault me with that, if you wish."

Adalet looks back at Afet and runs fingers through her hair. "He has not been there for me for so many years, but I have seen him. He is an old and beaten man now. I don't want him to suffer more than he is already—and that is quite too much."

"Try to see it as I think he sees it," Afet says leaning into the table to be closer to Nuray. "His life is over. In their eyes, he has bargained with the devil. Only a miracle will get him out of prison, a complete regime change, and that attempt did not go very well. The only good he believes he can do now is to help you. I believe he feels that if he can't even do that, his life is truly over." Afet reaches out to touch Nuray's hand by instinct, before she remembers that there is no physical contact and pulls her hand back. "He has already done whatever he has done," she says, "and so we will only waste his efforts if we do not go ahead."

"Do you know what that 'whatever' was?" Nuray asks.

"No. I have no idea."

"And I believe you, as you really are a terrible liar." Nuray laughs. "My life is not in my control."

"But it can be again, as much as anyone's life ever is. Let us try," Afet persists.

Nuray sits still for some time, and neither woman speaks. Finally, Nuray breaks the silence. "Okay, what's done is done. Since I cannot stop anything, we will go forward. If the appeal is granted, I will be forever in his debt." Nuray shakes her head in distaste.

Afet smiles. "We are in debt to our parents from the moment we are born. They have given us life."

Nuray motions to the guard that the meeting is concluded.

"Wait," Afet tells her. "This is for a sentence reduction. We won't be able to get you released."

"Any reduction beats ten years," Nuray shoots back, getting to her feet. "See you in two weeks."

"Yes, good. See you in two weeks."

The guard approaches with handcuffs to take Nuray back to her cell.

We'll just see, Nuray thinks as she stumbles along the hallway. I refuse to believe anything until it happens. How can I trust anyone? Even Afet? Let me get back to my fiction where I can play with some control, some little bit of control. As long as I force my mind to stay in the real world, I have none.

CHAPTER 50

It is almost midnight when Mark's cell phone begins to ring. He catches it on his nightstand just before it goes to voicemail. Adalet rolls over to see who might be calling at this hour. She hears him say, "I'm putting you on speaker so Adalet can hear."

Adalet identifies Afet's voice on the other line. "Sorry to call you folks so late, but as you know, it's daytime here. Nuray's hearing took about ten minutes this morning. We just finished, and I could not wait to call you. Her sentence was reduced to three years, and that includes all the time already served."

"That is wonderful news! We're so glad you called. How is Nuray? Is she happy?" Adalet wants to know how her friend is feeling.

"I don't believe she has taken this in yet. And she has a sense of disbelief. I think as long as they have Nuray in custody, she will never trust that she will be free. And perhaps even after she is released, she will never feel absolutely free again, not completely. Remember, she was released once and then taken back into custody. She has suffered so much trauma. But she is writing, and that is good."

"I wonder," Mark says into the phone, "do you think there is any chance of us bringing Nuray over here?" Adalet takes Mark's hand in hers. This is not something they have ever discussed. Adalet has not dared to imagine such a development.

But Afet quells this idea immediately. "She has no passport, and after all of this, she will not be granted one. And there is the matter of a visa for the Unites States. It will be impossible to get her out now."

"There must be a way," Mark retorts.

"Not one that I know," Afet insists. "Look, I must go now. Take care."

"Thank you, Afet." Adalet and Mark say this in unison.

"You should not have asked her that on that line," Adalet tells Mark. "She is probably being watched, and her lines are surely tapped. She represents the enemy."

"You're probably right," Mark admits. "But if her phone is bugged, it was smart of her to deny being able to help. And now at least she knows what we are thinking. And if she does know people who might be able to help Nuray, maybe she can do something. In the meantime, we can look into what we can do from here through the Embassy."

"That's true. Yes, let's do that," Adalet says. She rolls into Mark's arms. Her pregnancy is showing, and they now know it will be a girl. Both prospective parents have been bringing more pink items into the nursery. Two small, fluffy pink elephants, a gray hippo with a pink belly, a pink knit blanket one of the older Turkish women made especially for Adalet, the nursery grows.

As Adalet snuggles into Mark, in a state of half consciousness, her mind drifts to the wedding party that they held just a couple of weeks ago. Adalet smiles at the thought of her mother's wedding dress, still hanging unworn in her closet. Although she is not yet so big, she was not able to squeeze into the wedding dress. Instead, she went shopping with Meryem and Isha at the last minute to a wedding shop in a large shopping mall on Long Island. Actually, Adalet reflects, the shopping had been a lot of fun. Meryem and Isha had not restrained from much laughter at the various possibilities Adalet selected. They finally settled on a mother-of-the-bride silk, elastic-band pants, and an oversized top in a creamy peach color. Meryem had surveyed Adalet with amused scrutiny. "This is as good as it's going to get, and still, you do look beautiful."

The party was not what Adalet expected when she had imagined it from Istanbul. But when she looks back on it now, it was exactly as much as she could have tolerated at this point. As happy as she is in her pregnancy, she does feel nauseous at times, and tired, and out of sorts at others.

Adalet and Mark each prepared vows and read them aloud by the water. The wedding itself was symbolic, as they were already married, and so they did not have an official to declare them married. Mark just wanted something for friends, and as it turned out, Mark didn't really have so many. Most of the folks who came were acquaintances from the university. Azra and Ahmet came from the Raindrop Foundation. Adalet is pleased that Mark and Ahmet seem to be forming a friendship. Well, if not exactly a friendship, they do get along well. Her fears about Mark's reaction to the Raindrop Foundation folks has proved to be unfounded.

Mark lightly strokes Adalet's back. "There must be illegal ways to get her out. There are illegal ways to do most anything. People who've been in jail and in prison do get out of there."

Adalet is now more awake. "I don't know if Nuray would want to live here." I still don't know if I want to live here, Adalet muses to herself, not daring to utter such thoughts to Mark. After all, any doubts she has about her new life have nothing to do with him. She merely longs for her home.

"Didn't she plan to run once, but she didn't get away?" Mark asks.

"That is true. But I think that was desperation about going back to prison. And she didn't know for sure where she would be going. She was ready to go anywhere."

"But here is so much better than other places, don't you think?"

The question is disturbing to Adalet. She turns from Mark and sits up in bed. "I don't know if that is true for everyone. We can't know what is right for Nuray. She is the only one who can answer that."

Mark sits up beside her now, putting an arm around her shoulders.

"I think you sometimes wonder if living here is right for you," Mark says slowly.

Adalet is quiet. After a few moments, she turns to look into Mark's eyes. "I love you, my darling, Mark. Never doubt that. Do I love America? No, not yet. We live in a beautiful place. I love the ebb and flow of the water, the bird song, the smell of the air, the mixture of salt and green. This house is amazing. Our daughter is destined to have a wonderful life." Mark leans in and kisses her.

Adalet responds to Mark's kiss, and then continues. "But do I have fears—well, maybe not fears—maybe that is too strong a word, concerns is better—for the future here. I have to discover where I fit in. I am in a kind of limbo."

"How so?" Mark asks.

"I have no routine." Adalet pulls away from Mark and reaches for her bathrobe, flung over a chair near the bed.

"But that will all change with the baby." Mark reminds her.

"Yes, I know that. But I will need more than the baby. I will need meaningful work. I am thinking about getting an education degree here. I would like to do more of the work I did in Turkey, only expand it to the hearing population and work with the Raindrop schools."

"That's a fantastic idea, Sweetheart. You will be a wonderful asset to them. Do you think you will be able to do all of that?"

Adalet gets up, puts on her bathrobe, and ties it closed. "I have no idea what I can do or can't do until I try."

Mark leans on one elbow. "Where are you going?"

"I could never sleep now. I thought I'd have a cup of tea and maybe a walk out on the deck. My mind is too busy." Adalet puts on her slippers.

"What else is on your mind?" Mark persists.

Adalet hesitates for a moment. "Nuray, Erdoğan, Trump, all of these things. I keep thinking I might have run from one power maniac right into the clutches of another. I've seen how this kind of sickness can grow. I'm concerned for us, and honestly, I'm concerned for America."

Mark hoists himself up on the bed, leaning back into his pillows. "We don't have coups in America."

Adalet shakes her head back and forth. "Let's hope not."

Adalet leaves the bedroom and walks cautiously into the hallway, dimly lit by nightlights and the reflections of a full moon. She ambles down the stairway, not quite used to the wide stairs yet. She goes to the kitchen to heat water in the *çaydanlık*, but then changes her mind and goes directly out onto the deck. The night air is cool, fall is coming, some of the birds are already aware and abandoning their nests. Their little ones have learned to fly and to procure their own food.

Adalet wanders to the edge of the deck, leans over, and rests her elbows on the damp wooden planked siding. The moon is reflecting a pathway along the gently rippling current. If my heart could only lead me across these waters straight to Istanbul, she contemplates. If only Turkey and America were simply divided by a river, like Istanbul is divided by the Bosphorus. If only I could simply cross a bridge from one side to the other and back again. If only I could just see Nuray one more time, just to know that she is okay, that she is happy with her early release. I just wish I could hear her say that.

Adalet runs her hands over her stomach, finally resting them there. "Ahsan," She whispers. "My most beautiful, *benim küçük kızım*, my little girl."

Adalet hears footsteps behind her. Mark has followed her outside. His next words indicate he has heard her.

"Ahsan is a beautiful name." He comes up behind Adalet and puts both arms around her.

"Do you like it?" she asks. "It means beautiful, you know."

"I do know, and I like it. It's a perfect name." He pauses. "Adalet?" Mark sounds serious.

"What is it?" Adalet asks him.

"Whatever your fears, whatever your concerns, we will face them together. You have a partner for life now. Each of us is so much stronger now that we have each other. Whatever comes, we will face it together." He holds Adalet closer to him. She leans into his welcoming body.

They linger a few more minutes, gazing up at the moon, and then down at the moonlit pathway on the water. Moving as one, they link hands and walk back into their home.

. . .

Nuray places a large X over a paragraph she has been writing many times for the past two hours. She darkens the X until the paper under it begins to separate. Once she believes she has worked through her frustration, Nuray starts to write again:

Ezo wanders aimlessly through the market. No, Nuray thinks, and she crosses out *aimlessly*. Ezo doesn't do anything *aimlessly*. Here she is in Istanbul after a grueling journey, and she must find food and a place to sleep. She is close to being without any money. Leave out the adjective, Nuray decides. I can always add later.

Ezo wanders through the marketplace. She feels her hunger—no, I can make that stronger, Nuray decides—*Hunger pains strike her, like a dagger thrust repeatedly into her stomach walls. Her throat feels like it has been brushed with sandpaper. The world around Ezo begins to fade into darkness, and she sits down on an overturned carton to avoid passing out in the street. A little girl approaches her cautiously, and then calls to her mother, "Anne, anne, I think this girl is sick. Come help."*

Nuray stops here. Does anyone help? Should Ezo be rescued so quickly? Does she want her character to find comfort while she, Nuray, is facing years of prison time? Why should Ezo have it so easy? But then Nuray softens. Ezo is just a child who has lost her mother in an earthquake. Like my own Adalet, she thinks. And Fatma did assist Adalet, even if it did take some time. She picks up her pen again.

A young woman in hijab walks over to the child. "What is it, Ayla?" She sees Ezo with her head now in her hands, and she asks, "Are you all right, dear?" Ezo bursts into sobs that shake her small body like a baby tree in a violent wind. "I'm okay," Ezo manages between sobs. "I don't think so," the woman responds. "Ayla, here is some money. Go get a bottle of water and some snacks, anything."

Nuray recognizes that she is smiling. When was the last time she smiled? She cannot recall now. Ezo will have more challenges, as in any real life, but she will also find kind people who will support her.

In this way, she is like me, Nuray realizes. But I was more fortunate than Ezo, as I had my mother for many more years. And now, I know I did have a father who cared about me—no, I have a father who cares about me. There is my friend, Mohammed, who brought me this very pen and paper. And there is my dear Adalet. No, Ezo, even if you still have to struggle, I will let you have the help you need. I will not write you in total despair. Nuray continues:

The young woman takes Ezo's hands in hers, rubbing Ezo's filthy fingers in her own clean and manicured ones. "Whatever troubles you, my child, let it go for now. You must eat and drink something, and then maybe we can work something out together. Does that sound okay to you?" Ezo squeezes the woman's hands and nods her head weakly, yes.

ABOUT THE AUTHOR

Phyllis M Skoy published her first short story *Life Before* which appeared as the Discovery of the Year in Bosque, 2013.

In 2016, Ms. Skoy's first novel, *What Survives*, a novel about Turkey, was published by IP Books. *What Survives* was short listed for the Santa Fe Writers Project, was a finalist in the New Mexico/Arizona Book Awards and First Runner-Up in the Eric Hoffer Grand Prize Short List.

In 2022, Black Rose Writing reissued *What Survives* and published the prequel, *As They Are. A Coup*, is the third book of *A Turkish Trilogy*.

In *Myopia*, a memoir, published in 2017 (IP Books), Ms. Skoy describes what it was like to grow up with a refugee father still unknowingly consumed with the fears and struggles of his past.

NOTE FROM THE AUTHOR

Word-of-mouth is crucial for any author to succeed. If you enjoyed *A Coup*, please leave a review online—anywhere you are able. Even if it's just a sentence or two. It would make all the difference and would be very much appreciated.

Thanks!
Phyllis M Skoy

We hope you enjoyed reading this title from:

BLACK ROSE writing™

www.blackrosewriting.com

Subscribe to our mailing list – *The Rosevine* – and receive **FREE** books, daily deals, and stay current with news about upcoming releases and our hottest authors. Scan the QR code below to sign up.

Already a subscriber? Please accept a sincere thank you for being a fan of Black Rose Writing authors.

View other Black Rose Writing titles at www.blackrosewriting.com/books and use promo code **PRINT** to receive a **20% discount** when purchasing.